D1384001

Other Titles From Dev Love Press

The Boy Next Door
Harvard Hottie
Paradox
Devoted
(W)hole
Breath(e)

Love In Touch

Lucy May Lennox

LOVE IN TOUCH
1st Edition

A book by Dev Love Press, published by arrangement with the author

Copyright © Dev Love Press, LLC. 2013
Cover art by Michelle Marie H. Suan
Proofread by Janet Michelson

For information address: Dev Love Press,
6593 Quiet Hours
Suite 102
Columbia, MD 21045

Visit our website at www.devlovepress.com

ISBN: 978-0-9858263-3-8

CHAPTER ONE

"Are you sure this is a good idea?" Kassie asked as she slammed the car door shut behind her.

Erik smiled down at her, his brilliant white grin reassuring. "Of course. You'll be fine." He jogged across the parking lot while Kassie dawdled behind, even though the rain was increasing from a mist to a steady drizzle.

"I don't know. My signing still sucks. What if they don't understand me?"

Erik put an arm around her, hugging her to his lean tall frame. "Come on, you're not here as an interpreter. This is just a casual meetup. And since when have you been shy?"

Kassie grinned despite herself, then looked up at the low-slung building before them. A sign over the door read Seattle Deafblind Center. She glanced up at Erik again.

"OK, but you'll help me if I get stuck?"

"You'll be fine," Erik repeated as he pushed the door open.

To Kassie it seemed purely by accident that she ended up in this place at this time. She had moved to Seattle after graduating from college because she wanted to get away, to start over. She had chosen a small school in Indiana near home, but her father had gotten sick in her freshman year and died in her junior year, leaving her to sleepwalk through college in a haze of grief that prevented her from making any friends, let alone boyfriends. By the time she graduated she was ready to start over in a new place where she didn't know anyone. She found a job easily enough as an administrative assistant (well, secretary really) to the head of finance at the corporate office of a big name department store. The pay was alright, even if the job itself felt pointless and boring. The

atmosphere in the office was decidedly stodgy despite the
store's inept attempts to be edgy and hip.

It was because of her housemate, Erik, that Kassie started
taking American Sign Language classes at Seattle Community
College. Erik was a CODA, a hearing Child Of Deaf Adults,
and worked as an ASL interpreter. Learning ASL seemed like a
good way to get involved with something more meaningful
than her current job, but after over a year of classes Kassie
was, if anything, even more painfully conscious of how far
from fluent she was. From time to time she accompanied Erik
to pizza nights and meetups at the Seattle Deaf Community
Center, but while people there were nice, they always seemed a
bit mystified by her presence. Inevitably someone would ask if
she was training to become an interpreter.

No, I just want to learn, she'd reply, doing her best to make
her signs quick and natural. Usually the other person would
smile, but somewhat hesitantly, as if that wasn't really enough
of an explanation.

If she signed, *I'm Erik's friend,* people assumed they were a
couple, which seemed ridiculous to her because he was so
obviously gay. But apparently it was the only way people could
make sense of her presence there.

Still, she kept going with him every month or so. The
meetups, just casual gatherings to chat in ASL for a few hours
in the evening, were good practice. Then one day Erik
mentioned to her that he had been asked to attend a similar
meetup, but for deafblind people. Impulsively, Kassie
volunteered to go with him, but the thought of her inadequate
signing skills was making her uncharacteristically nervous.

Kassie followed Erik into a medium-sized meeting room
with round tables and plastic chairs arranged around the hard
linoleum floor, like a school cafeteria. A dozen or so people
stood or sat eating pizza, just like the Deaf meetups she had
been to before, except everyone sat much closer together,

signing in pairs. Erik greeted several people with great animation, hugging them and introducing Kassie. Most of them seemed able to see her signing well enough to understand her, even some of the people carrying white canes. Only one woman put her hands on top of Kassie's as she spelled out her name.

As Kassie started to relax and look around, she noticed a figure sitting off by himself, separated from the small knot of people. She watched for nearly half an hour, but no one approached him. She gauged him to be about her age. His eyes were closed and his brows pinched up in a frown, but even so he was strikingly handsome, with close-cut, glossy black hair contrasting with a pale complexion.

She nudged Erik, pointing toward him with her chin. "Who's that?"

"Oh, that's Jake," Erik replied. "Don't worry about him-- his intervener will be here soon."

"His what?"

"Intervener, it's like an interpreter for deafblind people. Like Mandy there," he added, waving to a woman who was signing into the hand of another woman seated beside her.

"I'm going to say hello to him," Kassie said. It seemed wrong to her that one person should be excluded from the group.

Erik looked slightly pained. "Kassie, you don't understand," he said. "Everyone else here has Usher's Syndrome. They've been Deaf all their lives--only started to lose their vision as teenagers or adults, and most of them still have some sight. They're all ASL native speakers. But Jake is profoundly deaf and totally blind from birth. I'm not sure he even knows ASL."

Kassie stared at him, her eyes growing larger. "How can he not know ASL? He must know something, right?" she asked, a little shocked.

Erik explained, "It's hard to learn the signs if you can't see them. I think he uses a different manual alphabet that's easier for him." Seeing the look of concern on Kassie's face he added, "Don't worry about him, he's fine."

Kassie turned to look at Jake again. He didn't look fine to her. He looked bored and lonely. She knew how it felt to be on the outside, to have no one to talk to. What if he was just waiting for someone to go over to him? It didn't hurt that he was cute too. If they were at a party she would find some excuse to talk to him. "I'm going to say hello to him," she insisted.

"Try printing block letters on his palm, he might understand that," Erik suggested with a shrug.

Kassie squared her shoulders and marched across the room, daring Erik to stop her, but he had already turned his attention to someone else.

Jake did not seem to notice her approach his chair. He sat with his back rigidly straight, but his head dipped slightly down and to the left. Up close he was even cuter, with his strong, slightly triangular jaw. The contrast between his glossy black hair, slightly grown out on top, and his pale skin was startling. His eyelashes were dark and thick too, although his eyes opened only slightly, showing a line of white.

Kassie waited for a moment, but when he still did not give any sign of noticing her she tapped him on the shoulder. Jake jumped so high she nearly retreated, overcome with guilt for having startled him, but he was already holding out his left palm toward her. Realizing it would be even more cruel to walk away, Kassie extended a trembling finger and wrote very slowly in the palm of his hand, H-E-L-L-O.

To her extreme surprise, he saluted her with the ASL sign for *hello*, then added, *My name is Jake*, in rather jerky, hesitant signs. At least that's what she assumed he meant; rather than spelling out his name, he made a name sign, tracing a sort of J against his chest with his pinkie finger.

Kassie made to introduce herself as well, with his hands resting on hers, realizing only too late that when she gestured towards herself, she brought his hand directly onto her breasts. Jake seemed to realize the same thing--he breathed in sharply and flushed from his neck to his hairline, bright pink splotches standing out against his white cheeks. Flustered, Kassie tried again, this time only moving her hand halfway. *My name is K-A-S-S-I-E*, she signed, fingerspelling her name then adding the name sign Erik had given her, a K at her right temple, a reference to her short, curly blond hair.

Jake did not reply, so she made the signs again, even more slowly, but he kept tugging her hands towards him. She gently tugged back, but that only seemed to agitate him. He brushed his fingers over her palm, then made some rapid signs she couldn't follow. She stared at him helplessly. He sighed in irritation as he repeated the signs, the splotches on his cheeks turning darker red.

This time Kassie picked out *C-A-R-T-E-R*, but that was all. What is carter, she wondered, feeling increasingly panicked. She glanced behind her, trying to spot Erik, but instead a small balding man with round glasses set atop a hooked nose suddenly appeared and insinuated himself between her and Jake. Before she realized what had happened, he pushed her aside and put his hands under Jake's. Immediately they began signing back and forth rapidly.

Kassie shifted from foot to foot, unwilling to end their conversation so abruptly. If you could even call it a conversation, but still, it seemed rude to walk away. "Umm...excuse me, but who are you?" she asked the interloper.

Without pausing his signing with Jake, the man gave her a sour look. "I'm Joel Carter, Jake's intervener," he snapped.

"Oh, of course!" It seemed so obvious now. "I'm Kassie," she said, fingerspelling her name again and adding her name sign at the end, so he could repeat it into Jake's hand. "I'm a friend of Erik's. I was just, um, saying hello to Jake."

Carter passed along the message, then said, "Jake says hello." Kassie watched their interaction curiously. Carter was not using any ASL signs or fingerspelling she recognized. Jake held out his left palm flat and at an angle, while Carter tapped and brushed it in different places with his fingers, sometimes straight or bent, sometimes one or more than one finger at a time.

"I'm sorry, Mr. Carter, but do you mind telling me what system you're using? Erik said Jake doesn't know ASL, but I guess he was wrong about that. Anyway it looks like now you're using something else. I'm just curious," she finished lamely, realizing she was starting to babble.

Carter was not pleased with her question. "He knows some basic ASL," he answered shortly, "but we're using the deafblind manual alphabet."

"Oh, I see."

Carter stared at her but did not say anything more. After a moment Kassie realized what was happening: Carter didn't want to talk to her. He wanted her to go away, but being an ethical interpreter he was not going to say anything to her he would not also sign to Jake.

"Well, um, ok, nice to meet you, Jake," Kassie said, and patted him on the shoulder as Carter interpreted. Again Jake jumped a bit, and Kassie fled back to Erik on the other side of the room.

For the remainder of the evening Kassie stuck close to Erik, signing briefly with a few people, but for the most part feeling like an observer. At the Deaf meetups there were always lots of people, and she rarely had a problem finding someone willing to let her practice her ASL. But here she realized it was hard to sign to more than one person at a time, and even harder to initiate small talk with a stranger. She never realized how much she relied on catching someone's eye to begin a conversation. She ended up chatting with one of the interpreters about her ASL class, although she knew her teacher would scold her for using her voice.

Back in the car , Erik asked, "So what did you talk about with Jake?"

"Nothing," she replied truthfully.

"I told you his intervener would show up," Erik said as he pulled out of the parking lot. "But he is kind of a hottie. I don't blame you for wanting to chat him up." He turned to wink at her.

"Oh my God, what are you talking about?" Kassie protested. "Not everyone is a horndog like you."

Erik just laughed. In the two years they had been living together they had grown close, even though initially they only met through Craigslist. Erik was the ideal housemate, a good cook and fastidiously clean, even if he was kind of loud and liked to play techno turned all the way up. After feeling alone for so long, Kassie was glad to have someone to joke around with. She liked going out with him to gay clubs where she could dance however she liked, and no one hit on her. Not that she was against dating--she had attempted a few relationships, but somehow the guys she met all seemed self-involved and shallow.

But even though Erik was fun, he definitely had his own life that didn't always include her, and she tried not to be too clingy. She tried to find activities that would get her out of the house more, and suddenly she found she was running around all the time.

Now she caught sight of the clock on the car radio."Oh no, is that the time? Do you mind dropping me off at my yoga class? I'll take the bus home."

CHAPTER TWO

One evening later that week, Kassie typed "deafblind manual alphabet" into Google, more out of curiosity than anything else. Several charts and YouTube videos popped up. She gathered that it was based on the British Sign Language system of fingerspelling. There was no doubt that was what Jake and Mr. Carter had been using. It looked easy enough--a tap on the tip of the thumb for A, then on the tip of each finger for the rest of the vowels. Some of the other letters, like C, J and D followed the shape of the printed letter. There was a note at the bottom explaining that two taps on the palm meant yes and a brush across the palm meant no. Kassie printed out the chart and tacked it up on the wall near her desk. It seemed like a useful thing to know, and she thought vaguely that she might mention it in ASL class.

First year ASL class had been fun. The teacher, Ms. Andrea, was a young hearing woman who also worked as an interpreter. Her classes consisted mostly of games and silly roleplays, and she never hesitated to use her voice as she signed, translating and explaining simultaneously. Some of the students complained that it was like kindergarten, but Kassie enjoyed the class and eagerly signed up for another year.

But the second year teacher, Ms. Hansen, was nothing at all like Ms. Andrea. A stern, middle-aged Deaf woman with a severe short haircut, she shocked them all the first day of class by informing them in swift, no-nonsense signs that there would be no speaking allowed. Instead of games, now there were tests, and Kassie found her grades slipping from As to Bs and once, to her shame, a C, despite the extra practice she got thanks to Erik and the occasional meetup. She redoubled her efforts and made it through the first semester with a B+. She considered quitting, but she enjoyed the intellectual challenge, something lacking from her job. And Ms. Hansen worked in little bits of information about Deaf history and culture, and about disability rights, as much as possible with their limited vocabulary. She was always encouraging them to get involved, learn more on their own. Kassie thought Ms. Hansen might be pleased if she brought up something about British Sign Language or the deafblind alphabet in class.

But a week went by, then another and another, and somehow Kassie never found an appropriate moment to mention it. Her grades were getting a little better, but Ms. Hansen still intimidated her.

One night over dinner Erik mentioned casually that the next deafblind meetup was the next day. "You wanna come along again, or was it too boring for you?" he asked.

"I dunno. I had plans to go running with Dave and the others."

Dave worked in her office; through him she had joined an informal group of runners, and at the moment they were training for a half marathon. The group was three guys and their girlfriends, and the guys were rather more competitive than she would have preferred, but they were the first friends she had made besides Erik, and she felt she couldn't be too picky.

Erik shrugged. "Whatever, it's up to you."

Kassie thought it over for a few minutes, then said, "No, screw those guys. I need the extra practice."

"Ok, cool." Erik gave her a sly grin. "But are you really coming along for ASL practice, or because you want to see a certain someone again?"

"Yes!" Kassie replied. Erik hooted with laughter, and Kassie quickly amended, "I mean yes to practice, no to the other thing. Jeez!" She stood up abruptly from the table and carried her dinner plate to the sink.

"I'm sure he'll be there!" Erik called after her. The image of a pale, black-haired figure flashed in her mind. She wasn't about to admit as much to Erik, but she had been thinking about Jake, what his life was like, what kind of person he was. Surely if they could actually communicate, he would have something interesting to say.

For over an hour that night and during her lunch break the next day, Kassie did her best to cram the deafblind alphabet chart, but she couldn't seem to remember all the letters consistently. As they were leaving the house, she folded the chart and stuck it in her jeans pocket before jumping in the car with Erik.

At the Center she found much the same scene as last time: the same people sitting or standing near the pizza, signing to each other in groups of two. And as before, there was Jake sitting off by himself, rigidly upright and toying with his cane. Kassie scanned the room but saw no sign of Carter. She greeted several people she had met last time, and had a slice of pizza. Still no Carter, and no one else was talking to Jake either.

Pulling her chart out of her pocket, Kassie walked over to Jake, then very slowly and gently touched his arm. He must have sensed her presence, because this time he didn't jump, but only extended his left hand toward her. She sat down facing him and balanced the unfolded paper on her knee.

H-E-L-L-O she signed. I A-M K-A-S-S-I-E. If he was surprised that she was now using the deafblind alphabet rather than printing the letters on his palm, he made no indication.

I K-N-O-W he replied.

Kassie found herself surprisingly pleased that he remembered her. H-O-W D-O Y-O-U K-N-O-W she asked.

Y-O-U S-M-E-L-L N-I-C-E.

Well, that was unexpected. She glanced up from her

hands to his face--that pointed chin, those curving lips. It was getting even harder to concentrate and remember all the letters. She tore her eyes away and slowly spelled T-H-A-N-K Y-O-U, pausing frequently to check the chart for some letters.

Y-O-U-R-E W-E-L-C-O-M-E he answered.

There was a lull, and she sat with her hands resting against his. It was exciting, but also a little unsettling to be this close, holding hands with someone who was still virtually a stranger. After all the anticipation, Kassie found herself at a bit of a loss. Casting about for a topic of conversation, she asked D-O Y-O-U L-I-K-E C-O-M-I-N-G H-E-R-E.

He snapped his two fingers down against his thumb vehemently, repeatedly: an ASL sign for *no no no*. Then with the other hand, he added I H-A-T-E I-T.

Kassie stared at him, not knowing how to reply. She wanted to ask him more, but spelling out each word seemed like a laborious way to go about it. Already she could see why ASL speakers preferred to use signs, and when they had to fingerspell, did so with blistering speed. Between having to glance down at the chart repeatedly and watch his replies carefully to ensure she really got it, even this very short conversation was slow going.

Before she could formulate a reply, Jake started signing again.

G-I-V-E M-E Y-O-U-R E-M-A-I-L. Evidently he had been signing slowly for her benefit, because now he speeded up, and she had to ask him to repeat it several times.

E-M-A-I-L, she confirmed, and he tapped the palm of her hand twice for yes. I D-O-N-T H-A-V-E A P-E-N, she signed back.

Seeming irritated, he brushed the palm of her hand, which she now knew meant *no*. T-E-L-L M-E I-L-L R-E-M-E-M-B-E-R he signed.

She tapped his hand twice: *yes, ok.* K-A-S-S-A-N-D-R-A-B-L-O-C-H-A-T-Y-A-H-O-O-D-O-T-C-O-M. She spelled it twice to make sure he got it, then added the ASL sign, *why?*

Y-O-U-R F-I-N-G-E-R-S A-R-E S-L-O-W S-T-U-P-I-D he answered.

"Hey!" Kassie exclaimed, once she had decoded the letters. "Did you just call me stupid?" She started to spell out an indignant reply, but in her agitation she kept losing track of the letters, and he was tugging on her hands again, increasing her irritation. She pulled back, and saw the color rise in his cheeks as they engaged in a tug of war.

"He's trying to tell you that he doesn't understand."

Kassie turned to see that Carter, looking sour as ever, had materialized in the chair beside her. "Here, let me," he said, and once again pushed his hands up under Jake's, displacing her. The signs began flying back and forth, as rapidly as if they were typing. Kassie slouched back in her chair, defeated.

"All right, fine," she said, standing up. "Tell Jake it was nice talking with him."

"Tell him yourself." Carter glared at her, challenging.

Kassie glared back at him, then spelled out B-Y-E in Jake's palm.

She was out of sorts the rest of the evening, but Erik did not enquire why. Nor could she have explained fully. Why did I bother to learn that alphabet, she wondered. He clearly doesn't want to talk to me, and he has an interpreter. How stupid to expect him to fall all over himself with gratitude just because someone said hello.

The next morning in the office Kassie was, as usual, putting off starting her work by drinking coffee and surfing the internet. Her boss didn't like to see her looking at random websites, but Kassie's desk faced the door to her boss's office, and she had gotten very good at clicking the browser shut in a flash. After reading the daily updates on the *Stranger* website, Kassie opened her personal email.

There was a message from Jake.

Dear Kassie,

This is Jake O'Malley from the Deafblind Center. I'm sorry if I was rude to you last night. Your signing really is slow, but I meant that as a joke. I'm sorry if I upset you. I didn't mean to.

I just wanted to let you know that I really appreciate your coming over to say hi to me. I've been going to those meetups for a long time, and hardly anyone ever talks to me because I don't know ASL very well. It was nice of you to learn the deafblind manual alphabet for me. I hope you can come again next month. You seem like an interesting person. I want to get to know you better.

Sincerely,

Jake

Kassie stared at the email, openmouthed. The contrast between the email and the way they had conversed in person was stunning. She felt as if she had been trying to talk to him through a brick wall, but now the barriers to communication fell away, leaving his real personality to shine through.

She was about to compose a reply when she noticed the smiley face icon next to his user name. He was online. She brought up instant messenger and typed in a greeting.

>Hi Jake this is Kassie

There was a pause of several seconds. Kassie waited nervously, then at last a reply popped up.

>Hi Kassie

She continued,

>I got your email. Thank you! But you don't have to apologize, it's ok.

>Whew, I was worried I pissed you off. The thing is, I thought you were Deaf. I didn't realize you're a seeing hearing person who had only just learned the deafblind alphabet. Carter said you had a chart. And he said you're pretty.

For the second time that morning Kassie was stunned.

> Carter said that? I was sure he didn't like me and didn't want me to talk to you.

>Why would he have said that if he didn't like you? He's just very direct. So will you come back next month?

>I thought you said you hated it there.

>I do hate it. Everyone there is so much older, and all they want to talk about is their kids or Jesus. Except for one woman who became a Buddhist last year and tried to talk to me about getting enlightened. I told her I don't feel heavy.

>Haha

>So now that's one more person there who doesn't want to talk to me. But it gets me out of the house. Besides, if I can talk to you there it won't be so boring.

>Even with my slow signs?

>If you practice, you'll get faster.

>OK, bossy. So if you don't like talking to people at the meetup, what do you like?

>I do like talking to people, just not those people. They sign too fast. I can't follow them. Besides, they're all old.

>How old are you?

>I'm 26. How old are you?

>24. You didn't answer my question. What do you do for fun? You don't look like someone who sits around the house all day. You're pretty fit.

>Ha, thanks! I go running with my dad, and he helps me with weight training at the gym.

>I like running too! Maybe we could go together sometime.

>Sure.

>What else?

>Mostly just internet. I like to read, newspapers, magazines, novels, anything. Sometimes I play chess online.

>Wait, how are you reading the screen right now?

>I have a Braille display. My computer is just a keyboard and a bar with pins that make the Braille cells, no bulky, useless monitor or speakers.

Kassie wanted to continue but at that moment she noticed her boss, Nancy, approaching with a threatening look in her eye.

>Oh no! I'm sorry, it's 11:00 and I still haven't done any work today, and now I'm in trouble. I gotta go, I'll write again later.

Kassie clicked the IM window shut, her mind reeling. After how hard it had been to say even the simplest things to him, she could hardly believe they were chatting so freely. Their short exchange made her even more curious to find out more about him.

"Kassie, are you listening to me? I want that spreadsheet finished before my 11:30 meeting." Nancy gave her a searching look, as if she doubted the work would be done.

"I'm on it, don't worry," Kassie assured her, trying to look attentive. She had only been Nancy's assistant for a few months, and she didn't want to make a bad impression.

Kassie had first been assigned to the marketing department as the administrative assistant to a woman named Dyanne with a y. At first Kassie was excited to work there with the creative, artsy people, but it soon became apparent that Dyanne was a screeching, ranting maniac, given to taking out her frustrations by yelling at Kassie. Eventually Kassie complained to HR, but instead of disciplining Dyanne, they quietly shuffled Kassie off to Nancy, head of the finance department.

At first Kassie was hugely relieved to be working for Nancy, who seemed in every way Dyanne's opposite. Where Dyanne was sharp and spiteful, Nancy was warm and motherly. But once they settled into a routine, Kassie realized just how boring her job was. Everyone in her division was so stuffy, and she felt like she was wasting her life proofreading reports and sending emails. It was hard not to let her mind wander.

In a burst of activity Kassie rushed through the spreadsheet, and after lunch finished a few other tasks Nancy had given her. At the same time, she was still thinking of her earlier conversation with Jake.

By the late afternoon, she was online again.

>You want to know why I am deafblind, Jake wrote, apropos of nothing.

>Yeah, I guess so.

>It's ok, I don't mind talking about it. My mom had rubella (also called German measles) when she was pregnant with me, that's what caused it.

>oh

>Yeah

There was another long pause, then Jake continued.

>It's pretty common for kids with rubella
syndrome to also be retarded. I think they were
afraid I was too for a while.

>Seriously?

>Well, when I was a baby. It's not like I
could tell them. Even now a lot of hearing
people seem to think there's something wrong
with my brain because I can't speak.

>A lot of people are jerks.

>Haha. But hardly anyone just starts
signing directly to me like you did. They
usually wait for Carter or someone to interpret.

> Really? why? Anyone can do the printing
block letters thing. They don't have to know
sign.

>Like I said, some people think I'm
retarded.

>I thought we weren't supposed to use that
word anymore.

>Oh sorry, should I say "differently
special"?

>Haha.

>But the truth is, I think people are
afraid of me.

Kassie stared at the blinking cursor on the screen,
thinking back to her own first reaction. She had been afraid,
although she wasn't ready to admit that to him. Instead she
wrote,

>You can't help what other people think.
Maybe they're just scared to confront a
disability.

>You're probably right. 90% of the
information humans get about the world is
through sight and hearing. Touch alone can't
compensate. It sucks not knowing what's going on
around you, and not being able to do things for
yourself.

"And then he said how much he hates being
deafblind," Kassie repeated to Erik over dinner.

He cocked an eyebrow at her. "Well, duh. What did
you expect him to say? That it makes his life better? This isn't
a TV movie, you know. Adversity doesn't necessarily make
you a happier, more enlightened person."

"I know. But he's just so matter-of-fact about it. You
know how most guys are not so eager to talk about their
feelings. Everything is about building up their image, whether
they're jocks or hipsters. But with Jake, it's like there's no filter.
He just puts whatever he's thinking right out there. It's
amazing. I've never met anyone like him at all."

Erik did not reply, but only gave her a blank, distracted
look.

Kassie stared back at him. "Hey, are you alright?" she
asked.

"Yeah, fine."

"You don't seem fine. Is something wrong?"

Erik groaned and rose from the table. "Ugh, it's just
work, okay?" He tossed his plate in the sink with a loud clatter.

"Sorry," Kassie whispered, kicking herself. Being an
ASL interpreter meant Erik had to intrude in his clients' most
private moments: child custody fights, bitter divorces, money
troubles, medical test results, all passed through his fingers.
But to maintain confidentiality, he was not allowed to share
any information about any client, no matter what. Kassie tried
not to press him for details, even though she knew some of
the things he saw ate away at him, and talking would be the

best way to get over it. All she could do was leave him alone, and trust that his usual sunny disposition would eventually return.

CHAPTER THREE

Over the next few weeks, almost every time Kassie opened up her email there was the smiley face icon next to Jake's name. She found herself IMing with him more and more, sharing every detail of her day with him: work, ASL class, yoga class, marathon training, brunch with women from her yoga class, drinks with the running group guys and their girlfriends, out to a gay club or a Deaf social event with Erik. Before she realized it, she could hardly imagine not IMing or emailing him about her day, and whatever she was doing, she was always composing a message to him in her head, planning what to tell him to make her ordinary life sound interesting.

>Oh my God, are you running off somewhere again tonight? You do too much, Jake teased her.

>Yeah, well, you do too little, she replied. She glanced up at Nancy's door--still closed.

>Deafblind people have to do things more slowly, he explained. You seeing hearing people are always running around, just so you can say how busy you are all the time.

>Whatever, my friends are even more busy than I am.

>You're only proving my point.

>Ok, but don't you want to get a job? Or at least finish school?

Jake had mentioned that he had taken a few classes at the University of Washington, but not working toward any particular degree. It had taken him until he was twenty to graduate from high school because he was so behind from years of special ed. He lived with his parents in the suburb of Bellevue, the same house in which he had grown up.

>Of course. I want to get a job and move out of my parents' house already, but it's not that easy.

>Why not?

>Well, for one thing, you may not have noticed, but I have this slight problem with my vision. And my hearing. It interferes with my life's ambition to be an airline pilot.

>Only because society has these stupid hang-ups about disability.

>Yes, stupid things like "safety."

>Haha. So come on, can't you at least finish your BA?

>I don't know. I enjoyed it, but I wasn't taking the kinds of classes that would lead to a job.

>So what were you studying?

>Astronomy mostly, and some physics.

>I thought you had to look at the stars through a telescope to study astronomy?

>No, only for observational astronomy, the boring kind. I'm interested in theoretical astronomy, aka, the awesome kind: for instance theories on how the universe was formed. It's all about thinking, not seeing. Human eyes are weak and can only sense a tiny fraction of what's out there.

>I guess I never thought of that before.

>It's true. Did you know that over 80% of the universe is probably dark matter?

>I think I heard that somewhere but I don't really know what it is.

>No one knows what it is, that's why it's so interesting. There are a lot of theories, but basically it's this thing we can't see or detect directly, but observations of other galaxies

shows there's something there. Just think, most
of the universe is made up of stuff no one can
see or hear. So it's not just me, haha.

>That is pretty cool to think about.
Astronomy always makes me feel so tiny and
insignificant, but I guess it doesn't have to.

>Not at all. String theory, quantum theory,
all those things suggest that what we think we
know through our senses may not be how the
universe works at all.

>So why did you stop taking classes?

>There was really only one teacher at UW
who I liked, Prof. Clark. His classes in
theoretical astronomy were great, and he was the
only teacher there who didn't freak out or
hassle me about accessibility. He made it so
easy to take tests or get Braille copies of
readings and lectures, even emailing me
explanations if there were charts or pictures.
And he would talk to me for hours in his office,
not even through Carter, but writing out the
letters on my hand. But then he was denied
tenure.

>Oh no, that's terrible!

>Yeah, he had to leave. He got a job at
some small college in North Carolina. We still
email sometimes but it's not the same. I took a
few other classes after that but it wasn't worth
it. The other professors were always forgetting
to get me the readings, and it was too expensive
to justify hiring Carter for all those hours for
what was basically a hobby.

>Wait, so how did it work taking classes
anyway?

>Painfully and with great difficulty.
Carter would come with me to all the lectures to
interpret. You think we sign fast now, but he
had to go like lightning to get everything the
professor was saying and also describe all the
charts and pictures and everything. Then for the

readings, if it was online I could read it on my
computer, or if it was a textbook I could order
a Braille copy, but if neither worked out, that
was more interpreting for Carter. If I could
submit all my homework and tests online, I could
do it myself, but some professors insisted on
writing longhand, so that was Carter again.

>Oh my God, that's a lot of hours.

>No kidding.

>Didn't UW have disability services?

>Yeah, they had ASL interpreters and
notetakers for the other blind kids, but none of
them knew the deafblind alphabet, and it was
just too hard communicating with them, even more
so if they didn't know the subject. When you're
taking a final exam, you don't want some idiot
who doesn't know what you mean by CMBR and
decides to "fix" it to "come" or "comb."

>Ok, I am also an idiot. What is CMBR?

>Cosmic Microwave Background Radiation.

>Did that really happen?

>Yes, with some kid who claimed he knew ASL
fingerspelling. The moral of that story is,
never use an untrained interpreter.

>Amen to that. But wait, we were talking
about jobs. So you couldn't get a job with using
astronomy?

>Haha, no, the only jobs are for university
professors with PhDs.

"Hey, whatcha doin'?"

Kassie jumped and nearly spilled her coffee in her
hurry to close the browser window. She had been keeping one
eye on her boss's door as she chatted with Jake. She never
even noticed Dave sneaking up behind her. Dave worked a
few floors down in the marketing department, and was the
first friend she had made when she started working there.

Since she was reassigned, he liked to come by and pester her when he was bored, which was often. He wore glasses with thick black frames, his curly brown hair slicked back with gel into a series of frozen waves. It was Dave who had kept her sane through the Dyanne days by cracking jokes and coming up with creative insults behind Dyanne's back.

"What's this about a PhD?" he said, squinting at her computer, even though the only thing visible now was a spreadsheet. "Are you thinking of going back to school?"

"No! Jeez, mind your own business." Kassie felt her face burning red. What if it had been Nancy?

"Okay! Calm down. You know, no one really cares if you IM or email on company time." Kassie glared at him, disbelieving. "Anyway I just came by to ask if you want to go to Angie's tonight after work." Angie's was a tiny dive bar in Belltown, one of the few that had not succumbed to gentrification, and for this reason a favorite of Dave and his friends. Kassie thought it was dank and depressing, but she knew that voicing her opinions would only get her a lecture on the bar's authentic qualities, as opposed to the fake hipster places that had sprung up around it.

"Sure, sounds good," she said.

"Cool. Hey, let's go get lunch," Dave said.

"Shit! Is it lunch time already?"

"Yeah, the food truck with the awesome tacos is only like ten blocks from here. Let's go."

"What, are you high? It's too far, and I'm behind on my work. I'm going to have to eat at my desk."

Dave narrowed his eyes at her. "How long were you on IM anyway? Who were you talking to?"

"No one! Never mind."

He looked like he was getting ready to interrogate her, but that moment Nancy's door opened, and he disappeared

down the hall, whispering "Tacos! You're missing o-ut!" in a
sing-song voice.

Once Nancy had left for lunch, Kassie brought her
sandwich from the break room refrigerator to her desk and
opened her email again. Jake was still online.

>Sorry! she typed with one hand, the sandwich in the
other.

>Where did you go?

>Someone came to talk to me. I thought it
was my boss. I probably shouldn't be doing this
at work.

>We don't have to chat now. I don't want to
get you in trouble.

>No, it's ok. I'm on my lunch break. Anyway
it was just a friend asking me to go out for
drinks tonight after work.

>See, you're running around again.

>It's what people do. Don't you have
friends you go out with?

>Yes, Carter.

>Carter is your intervener.

>He's also my friend. And you're not the
only person I talk to online. I've been playing
a long game of chess with a man in Russia.

>Does he know you're deafblind?

>No, I didn't mention it. There's some
others too. I sometimes write to Prof. Clark,
but he's even more insanely busy than you.

"And then he said he doesn't have any friends except
Carter! Seriously, what the hell? How can they just let him be
so isolated?" Kassie exclaimed to Erik as he served her a bowl
of hand-rolled pasta. She had only been able to stand an hour

of smoke and stale, oily peanuts at Angie's, and decided to bail early in favor of dinner at home.

"Jake, Jake, Jake, that's all I hear from you these days!" Erik burst out. "Hello! Did you even notice the new guy I brought home last night?" She had not. "He's so freaking hot, and the way he signs is like music. And he sent me a thank you text this morning." Erik dug into his pasta with gusto and favored Kassie with a self-satisfied grin.

"Not another one," Kassie groaned. "What, are you fucking every Deaf gay guy in Seattle?"

"Trying to," Erik replied, still grinning.

"Who is this one? Is he new in town? Please tell me he's not in high school." As a minority within a minority, Erik didn't have a big pool to fish in, and his prospects were quickly diminishing. People were starting to talk.

"He's nineteen and already graduated from high school, for your information, Miss Noseyface." Kassie rolled her eyes. "His name is Dillon." Erik continued. "Remember it! I have a feeling this is going to be more than a tawdry one night sta-and," he said, singing out the last words as he disappeared into his room.

Kassie hoped for his sake this was true. After cleaning up the dinner dishes, she helped herself to a peanut butter cookie and settled down in front of her computer. As usual, Jake was online.

>I thought you were going out with your friends tonight, he wrote.

>Nah, I got tired and came home early. Maybe you're right, I do run around too much.

>So why go out if you don't really want to?

>I don't know, it just feels like what someone our age should be doing.

>That seems like a silly reason to do anything.

>Yeah, when you put it that way.

>I think you do it because you're lonely and sad.

Kassie felt her face heat up as the text scrolled across the screen. Her first reaction was to type a sarcastic response, but something made her hold back. Jake could be disarmingly direct but he wasn't intentionally cruel. She had just finished telling Erik how much she liked Jake being so emotionally open. That meant the bad as well as the good feelings, and hers too, not just his.

>I think there's some deep sadness inside you, Jake continued when she did not reply.

>How do you know that?

>You can tell a lot about someone through the hands. The face can lie, but the hands always tell the truth.

>So what can you tell about me?

>That you're pretty.

>Carter told you that.

>Well, there was some...physical evidence as well...

>Hey!

>Hey what? You're the one who put my hand on your chest when we first met.

>Are we having a serious conversation here or what?

>I am being serious. You're good-looking, and on the surface you're lively and energetic, Jake continued, but it's like there's something kind of uncertain or weighed down behind that.

Feeling extremely exposed, Kassie looked at her fingers on the keyboard, wondering how to respond to this. A few cookie crumbs lay scattered around the keys. Slowly, she wiped them away.

>Hello? Are you still there? Jake wrote.

>Yes.

>I'm sorry, did I say something wrong?

>No. You're right. It's just kind of shocking to see myself described like that. I thought I had gotten past it.

>Gotten past what?

>My dad died a few years ago.

>Oh no, I'm so sorry.

>Yeah, it was horrible. And him dying wasn't even the worst, you know?

>What happened?

>It was all when I was in college. Right when I started my freshman year, just two months in, he had a stroke.

>Why? Was he old?

>No one really knows why, maybe because he smoked when he was younger, maybe just bad genes. He wasn't that old. Anyway even after the hospital released him, he couldn't talk, or walk, or do anything for himself. My mom's an RN so she took care of him at home. Therapists came and went, but nothing seemed to help. For over two years, he was like that. Then he had another stroke, and another, and that was the end.

>I'm sorry, that's really terrible.

>The truth is, I was relieved when he died. I've never admitted that to anyone. Do you think I'm a horrible person?

>No, of course not. Why would you even think that?

>Because I could barely even stand to go home to visit. It was so awful to see him like that. Then back at school I couldn't really talk about it with anyone. No one wanted to hear it. It was too huge, too depressing. People avoided me. I hardly had any friends at all.

>So that's why you run around so much now?

>What? No! That has nothing to do with it. I do have friends now, but I still never talk about any of this.

>You can talk about it with me. I don't mind.

>Thank you. That means a lot to me.

They chatted for a few more minutes, but it was late and before long Kassie signed off and rolled into bed. But even after she switched the light off she lay staring into the darkness for a long time. It was such an old pain, thinking about her father. Maybe it was just because more time had passed, but somehow talking to Jake, it felt at last a little easier to bear.

CHAPTER FOUR

Before long the monthly deafblind meetup rolled around again, and this time Kassie arranged to borrow Erik's car and go on her own, while Erik went out with Dillon.

"So do I call this a first or second date?" Erik asked her, staring at himself in the bathroom mirror as he sculpted his short wiry hair into a geometric shape with a handful of gel.

"I don't think you can call a drunken hookup in a club a date. But thanks for letting me use your car."

"No problemo. Have fun on your date with Jake!"

"Oh, please. It's a social services event, not speed dating," she said, plucking fruitlessly at her mass of curls, frizzy with the humidity. Erik just winked at her in the mirror.

The truth was she was looking forward to seeing Jake in person again, now that they had shared so much online. She had been practicing his alphabet. She was still slow, but at least she didn't need to keep checking the chart anymore. Her first instinct had been to put on makeup and the little ass-hugging miniskirt she wore out clubbing, but she realized with a start that it wouldn't matter. Instead she opted for no makeup, jeans and a t-shirt, but her most flattering jeans, and a low-cut t-shirt. She didn't intend to drag Jake's hand onto her boobs again like a shameless hussy, but the thought of sitting so close to him again was kind of exciting.

She arrived early to find Carter in attendance, but no Jake, unfortunately. Carter assured her that Jake would be along soon. Kassie greeted some of the other people there, but before long Carter circled back around to give her some lessons on talking with Jake.

"When he pulls your hands toward him, that means he doesn't understand you," Carter started off, fixing his beady gaze on her as he helped himself to a slice of pizza. "So don't start pulling back--that just makes him more frustrated."

"Yes, okay," Kassie replied. She had truly gotten the message on that one.

"Try spelling the word again. If he still doesn't get it, phrase it a different way. And remember he can't see your face or hear you laugh, so if there's some emotional content, be sure to tell him," Carter continued, picking up steam. "And for God's sake, whatever you do, don't grab his hands and pull him somewhere or force him to touch something. It would be like if someone grabbed you by the back of the neck and forced your head around. Have respect for his hands. Always reach up to them from below. If you want to show him something, just put your hand under his and guide him, he'll follow. You don't have to pull."

"Okay, okay, I never did that," Kassie protested.

Carter then showed her some more signs they used, like how to indicate a question, or spelling out H-A-H-A for laughter. Kassie was grateful for the tips, but why did he have to be such a jerk about it? Didn't he want Jake to have a friend?

Finally about half an hour later, Jake showed up on the arm of an older man who looked a lot like him: same black hair, only tinged with gray, and bright blue eyes. It could only be his father.

"I'll tell him you're here," Carter said, wiping his hands on a paper napkin.

"Sorry we're so late. Traffic was all backed up," Mr. O'Malley apologized, as Carter spelled the letters out to Jake. "Carter, you can take him home, right?" Carter nodded, still interpreting. Mr. O'Malley turned to leave, but Jake tugged at his sleeve and made an inarticulate noise. Kassie realized it was the first time she had heard Jake use his voice. It was low and muffled.

"He wants you to meet Kassie," Carter explained.

"Hi, nice to meet you," she said, extending her hand with her friendliest grin.

Mr. O'Malley shook her hand seriously, giving her a searching look. "So this is the famous Kassie!"

Oh no, Kassie groaned inwardly. How does he know me? What did Jake tell him? Do his parents read his email and IM logs?

"I've, um, heard a lot about you too," Kassie said, trying to sound cheerful rather than defensive. "Jake says you go running. I'm training for a half-marathon right now. Maybe we could all go for a run sometime."

"Uh-huh." Mr. O'Malley continued to stare straight at her, unsmiling. "I don't recall ever seeing you here before. So what brings you to the Center?"

"Well, um, my friend Erik Larson is an ASL interpreter, and sometimes he attends meetups here, and, uh, I've been taking ASL classes so he invited me to come along." She stopped short of mentioning that Erik was not there that night, hoping Mr. O'Malley wouldn't ask to meet him too.

"So you're training to become an interpreter?"

"Um, yeah," she offered, feeling Carter glaring at her. It wasn't really true, but somehow it seemed easier than saying she was learning ASL just as a hobby. "I mean, maybe, if I ever get good enough to be certified."

Mr. O'Malley looked as if he wanted to say more, but instead he took Jake's hand and spelled something Kassie couldn't make out. Whatever it was, it made Jake flush red, then give his father a sort of shove, as if he wanted him to leave.

"Well, okay, you kids have fun," Mr. O'Malley said as he left.

Carter led Jake over to his usual seat, then pulled another chair directly in front of him and gestured to Kassie. "Go ahead."

She sat down, feeling like she was under surveillance. This was not how she had imagined the evening going, not after all their online chatting. She glanced at Carter, then at Jake, who already had his hand out, waiting for her. Not for the first time, she was struck by how handsome he was, even with his half-closed eyes. His dark hair and smooth white skin with traces of a carefully shaved beard, his strong, sharp features and red, curving mouth...suddenly her heart started beating faster as she laid her hand against his, hoping to get back to the way they had been talking online.

Y-O-U-R F-A-T-H-E-R G-A-V-E M-E A F-U-N-N-Y L-O-O-K, she spelled, but already he was pulling away again: *I don't understand.*

Her heart sank. Was it her signing, or the words, or her meaning? She tried again, even slower. Y-O-U-R F-A-T-H-E-R, then paused. He tapped the palm of her hand impatiently, *yes yes.* She intended to add, *I think he's suspicious of me,* but she only got as far as S-U-S-P before she realized she couldn't remember how to spell "suspicious." She paused, and again he tugged at her hands with increasing irritation.

Kassie turned to Carter. "I think you'd better take over."

She had expected Carter to push her aside like before, but instead he sat back in his seat and folded his arms across his chest. "If you want to talk to a deafblind person yourself, you're going to have to try harder than that. Go on, be creative," he said. The look in his eyes said, *I dare you.*

"Okay, fine." Kassie turned back to Jake and squared her shoulders. If he was going to be like that, she would do things her way. Instead of spelling, she signed in ASL, *Your father doesn't like me.*

At least he didn't pull his hands away this time, but he signed back to her *no no no.*

She turned to Carter again. "Does he mean he disagrees, or that he didn't understand?"

"Ask him yourself." But Kassie was already tired of this one topic; she was sorry she even brought it up. Carter added, "And if you're going to use ASL, make sure you put your hands on top of his while he's signing to you. It's the only way he knows you're paying attention to him."

She tried again, with an easier topic. W-H-A-T D-I-D Y-O-U D-O T-O-D-A-Y?

N-O-T-H-I-N-G.

She slumped back in her chair, letting her hands fall to her lap. Her back ached from leaning forward, and her shoulders were all knotted up. This wasn't working at all.

Jake reached forward, searching for her hand, and she braced herself for a rebuke from Carter for having broken contact, but he didn't say anything.

Y-O-U-R F-I-N-G-E-R-S A-R-E A L-I-T-T-L-E F-A-S-T-E-R T-O-D-A-Y, he said.

Kassie sat up straighter. R-E-A-L-L-Y?

O-N-L-Y A L-I-T-T-L-E, he replied.

T-H-A-N-K Y-O-U. Kassie paused, then added I-M S-M-I-L-I-N-G.

From there, things got slightly easier. He asked her about her day, and she told him about Erik's new boyfriend. It was still slow going, but at least they understood each other. After a while she traded places with Carter, and as she sat rubbing her stiff shoulders she noted with dismay how much faster they were going.

"He's still slowing down his signs for me," she commented.

Carter barely glanced at her. "He's adjusting to your capabilities," he said pointedly.

The next morning, Kassie opened up her IM as soon as she got to work. Jake was waiting for her.

>Sorry about yesterday, she wrote.

>Why are you sorry?

>I thought we could talk like we do online, but I still suck at signing. Maybe we should just be online friends.

>But I like talking to you in person.

>You do? I thought I was just annoying you. I feel bad when you can't understand me.

>It will get easier once we get used to each other. But you have to be patient. I told you, deafblind people do everything slowly.

>I know. I'm sorry.

>So what were you trying to tell me about my father?

>I don't know, he was looking at me in a strange way. I think he doesn't like us being friends.

>He said he thinks you have an agenda.

>He said that? What does that even mean?

>I don't know. Sometimes my parents get super protective like I'm still a kid. It's annoying. Just ignore them.

>Do you think I have an agenda?

>No. Really, forget I said anything.

>Oh shit, I think I hear my boss. Later!

Kassie quickly signed off and switched over to a spreadsheet as Nancy emerged from her office, wearing the saccharine grin that meant she was irritated but didn't want to show it. Kassie did her best to concentrate as her boss detailed the report she wanted compiled by noon, but her mind was still on what Jake's dad had said. After dutifully receiving the depressingly thick file, she slipped off to the break room for more coffee. There she found Dave loafing in one of the hard plastic chairs, fiddling with his phone and drinking coffee.

"Oh hey girlie, what's up," he greeted her with an upward jerk of his chin.

Kassie hated the way he called her girlie, especially since she was the only girl in their group without a boyfriend, but she didn't say anything. "Nothing."

Dave narrowed his eyes at her from behind his thick-framed Buddy Holly glasses. "That's a lie," he drawled. "You've been really out of it lately. Something is definitely up." He straightened up suddenly. "Oh my God, are you seeing someone? That's it, isn't it?"

Kassie scowled at him. "What? No, don't be ridiculous. It's just that I have a ton of work." She had no intention of telling Dave anything about Jake. Not that there was anything to tell, at least not anything that he would be interested in. When she started the ASL class he had teased her constantly, until she just stopped talking about it. She helped herself to coffee and went back to her desk.

That evening after work she explained to Erik everything that had happened, the way Jake's father had stared at her, and their later conversation. "And then he told Jake he thinks I have an 'agenda'! I mean, what the hell?"

She was chopping vegetables for stir-fry. Erik threw the onions into the pan, and they sputtered and sizzled. "If it's true what you said that Jake doesn't really have friends, he's probably wondering why you're making such an effort to get to know him," he said, stirring the onions. He looked up at her across the counter. "Seriously, Kassie, where is this all headed?"

Kassie paused in chopping the sweet red pepper to put a sliver in her mouth. "Why does that matter? You're the one who said he's cute."

"Sure. So what's the goal? What do you want to have happen?"

Kassie just shrugged and toyed with the knife. "I don't know, just get to know him better, I guess. You have no idea. He's like, super smart and has all kinds of interesting things to say when he can type online. It's just talking in person that's hard."

Erik's eyes widened suddenly, and he waved the spatula at her accusingly. "Oh. My. God. You LIKE him like him!" Bits of onion fell to the floor.

Kassie turned bright red and looked away. "Maybe, I don't know. Jeez!" she muttered.

Erik just shook his head disbelievingly as he took the cutting board from her and tipped the rest of the vegetables into the pan. "He is cute, I'll give you that. But girlfriend, you've chosen the hardest of the hard cases. Just be sure you think about what you're getting into."

"I know," she said quietly, bending over the chopping board as she finished her task. They didn't say much over dinner. Kassie really had been thinking about where things were going with Jake, even if she couldn't quite put it into words. It had started as curiosity, but the more they talked online, the more she wanted to get to know him. He was so different from anyone else she had ever met. She knew what Erik meant, that she shouldn't lead Jake on unless she was serious, but how could she decide that until she got to know him better?

Just as they were starting their meal there was a loud banging on the front door.

"It's Dillon," Erik explained as he jumped up and bounded through the living room to open the door. "We're going for drinks at the Re-bar."

"You're going to get in trouble when he gets busted with that fake ID," she called after him, but Erik ignored her.

Kassie turned away as they made out noisily in the living room.

Their make-out session finally ended, Dillon swaggered over to the dining table squeezed into a corner between the living room and the kitchen. He was wearing pale yellow sunglasses pushed up on his head even though it was nighttime and a neon green shirt so tight his nipples stood out.

Hey, what's up, he signed to her. Kassie waved, trying to be polite.

As Dillon threw himself into a chair, Kassie felt an almost visible wave of AXE body spray scent float towards her.

Smells gross, Dillon said, indicating the remains of dinner on the table. Erik shrugged sheepishly, and quickly finished the rest of his meal as Dillon waited impatiently, the signs flowing rapidly between them. Kassie couldn't catch all of it, but she gathered Dillon was complaining that his parents were hasseling him about going to college.

I'm so sick of going to hearing schools, he signed angrily.

What about Gallaudet? Kassie suggested.

Dillon turned to her and jabbed a petulant finger in her direction. *Who asked you? None of your business.*

Kassie stood up sharply. *Fine. Enjoy R-E-B-A-R*, she signed, then cleared the plates off the table and carried them into the kitchen.

She was trying to be nice to Dillon for Erik's sake, but it didn't seem to be working. Dillon had been coming by more often lately, but the more she saw of him the less she liked him. She started vigorously scrubbing the dishes. Whatever, there's no way he was smart enough to get into Gallaudet anyway, she thought. She could understand why he objected to a hearing school, but at the same time she had a feeling his avoidance of college was because he didn't want to give up his party lifestyle, not because of discrimination.

As Kassie stacked the clean dishes in the rack, her thoughts wandered back to Jake. It was even harder for him, but he had tried to go to college, despite everything. The fact that he hadn't finished certainly wasn't due to lack of intelligence or to laziness. She wondered how long it was going to take Erik to realize that Dillon was all wrong for him, that he deserved so much better.

After she finished in the kitchen, she went back to the dining table to gather up the remaining plates and glasses. It was apparent that Erik and Dillon had given up on the idea of going out, and had decided to stay in. There wasn't much privacy in the tiny one storey house. Both bedrooms were just off the living room. Erik had shut his door, but she could still hear them all too clearly.

Leaving the rest of the dishes in the sink, Kassie shut herself in her room, turned up her favorite online radio station as loud as it would go, and clicked open IM.

As usual, Jake was online.

>Hey, he typed. what's up?

>I don't know what's worse, Erik going out with Dillon using a fake ID or the two of them going to town on each other right across the hall.

>Again?

>It's like they're shooting a gay porno in there.

>If the doorbell rings and it's some guy delivering pizza, don't let him in.

>Haha. I turned up the music and I'm trying to block all sounds and images from my mind.

>Wow, being a seeing hearing person seems exhausting.

>You have no idea.

As soon as she saw the words flash on the screen she wanted to take them back.

>Ugh, that came out wrong, she typed. I'm sorry! I didn't mean that in a bad way.

>No, it's cool. I'm not that easily offended.

>So can I ask you something?

>Sure, ask me anything.

>Do you ever open your eyes?

>Not really. There's no reason to. I never really learned to control those muscles. I don't ever think about it, so mostly they just stay closed, I guess. Does it look bad?

>No, not at all! It makes you look kind of serious and peaceful, like the Buddha.

>Ok, that's a little weird. So does that mean people will start leaving offerings at my feet?

>Oh no! I meant it as a compliment. You're totally cute.

>I don't think that's true, but ok.

>Uh...since I'm on a roll can I ask you
another awkward question?

>Why not.

>Erik said that some deafblind people use
abbreviations with fingerspelling, like leaving
out vowels or shortening words. How come you
don't do that?

>I don't know, I just don't like to. When I
was little, my mom made a point of always
spelling whole words in complete sentences to
me, and it got to be a habit. So how come you
don't use abbreviations when you IM?

>I guess it just feels lazy and wrong to
me. I prefer to type out the whole word even if
it takes longer, even when I send a text. My
friends make fun of me.

>See, it's the same thing.

>Haha, I never thought about it that way,
but I guess you're right. I'm a language nerd.
English was always my best subject.

They talked more about books--Jake was a voracious
reader, of news sites, science journals, literature, the more
dense the language the better. He liked to read classic novels
online because they were free and easy to find, with no
annoying HTML frames or ads. At the moment he was
working his way through *Frankenstein*, which Kassie had read
in college.

>Is it wrong that I feel sorry for the
monster? Jake wrote one evening. It was getting late, but
as usual Kassie had locked herself in her room for an
extended IM chat.

>No, I think you're supposed to. Kassie paused,
struck by a sudden thought. She was flipping through her copy

of the book while they were chatting. The line "The human senses are insurmountable barriers to our union" jumped off the page. She typed slowly,

>Do you identify with the monster?

>What? I don't know, I didn't think about that. Maybe a little. Like when he was hiding in the woods and watching the poor people in the hut. Wait, let me find the quote:

> I found that these people possessed a
> method of communicating their experience
> and feelings to one another by articulate
> sounds. This was indeed a godlike science, and
> I ardently desired to become acquainted with
> it. But I was baffled in every attempt I made
> for this purpose.

>I know how he felt. Learning to talk, that really was a "godlike science."

>I thought you said you couldn't talk?

>They made me try, hours and hours for years with speech therapists. But it didn't do much good. People don't seem to understand me and I can't hear what they say back anyway. It always seemed like a waste of time to me. Sign is so much better.

>You should learn more ASL signs.

>No, it's too fast, I can't follow.

>But if I promise to go slow, would that be ok? I can't sign fast anyway.

>Maybe. But I still prefer English. Half of ASL meaning is in facial expressions and body language. To me English is more expressive.

Kassie realized that was true--ASL is a visual language. Some signs change meaning depending on the facial expression. Not to mention classifiers, the concept she

struggled with most in her classes. So much of being really
fluent in ASL means giving visual descriptions, but since it is a
language and not pantomime, those descriptions are all
codified, based on handshapes of the alphabet or numbers,
and used to describe classes of things, like flat or round or
fast. Erik was a master at using a well-chosen classifier, but
Kassie could barely remember what they all meant, let alone
remember to use them herself. Since classifiers are all based on
visual cues, she could see how much harder it would be for
Jake to learn them.

Jake continued:

```
    >I really like how complicated the language
is in these old novels. In the next chapter, the
monster says the old man "compassionated" him.
Why don't people write like that anymore?

    >Haha, you're right, it is too bad. I guess
people are impatient with big words or
complicated sentences.

    >People are impatient with everything. In
these utilitarian modern times, no one wants to
slow down to think about the meanings of things.

    >You do.

    >I don't take any communication for
granted.
```

Even after they said goodnight and signed off, Kassie
sat staring at the blank computer screen, thinking over what he
had said about going slow and not taking things for granted.
No one else she knew ever talked about things like that. It was
refreshing, exhilarating, even, to think about the world in a
different way. She enjoyed getting Jake's perspective, she
thought, as she stood up from the chair and stretched, but
there was more than that. As she lay down in bed and turned

out the light, she recalled what Erik had asked her about where all this was leading. She didn't have an answer. All she knew was she wanted to see him in person again.

CHAPTER FIVE

The half marathon took place on Mercer Island, halfway between Seattle and Bellevue. Kassie got a ride across the floating bridge on Lake Washington with Dave and his girlfriend, Sandra, a shy, wispy girl. Sandra never had much to say, but that morning she sat the whole ride with her face turned to the window. Kassie wondered if they had been fighting, but she really didn't want to know. Dave was ranting about his latest discovery, a local band called Degrees of Doug.

"They're going to be HUGE!" he declared, stomping on the gas pedal to emphasize his words. The car lurched forward. Sandra ignored him, and he ignored her ignoring him.

"So where have they played?" Kassie asked, trying to be polite.

"Nowhere yet," Dave replied. "They're still working on a full set."

"So this is just your friend's band that you're trying to pump up?" Kassie felt vaguely disappointed. He had been talking as if they were already rock stars he happened to know, not regular people he was trying to make into rock stars.

"They're going to be HUGE," he repeated. "What they really need is a kick-ass t-shirt. I bet Marty could do it."

"Oh, good idea," Sandra chimed in. "Marty's a brilliant artist," she whispered in awed tones. Kassie rolled her eyes. She found Sandra's big-eyed, little girl affectations profoundly irritating.

When they arrived at the starting line, Marty and Adam were already there with their girlfriends, Tara and Jenny. The guys also worked in their office, in the marketing division with Dave. Jenny was in law school, and Tara worked at another office downtown, doing marketing research. They all greeted Kassie warmly with big hugs, but once the race started she found herself drifting away from the group. Dave was still going on about Degrees of Doug, trying to badger Marty into making a t-shirt to his exact specifications. Jenny and Tara split off together right away. By far the most athletic, they soon left the rest of the group behind.

Kassie jogged along slowly, several paces behind Sandra who was usually the slowest. The sky was overcast but the cool air felt good, and once the pack spread out after the start it was relatively quiet and peaceful. The course was along the northern coast of Mercer Island, and at a few points along the road she could see Bellevue across the lake, looking close enough to touch. Jake is right over there, she realized, wondering exactly where his house was. She knew it was pretty close to the coast. Maybe she was looking at it now without knowing it.

What if Jake were here now, she thought. Could he be running with her? She didn't see why not. He had explained how he ran with a guide, holding a short piece of rope. It was easier than holding a hand or elbow, because with the rope they didn't have to match strides exactly. She imagined him running next to her, with the rope in her hand, then glanced up ahead at her friends. She could only see Sandra and Marty; the others had surged ahead, not wanting to be last.

How different it would feel to be with Jake rather than them, she thought. They could run quietly side by side, rather than prattling on about nothing, or racing to be the first over the finish line. She closed her eyes for a moment, concentrating on the damp, mossy scent in the air, the feel of the breeze on her face. She opened her eyes again and looked over the water to the tiny houses on the other side, wishing Jake was with her.

The evening of the monthly meetup, Kassie came home from work to find Erik and Dillon lying on the couch, watching TV with the closed captions turned on.

"Aren't you going to the meetup?" she asked Erik, doing her best to sign as she spoke, because Dillon was there. It seemed like he was always there lately.

Erik snapped his two fingers onto his thumb. "No, we're going out to dinner."

"What? But I promised Jake I'd be there! Come on, can I at least borrow your car?"

What's she so upset about? Dillon signed, jabbing a finger in Kassie's direction.

She wants to go to the Deafblind Center for a meetup. There's a guy there named J-A-K-E who she likes, Erik explained.

He's deaf and blind? Dillon poked his two crooked fingers in a v towards his eyes and pulled down sharply, his lip curled in undisguised disgust. *Yuck.*

Erik had taught Kassie some crude signs, and now she used one, then added, *How can you say that? You're deaf too.*

Deaf is S-E-X-Y, Dillon spelled with a dramatic flourish. *Deafblind is yuck.* He pursed his lips at her, daring her to argue with him.

Kassie was still formulating an indignant reply when Erik stepped in. "Look, there's that good Thai restaurant right nearby," he spoke and signed at the same time. "We'll drop you off, and you can call when you're done. Okay?"

In the car on the way over Kassie was itching to put Dillon in his place, but she was squeezed in the back seat, and he pointedly remained facing forward as he turned the music all the way up so he could feel the beats. Erik and Dillon signed to each other animatedly; the car swerving slightly as Erik repeatedly took his hands off the wheel.

"Call me when you're done," Erik shouted over the music as he dropped her off.

Have fun with your gross boyfriend, Dillon added at the same time.

Ignoring them, Kassie turned on her heel and hurried up the stairs to the entrance, a light drizzle falling on her hair and jacket. She was already late. Inside, she didn't bother greeting anyone else, but walked straight over to where Jake and Carter were sitting together.

"Kassie." Carter greeted her with a clear note of disappointment as she sat down and pulled off her damp jacket. "We thought you weren't coming."

You mean you were hoping I wouldn't come, she thought, but she tried to sound cheerful as she replied, "Sorry I'm late. I had to wait for Erik to give me a ride."

"Jake is glad you're here," Carter said as he slid over, allowing her to pull her chair up in front of Jake. She put her hands in his, sitting so close she could feel his breath on her face. She took a deep breath and willed herself not to look at Carter, then started signing.

Hi sorry I'm late.

If he was surprised she was using ASL rather than the deafblind manual alphabet, he gave no indication, but only spelled back to her T-H-A-T-S O-K.

Kassie stared into his face: the smooth planes of his cheeks, his pointed chin and high Roman nose. So what if his eyes stayed mostly closed? He was handsome, surely anyone could see that. Dillon's insult still rankled, but she had no intention of telling Jake. There was no reason to repeat such hurtful words, and besides, he seemed to know he sometimes got that reaction. Hadn't he said, *people are scared of me*? She thought briefly of the monster lurking in the woods, desperate to join human society. But that was all far too heavy to talk about while sitting on folding chairs under the fluorescent lights of the community center, with Carter staring at her.

A-R-E Y-O-U O-K? Jake asked, when she did not begin signing immediately.

Yes, she made a fist and nodded it like a little head. *I'm still sore because of* H-A-L-F M-A-R-A-T-H-O-N. She fully expected Carter to scold her for mixing ASL with the deafblind manual alphabet, but Jake seemed to understand, and it was so much easier for her. At least they were communicating.

She told him more about the marathon, how much Dave had gloated and danced around because he finished first in their group. The deal was that the person who finished last had to buy beer for everyone else. Kassie thought it was a little gross how much they would drink after a run. After hanging back for most of the run, she purposely pushed ahead at the end, so she had only been second to last. The last was Dave's girlfriend Sandra, so in the end he called off the bet.

Jake was in the middle of asking her a question when her cell phone rang.

W-A-I-T P-H-O-N-E, she struggled to spell with one hand while fishing her phone out of her purse and flipping it open with the other. Jake waited patiently with his hands on his knees until she was done. She tapped the back of his hand to get his attention.

S-O-R-R-Y, she spelled. E-R-I-K C-A-L-L-E-D.

Y-O-U A-R-E U-P-S-E-T, he stated.

Kassie stared at him, remembering what he said about hands telling the truth. Who else would have noticed such a subtle shift in her demeanor? *Erik is going to a club with Dillon. He said go home by* B-U-S.

J-E-R-K.

Kassie laughed. H-A-H-A. I-T-S O-K.

B-U-T Y-O-U W-A-N-T T-O G-O T-O Y-O-G-A C-L-A-S-S he replied. Kassie was touched to detect a trace of concern in his wrinkled brow.

No, I changed to a different night so I could stay longer here, she explained.

G-O-O-D Y-O-U D-O T-O-O M-U-C-H, he spelled. Then he paused and added, C-A-R-T-E-R C-A-N D-R-I-V-E Y-O-U H-O-M-E.

She traded places again, and waited while Carter and Jake signed back and forth rapidly. "Really, I'm fine," she insisted. "I can take the bus."

"No, it's not safe this late at night," Carter said while still signing. "It's okay, I can drop you both off."

But Kassie knew it was a kind of a detour for him to take her all the way to Ravenna before getting back on the highway to Bellevue. She felt horribly self-conscious as she followed them out to the parking lot, Jake holding Carter's arm with one hand and his white cane with the other. They stood aside as Kassie squeezed into the back seat of Carter's aged two-door Honda Civic. It was musty and the seat was rock-hard, jarring up her spine with every bump and crack in the road.

The silence in the car was broken only when she gave Carter directions to her house. She looked at the back of Jake's head as he sat stiffly in the front passenger seat. She wanted to touch him or sign to him, or something, but it seemed awkward, and she worried about what Carter might say.

"There, it's that light blue house there on the right," she said, pointing. Carter pulled over, and signed something to Jake, prompting him to get up to let her out.

"Thanks, I really appreciate it," she called to Carter through the open door. He waved dismissively.

I H-A-D A N-I-C-E T-I-M-E, she spelled out to Jake as he stood on the sidewalk beside her.

M-E T-O-O, he answered, then raised his flat hand to his lips and lowered it: *thank you*. She still had her hands on his, and for just a brief second, the edge of her little finger touched his lips. Kassie watched him get back in the car and wave to her. Impulsively, she waved back, even though he couldn't see it. With the other hand, she rubbed her thumb against her little finger, which still retained the lingering sensation of his lips, soft and smooth.

The next morning Erik stumbled bleary-eyed into the kitchen for a late breakfast just as Kassie was about to leave for work.

"Hey, sorry about last night," he mumbled, helping himself to the coffee she had made.

"Whatever." She put her dishes in the sink then turned around, glaring at him. "Your boyfriend's an asshole. You know that, right?"

Erik groaned and slid onto the bench behind the kitchen table. "Kassie, please don't start. It's too early, and I'm too hung over."

"I don't care about the ride, but it's not cool for him to say those things about Jake. You'd think that being disabled himself he would be a little less prejudiced."

Erik rubbed his face wearily. "It's not the same and you know it."

"Yes it is!" she exploded. "I know Dillon thinks he's not disabled, like he just speaks a different language, and it's not his problem if other people don't know it. Whatever, that's fine with me. But he thinks he's better than those other disabled people who are gross and *yuck*." She copied his sign sarcastically. "Fuck that shit, man." She stomped across the living room, her chunky heels echoing on the wood floor. Pausing before the front door she called out, "I have a test in ASL, so class might go late. Don't wait for me for dinner."

Erik did not answer.

At work that day, Kassie traded her covert IMing with Jake for covert studying for the test in her ASL class. Her grades were finally starting to improve, and she didn't want to mess it up. Ms. Hansen had become less intimidating and more encouraging. Whenever Kassie had a spare moment at her desk, she clicked over to ASL videos on YouTube, signing to herself low, under the desk where no one walking by might see.

The class was downtown, not too far from her office, but by the evening it was raining hard. Kassie rushed through the wet streets, her shoes quickly becoming sodden. She slid into her desk just as the class was starting. First year ASL had been a big class--lots of students who were just curious, like her, and fulfilling their language requirement. There were a lot of older people too, mostly involved with Deaf churches. They were always asking how to sign words like "atonement" and "covenant." But the second year class was a lot smaller, mostly people with Deaf family members, or aspiring interpreters or social workers.

Ms. Hansen spent the first half hour of class drilling them on fingerspelling, trying to get them to go faster and to avoid looking at their own hands. From there she moved on to discussing appropriate uses for fingerspelling, and Kassie at last found her opportunity to mention the deafblind alphabet.

Deafblind people should learn ASL, Ms. Hansen asserted with precise, forceful signs.

I understand, Kassie replied. *But ASL is difficult for some blind people. They should do what?* She worried for a moment that she had made a mistake, but Ms. Hansen let it slide.

Very few people know the deafblind alphabet. Not enough to be useful. Deaf people should all know ASL, be part of the Deaf community, Ms. Hansen signed with finality. Then glancing at her watch, she signed in bigger gestures, *O-K, test time!*

Kassie slowly rose and shuffled into the hallway with the other students to wait her turn. The class was small enough that Ms. Hansen could quiz each of them individually. Kassie tried to rehearse the conversations for the test as she waited, but she couldn't stop thinking about what Ms. Hansen had said. Everyone seemed to have such definite opinions about Jake and how to talk to him. Carter expected her to use only the deafblind alphabet. Ms. Hansen thought they should use only ASL. But Jake himself didn't seem to mind when she mixed them up. Wasn't that the point, to communicate however you could? But maybe she was doing something wrong.

When it was her turn, Kassie sat nervously at a desk across from Ms. Hansen. The lesson was on question words.

How long have you and your best friend been friends? Ms. Hansen asked.

Kassie understood the signs, but for several moments was unsure how to answer. Who was her best friend? Was it Erik, despite their argument? She felt like she was losing him to Dillon. Certainly not Dave. Could it be Jake? Again she recalled Erik's question--where was this all heading?

Finally she realized she was overthinking, and lamely signed, *Two years,* but she had been too slow. Ms. Hansen probably assumed she hadn't understood. And she knew she was supposed to give a more complex answer, but her hands stalled out. Now Kassie was completely flustered, and her responses to the other questions were just as slow and hesitant.

When she got home from class Kassie found Erik in the kitchen. Luckily Dillon was not around that evening, for once.

"I made sausages and potatoes for dinner," Erik said by way of greeting. "Let me reheat some for you." He bent his tall lanky frame to reach into the refrigerator.

Kassie sank onto the bench behind the kitchen table. "I'm sorry I yelled at you this morning."

"It's okay." He tipped the sausages and mashed potatoes from the plate into a frying pan. "I'm sorry Dillon said that about Jake. He didn't mean anything by it." Kassie cocked an eyebrow at him, disbelieving. "You have to understand, it's a scary thought for a deaf person to be blind also."

"I should think it's a scary thought for anyone," Kassie insisted stubbornly. "It doesn't mean you can be a dick about it."

Erik just shrugged, not wanting to argue. "So how was your ASL test?"

Kassie was touched that he remembered. "Ugh, I totally blew it. Ms. Hansen still scares me. I get freaked out and the signs come out all slow and wrong."

"Yeah, she can be a bitch. She once told me I'm a man-slut. Can you believe that shit?" Kassie did her best to keep her face expressionless. "But anyway she's a great signer, and one of the best teachers around. Don't let her scare you." He expertly flipped the mashed potatoes like a pancake so the bottom would form a crisp.

"Yeah, I guess," Kassie conceded. "But I mentioned the deafblind alphabet in class today, and she said it's better not to use it because not enough people know it. She thinks

Jake should learn ASL. I tried using more ASL with him last night and we finally seemed to communicate better. Is it bad to mix things up? I don't want to do the wrong thing."

Kassie watched Erik slide the sausages and mashed potato onto a plate, hoping he would tell her of course she wasn't doing anything wrong. Instead, as he laid the plate in front of her, Erik gave her the same long, considering stare she had gotten so often from Carter. "Well, just make sure you use real ASL signs," he said at last. "Don't make anything up."

"What? What are you talking about?" Kassie instantly felt defensive.

"If you're going to use a different system with him, at least make sure it's one that other people could use too, otherwise you're just devising a private code."

"So what?" she mumbled around a mouthful.

"You keep complaining about how isolated he is, but if you make up signs, then you're down to a community of only two," Erik explained.

"Okay, I wasn't anyway! Jeez! And he's already in a community of two, just him and Carter," she muttered.

Later that night she logged in to IM.

>It was nice of Carter to drive me home, but he doesn't have to do that every time. I'll make sure Erik can lend me his car next month.

>Sorry, I meant to tell you, I can't go next month.

>Oh no! Why not?

>We're going to visit my grandparents. They live in Bend, Oregon. I'm sorry. I don't want to go, but it's family. I can't say no.

Kassie paused. Two months seemed like an awfully long time to see him again. She definitely didn't want to wait that long. But maybe he did? She didn't want to come on too strong.

When she didn't reply, Jake continued,

>You know, we could meet at some other time. We don't only have to meet at the Deafblind Center.

She felt a little thrill at that thought.

>Yeah, I'd like that. What do you have in mind? Almost immediately her excitement was followed by doubts.

What would be fun for him, and also give them a chance to talk? She remembered him saying he liked to follow baseball statistics, and sometimes went to games with his father.

>We could go to a Mariner's game. My friend Dave knows a guy, and he's always saying he can get me cheap tickets.

>Yes, that sounds great. I'll ask Carter when he can come.

Carter, of course, she had temporarily forgotten. Why had she imagined they would be on their own? It wasn't like it was a date. Besides, she didn't have a car to pick him up. And there was the whole communication thing. Okay, Carter too, then. She would have to ask Dave for three tickets.

CHAPTER SIX

"Three tickets? You sure?" The next day at lunch, she ran into Dave in the break room again. He stared at her as he tipped his chair on the two back legs, his arms resting on the table. His sleeves were rolled up, revealing the tattoos that covered his arms to the wrists in dense patterns of color. But a closer look revealed disturbing images: dismembered baby dolls, a shark attacking an astronaut, a nun opening her habit to reveal enormous breasts. Someone in the office had complained, and he was supposed to keep them covered up at work. Lately he had been rolling his sleeves back a bit more each day, waiting to see how many inches it took before there was another complaint.

"Two friends of mine want to go," she said, purposely not elaborating.

"Those flaky women from your yoga class don't seem like baseball fans," he commented, rocking his chair back and forth.

"Not them."

"Oho!" He brought the chair down with a bang. "So two guys, then? Damn, girlie!"

Kassie scowled at him. "Are you going to get me the tickets or not?"

"Okay, but I want full details afterwards."

"Fine," she lied.

Making the arrangements was surprisingly easy. Dave got her tickets for a Saturday afternoon game. Kassie took the bus down, while Carter picked up Jake in his car, and they met her in front of the stadium. Jake looked the same as always-- jeans and a plain t-shirt under a light windbreaker, long rigid white cane held at his side. As ever, his expression was blank and distant, but when Kassie took his hand to greet him, his face seemed to light up. As he thanked her for getting the tickets, he brushed the fingers of his left hand lightly over the back of hers. Was that a caress? To cover her confusion, Kassie turned away. Before she could respond he was back on Carter's arm, and they were swept up in the crowds heading inside the stadium.

"Good seats," Carter commented as they slowly climbed the stairs.

"Do you like baseball?" Kassie asked, feeling forced to make small talk with him because she couldn't sign to Jake, not with him standing behind Carter and the crowd pressing in on all sides.

"It's okay," Carter shrugged. He was no longer glaring at her angrily, but that didn't mean he had warmed up to her.

When they reached their seats Carter guided Jake in, putting his hand on the back of the chair and helping him stow his long cane underneath, then sat down next to him. Kassie found herself sitting in the outside seat, next to Carter. Her hand still tingled where Jake had touched it. She wanted at least sit near him to see if he would do it again, so she could tell if he really was flirting with her, or if she was imagining things. But with Carter between them, she couldn't even talk to him directly. Relax, she told herself. Just talk normally and let Carter interpret. But she couldn't think of anything to say.

She sat silently, barely watching the game. Carter was signing something to Jake, she assumed telling him the plays, but he didn't seem to be telling him much. Mostly the three of them sat facing forward, alone with their own thoughts. At the first home run, the crowd surged to their feet and cheered. Only the three of them remained sitting down.

Into the third inning, Kassie gradually became aware that there seemed to be an argument going on beside her. Jake was turning red, and signing with sharp, angry strokes, while Carter remained impassive. Jake started yelling something, but it didn't sound like recognizable words. There was a lull in the game, and his strangely muffled voice carried over the din of the crowd. The people in front of them turned around and stared.

Carter stood up suddenly.

"Is everything okay?" Kassie asked timidly.

"I'm going to get some food. You want anything?" he asked as he stepped over her into the aisle.

"Um, a hot dog would be great." She really was getting hungry.

As soon as Carter left, she slid over and tapped Jake's hand. H-I Y-O-U O-K?

I-M H-U-N-G-R-Y he spelled back. Was that really all? He was still flushed, his brows pulled down. He looked angry, but why?

A-R-E Y-O-U O-K? she repeated.

He seemed to hesitate before answering. Y-O-U D-O-N-T W-A-N-T T-O T-A-L-K T-O M-E.

She snapped her fingers and thumb together. *No, I want to but Carter sat in between you and me.*

Jake seemed unconvinced. Y-O-U-D R-A-T-H-E-R W-A-T-C-H T-H-E G-A-M-E.

Did Carter tell you that? she asked. He didn't answer.

At last he said in his looping, uncertain signs, *If you sit over there, don't sign to me, feels like you're not here.*

But I am here, she signed back, emphasizing *here*. *I want to sign to you, no interpreter.*

When Carter returned with hot dogs and soda, Kassie thanked him but didn't get up, forcing him to take the empty seat on her other side. He placed a hot dog in Jake's hand and sat down, giving her a dubious look but not saying anything.

Kassie pointedly turned away form Carter and back to Jake. She attempted to eat her hot dog with one hand while signing with the other, noticing too late that ketchup was dripping onto her lap. She dabbed at it with a napkin, letting go of his hand.

Immediately, Jake started yelling again, and tugging at her sleeve. She dropped the napkin and found his hand again. W-H-A-T?

T-E-L-L M-E T-H-E P-L-A-Y-S, he demanded. Kassie snapped her eyes back to the field. She had totally missed the last few minutes, but something seemed to be happening. The crowd was cheering. She tried explaining, but almost immediately he starting tugging backward.

I-F Y-O-U D-O-N-T T-E-L-L M-E I D-O-N-T K-N-O-W W-H-A-T-S H-A-P-P-E-N-I-N-G. She could feel the waves of frustration radiating off him, as he made an effort to control his anger. Despite herself, she glanced around at Carter.

"Maybe we should trade places," he suggested coolly.

Kassie stood up abruptly, ketchup-stained napkins and crumbs cascading to the ground. She was about to yell something herself, but instead she clenched and unclenched her fists, took a deep breath, then suggested as calmly as she could, "Maybe Jake should sit in the middle."

With great difficulty, they all traded places as the people around them gave them dirty looks and shouted at them to sit down. The game continued, and Carter took over signing the plays to Jake. Every once in a while Kassie tapped his arm to get his attention and tell him something, but he couldn't talk to both of them at once, and she felt awkward interrupting Carter.

At the beginning of the seventh inning stretch Carter stood up and announced, "Jake wants to go home."

Kassie wondered just who had expressed this desire first, Jake or Carter, but she didn't argue. It was getting late, the Mariners were losing badly, the rain had started up again, and she was stiff from sitting in the hard stadium seat. They might as well leave now before getting stuck in the crowd at the end of the game.

Outside the stadium, Kassie waved to them. "Well, okay, the bus is that way. Thanks for coming out. I hope you had a good time."

Carter only nodded, but didn't offer her a ride. She took Jake's hand. O-K B-Y-E she spelled. He waved back.

She slumped down in her seat on the bus ride home, watching the drops of rain slide down the glass, overtaken by a vague sense of defeat. What were you expecting anyway, she berated herself. What does it mean to be friends with Jake? Maybe she should stop trying so hard.

CHAPTER SEVEN

Kassie stayed off IM the rest of the weekend. The days felt lifeless without their chats. To fill the time in the evenings she watched hours of TV, one crappy reality show after another until she finally dragged herself to bed, feeling empty and exhausted.

But Monday morning when she started up her computer at work, there he was.

>Hey Kassie, where have you been? I wanted to talk to you.

>I thought you were angry at me.

>No, you were the one who didn't want to talk to me.

>What are you talking about? I kept trying to talk to you at the game but you got angry. I'm sorry I suggested going to a game. It was a bad idea.

>But I had a good time. Thanks for getting those tickets.

>You had a good time?

>Yes, but I wanted to talk to you more. You have to be more patient with me.

>Me? You're the most impatient person I know! The second you don't understand something or I don't tell you something right away you start yelling and turn all red.

>Sorry. But when I can't communicate I just get so angry. I feel like an astronaut, floating out in space. You have no idea how frustrating it is.

>I know.

>Sorry.

>I wanted to talk to you more too, Jake.

>I kind of suck at crowds. Maybe next time
we could do something simpler.

>Ok.

>I really want to see you again, Kassie.

>Yeah, me too.

The next Saturday Kassie bounced out of bed early,
the sun streaming in through her window. It was the first
sunny day in three weeks, and with a Seattleite's instinct she
knew to take advantage of the nice weather while it lasted. Still
in her pajamas, she logged in to IM. As usual, Jake was already
online.

>Hey Jake good morning!!

>Wow, you're cheerful this morning.

>It's a beautiful sunny day.

>I know.

>Oh yeah? How do you know?

>The air just smells different when it's
sunny.

>For real?

>Also my mom told me.

>Haha. Let's do something fun.

>Ok, like what?

>You said something simple, right? We
could go to the beach. Is there one nearby you
usually go to?

>Chism Park is pretty close. I'll see if
Carter is free.

>No Carter, just the two of us. I'll bring
lunch. We can have a picnic.

>Are you sure?

>Yes, if you promise to be patient with me.

>Haha, yes, ok, I promise.

>Yeay! Ok, I'll ask Erik if I can borrow car.

Kassie cracked her door open and peeked into the living room. Erik and Dillon were sprawled on the couch eating sugared cereal and watching cartoons.

"Hey Erik," she called from the door, "What are you doing today?"

He swiveled around to face her. Dillon stayed focused on the TV. "I don't know. It's my one day off this week. I think I'm just going to lay around, maybe do some yard work. Why?"

"If you're not going out, can I borrow the car for the day? I'll bring it back with a full tank. Please?" She put her hands together and stared at him imploringly.

"What do you need the car for?"

"I want to go to the beach with Jake."

"Can't Carter drive you?"

"No, it's just the two of us."

Erik raised an eyebrow at her. "Are you sure you're ready for that?"

Kassie sighed in irritation. "Come on, we're just going to the beach for a walk. It'll be fine."

"Okay, knock yourself out." He picked up the keys from the coffee table and tossed them to her. "Just come back by the evening. We want to go out later."

Kassie thanked him profusely, then returned to her computer.

>Ok! Erik said yes! We have wheels.

Jake gave her his address, and she printed out a map. She buzzed with excitement as she showered, dressed, and hastily threw together some sandwiches.

"Damn, girlfriend! What's gotten into you?" Erik teased her as he put the cereal bowls in the sink.

"What's gotten into you?" she countered. "Why are you eating that crap? You hate that processed shit." He only shrugged.

It wasn't until she was driving over the floating bridge toward Bellevue that she started to feel uncertain. The thought of being alone with Jake felt a little like crossing the high wire without a net. What if they couldn't understand each other? What if he got angry again? She pushed her doubts aside as she pulled out the map she had printed out, trying to glance at it without swerving into the next lane.

After only two wrong turns Kassie pulled up in front of a smallish gray clapboard house. Bellevue was a wealthy suburb, but Kassie guessed the O'Malleys had moved here before property rates shot up. The house looked old and unassuming. Feeling extremely nervous, she walked up the step and rang the bell.

A large heavy-set woman answered the door. She had a cloud of white hair, frosted gold at the tips, and sprayed up into stiff waves. Her blowsy polyester outfit was embellished with heavy gold jewelry, and a liberal dose of White Linen. She had probably been quite glamorous when she was younger.

"You must be Kassie," the woman said, giving her a critical once-over. Kassie was painfully conscious of her unstyled curls hanging limply over her forehead, her plain pink t-shirt and jeans skirt.

"Nice to meet you, Mrs. O'Malley," she said, sticking out her hand and trying to sound confident.

"Please, call me Irene." Kassie shook her hand, thinking there was no way she could call Jake's mother by her first name. "Do come in." She turned and shouted down the hall, "Bill! She's here!"

Kassie stepped into the entryway just as Mr. O'Malley emerged from within the house, with Jake behind him. Jake's father greeted her, then for a moment no one said anything. Kassie felt horribly self-conscious--it was worse than having Carter stare at her. Leaning forward awkwardly, she took Jake's hand.

H-I L-E-T-S G-O, she spelled.

O-K he answered, I-L-L G-E-T M-Y S-H-O-E-S. He disappeared upstairs.

Kassie tried to look surreptitiously into the living room, half-expecting to see the furniture covered with plastic. It wasn't, but the plaid couch and two-tiered end table were sadly out of date. She guessed they avoided moving the furniture around to make it easier for Jake, but surely he wouldn't care if they changed the flocked wallpaper?

"So Carter tells us you're studying to be a sign language interpreter?" Mrs. O'Malley asked loudly.

Kassie snapped her attention back to Jake's parents. They were still looking at her suspiciously, but with perhaps slightly less hostility.

"Umm, yeah," Kassie mumbled. "But I'm not very good. Who knows if I'll ever qualify?"

"That's not true. Carter said you're quite good," Mr. O'Malley said. Kassie blinked at him in surprise. Carter said that? Had he vouched for her? It was hard to believe that sour man saying anything positive about her.

Jake bounded back down the stairs, now in sneakers and a jacket, and holding his long white cane. Kassie noticed how much more smoothly and confidently he moved in his own house. When he reached the bottom of the stairs, he put his hand out, seeming to sense roughly where she was. She put her hand in his.

L-E-T-S G-O she signed, just as his mother said, "Would you like to come in and sit down for a while? Can I get you anything to drink?"

Your mother wants us to stay, she signed quickly.

Jake shook his head firmly. "Okay, bye Mom," he said. Kassie's jaw dropped open. His voice was low and harsh, strongly nasal, and his enunciation was far from clear--she could barely make out the words, but he had definitely spoken. She had never heard him talk before.

His parents did not seem surprised, but shared a significant look. His mother seemed to be expecting his father to say something, but instead he only shrugged.

"Okay, have a good time," he said to Kassie, then signed something into Jake's other hand. His mother gave him a quick peck on the cheek, and at last they were out the door, Jake holding her elbow with one hand and his cane with the other. She walked slowly to the car, then guided his hand to the door handle. As she turned to get in on the driver's side, she noticed Jake's parents watching them from the doorway. She gave what she hoped was a reassuring wave.

They couldn't really sign to each other while she was driving because she had to keep changing gears, but at least the drive to Chism Park was a short one. Kassie kept glancing over at Jake as she drove. He was sitting very straight, running his hands over and over the tops of his thighs. Was he nervous too?

At the park she pulled the bag with their lunches out of the trunk, then led Jake to one of the picnic tables. She laid out the food and sat down next to him on the bench. Again she felt strangely intimate sitting so close to him, but it would be hard to reach his hands if she sat on the opposite side of the table.

P-E-A-N-U-T B-U-T-T-E-R J-E-L-L-Y O-K? she asked. He nodded his fist, *yes*, and she guided his hands to the sandwich she had laid out. There was so much more she wanted to say, but it seemed difficult to sign and eat at the same time. Starting her own sandwich, she watched him as he took a bite, then another.

His face lit up. *Tastes good*, he signed.

She took his hand. *Thanks. I made the bread.*

He pointed his finger at her. *You?* then added Y-O-U B-A-K-E-D I-T Y-O-U-R-S-E-L-F?

Yes, Erik and I cook all the time.

They alternated between bites and signing, their hands soon sticky with jelly. She had also brought slices of Fuji apples, and chocolate chip cookies, also homemade.

B-E-S-T I E-V-E-R A-T-E, Jake declared when they had finished.

Kassie poured some water onto a napkin to clean off their hands.

Thanks. Then she added, *I was surprised when you spoke to your mother. You said you can't speak.*

You understood me? he asked, and she nodded her fist. *Only a few words, only Mom understands me*, he added. *I don't like to talk.* Then he spelled out, B-E-S-T W-A-Y T-O G-E-T M-O-M-S A-T-T-E-N-T-I-O-N.

Kassie wasn't sure if he was joking, but still she replied H-A-H-A.

After lunch Jake suggested they walk along the trail by the water. There was a sandy beach where children splashed in the frigid water while their parents lounged in the sun, and a playground further back from the water where more children were playing. Kassie did her best to describe it all to him as they slowly walked along. It was hard to walk and sign at the same time, so she mostly spelled the words out, but he seemed to understand her. Most likely, she supposed, because he knew the park well already. He seemed to know also where the trail passed by a low concrete wall, and indicated that they should sit down.

Kassie leaned against the wall, luxuriating in the warm sunshine, and the calming sound of the low waves hitting the beach. Normally on a Saturday she would be running around doing housework, shopping, cooking, a thousand tiny errands. It was pleasant to relax like this, to just be in the moment.

T-H-E S-U-N F-E-E-L-S N-I-C-E, she spelled to him He tapped her hand in agreement but did not reply right away, only sat for some time holding hands.

Then suddenly he asked, I-S T-H-I-S A D-A-T-E?

Kassie froze. Was it a date? Did she want it to be a date? I D-O-N-T K-N-O-W she spelled out slowly, then added M-A-Y-B-E?

There was another long pause, then Jake said, I W-A-N-T T-O K-N-O-W W-H-A-T Y-O-U L-O-O-K L-I-K-E.

O-K. That seemed only fair, Kassie thought. *My hair color is* B-L-O-N-D, she started. *Eye color blue.*

Jake took her hands and gently stopped her signs. *No.* I D-O-N-T C-A-R-E A-B-O-U-T C-O-L-O-R. He gave a little impatient sigh, hesitating for a moment before he asked, C-A-N I T-O-U-C-H Y-O-U?

Kassie felt a flush of heat. It was hard to believe he was asking her this, but at the same time it felt so natural. She looked at his sensitive fingers resting against her hands. Her heart started racing.

She tapped his hand, then brought his hands toward her face. He started with the top of her head, feeling her short curls, then slowly ran his fingers along each of her features, taking in every detail with intense concentration: the curve of her ears, down to her tiny stud earrings, then her high forehead and thin brows, her small nose, round cheeks and pink lips, then further down to her slender neck. He lingered over her necklace, a delicately beaded chain, then lower still, and she was suddenly conscious of how low-cut her v neck t-shirt was. Jake seemed to become aware at the same moment, because he suddenly pulled back, blushing hotly.

She took his hand again. I-T-S O-K, she reassured him. He still leaned in close to her, his long dark eyelashes resting against his pale cheeks. There was something intoxicating about being the object of such concentrated attention.

He put his hand on top of hers. I W-A-N-T T-O K-I-S-S Y-O-U. Kassie stared at his lips, so full and curving, but for just a second, she held back. It seemed wrong somehow-- she wasn't supposed to have these feelings for someone like Jake. What would people say? Erik's words echoed in her mind. Where was this all going?

He placed his hand on her cheek again, rubbing her lips with his thumb, and just as quickly as her doubts had occurred, they disappeared, overcome by desire. She leaned toward him, and suddenly his mouth was covering hers, his soft, warm lips. She kissed him back, then slowly pushed her tongue through his lips. He responded immediately, kissing her more deeply, carefully probing her mouth with his tongue.

The kiss seemed to go on and on, but at last he leaned back with a little sigh. F-I-R-S-T K-I-S-S, he signed to her.

Kassie felt a stab of pain in her gut. His first kiss ever? It seemed so unfair. Of all he was denied, all the experiences he missed out on, to be so cut off from such primal human interactions seemed the most cruel. And what did this mean for her? She already knew he was nothing like the shallow poseurs she tried to date over the past few years, those slick players who went from one girl to the next, pretending to care only long enough to get laid. But for someone with no experience of dating at all, what would he expect of her? There could be no game playing, no hooking up then moving on, she realized. She had to be completely sincere with him.

She slid her two hands together: *Good?*

A slow grin spread over his face, revealing even white teeth. *Yes.* Kassie realized it was the first time she had ever seen him really smile. *I like you.*

She put her hand on his cheek, then leaned in to kiss him again. *I like you too.*

"What's gotten in to you?" Erik looked down at Kassie, who was sprawled out on the couch. He nudged her feet, and she bent her knees up to give him room to sit down. It was past noon on Sunday, but he had just gotten up. Erik sat down with a groan and slowly sipped his coffee. "So how was your date with Jake? We were in such a hurry last night, I didn't get to ask you."

Kassie just stared up at the ceiling with a dreamy look on her face, avoiding his gaze.

Erik poked her knee. "Wait, you're not going to protest? So was this an actual date?"

She lowered her gaze to him finally. "We kissed."

"Holy shit!" he spluttered, choking slightly on his coffee. "Seriously? What were you thinking?"

"It was freaking amazing," Kassie insisted, then added shyly, "I really like him."

"Kassie--"

"What?" She sat up suddenly, folding her arms defensively across her chest. "Are you going to say I shouldn't date him? You of all people?"

"Just, you know, it's not like dating other people. It's going to be difficult."

"It's already difficult," she snapped. "I would have hoped my friends would be more understanding." She heaved herself up off the couch and retreated to her room.

CHAPTER EIGHT

The next Saturday Erik planned to spend the day picking blackberries that grew wild along the bike trail by the university, then making them into jam and canning it. This was a major yearly project, but Kassie noted that he had waited until Dillon was out of town to suggest it.

"I want Jake to come with us," Kassie said.

Neither of them had mentioned their argument of the previous week. Instead, Kassie simply carried on as if Erik had not said anything. She was dating Jake, and that was that. Everyone else would just have to accept it. She tacked up her chart of the deafblind manual alphabet on the refrigerator.

Erik looked at her with dismay. "Seriously? You really think he could help?"

Kassie eyed him defiantly. "I don't see why not. If he can't come, then count me out. I'll do something else with him today."

"All right, fine, whatever. But Carter can drive him over here, right?"

Kassie shook her head. "No Carter, we don't need him." Erik looked doubtful. "No, it'll be fine," she insisted. "You can use ASL with him. If you keep it simple, he'll understand. Or you could, you know, learn..." she glanced meaningfully at the chart on the refrigerator.

Erik groaned. "Does that mean we have to drive out all the way out to Bellevue to pick him up?"

"I'll pay for the extra gas," Kassie offered. "But thank you, I appreciate it. I want him to be part of my life. This really means a lot to me."

Despite her bravado, Kassie's heart was pounding by the time they arrived at Jake's house. He didn't say anything about telling his parents that they were more than friends, and she couldn't bring herself to ask.

But Jake was ready to go the minute she showed up at the door, and arranged a hasty retreat from the house. No awkward small talk this time, he had them both out the door before Kassie had even finished her greeting. If Jake's parents were hesitant about him going out with Kassie again they didn't say anything, just waved and told them to have a good time as she guided Jake back to the car where Erik was waiting.

Erik seemed a bit shy around Jake at first, but once they arrived at the trail and got out of the car, at Kassie's prompting he introduced himself. Kassie was touched to notice that Erik had learned the deafblind alphabet, and Jake seemed to understand him.

W-O-W E-R-I-K S-I-G-N-S F-A-S-T, Jake commented to her. F-A-S-T-E-R T-H-A-N Y-O-U.

Kassie pushed playfully against his hands. M-E-A-N, she spelled, then added H-A-H-A.

Kassie showed Jake how to pull the fat berries from the branches and place them in a sieve. The bushes were so covered with berries the canes hung low, and it wasn't hard for him to find them.

Be careful of T-H-O-R-N-S, she warned.

For a long time, each of them was occupied with picking berries. It was another beautiful, rare sunny day. The only sounds were the occasional whirring of a bike passing, and the buzzing of the insects. Kassie glanced over at Jake, who was slowly, slowly feeling along the canes. Further down the trail, Erik was beatboxing to himself and dancing around as he filled his basket at lightening speed.

When all the containers were full, they headed back home. While Erik set up in the kitchen, Kassie showed Jake around the house; first the living room, then to the left the narrow hall leading to the bathroom and two bedrooms. When they stepped into her bedroom, Jake moved his hand from her elbow to her waist, pulling her into an embrace. She gasped a little as she felt his strong arms encircle her, then stretched up to kiss him. They were both still slightly sweaty, smelling faintly of grass and berries, and the kiss was sweet and earthy. Kassie wanted to go further, much further, but the sound of Erik clattering around in the kitchen stopped her.

Later, she said. *Erik is waiting.*

D-E-F-I-N-I-T-E-L-Y L-A-T-E-R, he replied. He seemed like he was about to say something more, but at that moment Erik turned on his music, cranked to full volume, and Jake immediately noticed the vibrations. They went back out to the living room, and Kassie guided Jake's hands to the oversized vintage box speaker.

Jake laid his head right down on top of it and smiled, that slow, wide grin.

Cool, he signed.

Erik slapped him playfully on the back. *I like this guy*, he said, letting Jake feel his signs, then led him into the kitchen.

In the kitchen Erik boiled the berries and sugar down to a thick syrup, then instructed Jake to stir it to keep it from burning. Kassie mixed together a quick dough for scones, and while Erik prepared the jars for canning, she showed Jake how to roll out the dough, cut it into rounds with a cookie cutter, then transfer the rounds to a baking sheet. She left him to this task, slowly creating each circle of dough, while she helped Erik fill the hot jars with jam, wipe the rims, seal the lids, and set them in the huge pot of boiling water.

When everything was finished, they sat down at the built-in benches by the kitchen table to eat the jam on fresh-baked scones with butter, while the jars sat cooling on the counter, popping softly as they sealed.

Again Jake's face lit up, as if the first bite were a revelation. *Delicious,* he signed.

You never had before? Kassie asked him, and he shook his head, feeling around his plate for more.

Erik spelled something in his hand that Kassie couldn't follow, and Jake smiled again, followed by a strange, gasping kind of sound. Kassie realized with a start that he was laughing.

"What did you say to him?" she demanded, but Erik only winked at her.

Train gone, sorry, he signed with Jake's hands still on his, and at the same time said, "Wouldn't you like to know?"

After all that, they only had time to sit on the couch for a little while before Kassie had to drive Jake back home. He kissed her again, slowly at first, then more vigorously. Kassie placed her hand on his cheek, looking into his face. So often his expression was either blank or stormy, with his brow furrowed in a perpetual frown. But now he was smiling again, and it lit up his whole face. As she kissed him again, it seemed they both wanted to go further, but were holding back. It was all so new and unfamiliar.

W-H-A-T D-O-E-S I-T M-E-A-N *train go sorry?* he asked, imitating the signs Erik had used.

I-T-S A-N A-S-L I-D-I-O-M, she explained. *It means you missed it, I won't say again.*

Funny, he said, and repeated the idiom.

Sorry, does Erik use too much A-S-L? she asked.

No, his signs are fast but I understand, he replied. *I had fun today. Thank you.*

Kassie was hoping that she could spend the next weekend with Jake as well, and maybe arrange it so they could get more alone time, but before she could suggest anything, Jake passed along an invitation from his parents: they wanted her to come over for dinner. This was not what she had in mind at all, and besides, they were so square. She couldn't blame Jake for living at home still, but did his parents have to be so involved? She only talked to her own mother on the phone every few weeks, and she never shared any details about her dating life, figuring it was better to wait until things got serious. So far no one had rated more than a passing mention. She had no idea what her mother would think of Jake, and she didn't intend to tell her anytime soon.

"Ugh, this dinner is going to suck!" Kassie lamented to Erik as she lay on his bed while he folded his laundry.

"Just go! I thought you liked him. This is good, right? And get off my shirt--you're wrinkling it." He tugged the shirt out from under her, and she rolled over with a groan.

"I don't know! His parents make me so nervous, and Carter will be there too. We have so much more fun when he's not around. Why can't we just keep hanging out like last weekend?"

"Look, I can see why you like him, and you two seem pretty great together, so I'm not going to tell you not to try out this relationship thing. But if you're really serious about this, you've got to meet him where he is."

Kassie frowned. "Why do I have to meet his parents like we're teenagers?"

Erik gave her a serious look, and she immediately regretted the whine in her voice. "Kassie, you can't separate Jake from the only people he's close to. I get that you want to be alone, but don't try to come between him and his family, or between him and Carter. They probably just want to get to know you."

"Okay, fine." She knew he was right, but it was hard to admit. "So when is Dillon coming back?"

"Tomorrooooow!" Erik sang out, instantly switching from serious to fluttery. "So take your time in Bellevue--don't come back too early!" He pumped his hips around in a circle.

"Ugh," Kassie said, jumping up off the bed. "Honestly, I don't get what you see in that douchebag," she muttered.

"I heard that! That's it, get out!" he said, playfully swatting her behind with a t-shirt.

CHAPTER NINE

Kassie stared at her reflection in the mirror and tugged hopelessly at the hem of her skirt. Behind her, remnants of at least ten discarded outfits lay scattered on the bed. She just couldn't seem to strike the right note. Not too slutty, of course, but she felt that it was important to dress cute, even if Jake couldn't see her, to let his parents know she was girlfriend material. And that she wasn't a desperate loser. Normally she didn't pay much attention to her clothes, but now somehow everything seemed wrong. Her work clothes were too bland, and her club clothes too revealing. At last she settled on a fitted brown skirt and light blue sweater, which gave her a kind of classic retro 1940s look. She added some chunky shoes and clipped a silk flower in her hair. Good enough.

Erik gave her a thumbs-up as he tossed her the keys to his car, which raised her confidence slightly. But still her nerves were jangling all through the ride to Bellevue, and again she made two wrong turns. It was raining steadily.

Jake's parents greeted her politely, but Kassie instantly noticed that no one else was dressed up. She slid her jacket off reluctantly, feeling horribly overdressed.

"Hello, Kassie." It was Carter, emerging from the hall with Jake on his arm as Mrs. O'Malley went to hang up her jacket. "Don't you look nice?" Was he being sarcastic? She couldn't tell. Reaching around Carter, she took Jake's hand and spelled out H-I.

D-O-N-T B-E N-E-R-V-O-U-S, he told her, giving her hand a reassuring squeeze. His hand was warm and strong. Her heart gave a little leap at this gesture, and her gaze lingered for a moment on his broad chest under a plain white t-shirt. She wanted so much to put her arms around him, to feel his arms around her, but his parents were staring at them.

Mrs. O'Malley ushered Kassie into the large combined kitchen/dining room opposite the living room, also appointed with the same vintage 1980s décor. A wallpaper strip of beribboned geese, now somewhat darkened with age, ran along the upper edge of the walls and around the faux walnut cabinets. Mrs. O'Malley offered her a glass of Coke, and they all sat down at the table.

Dinner was meatloaf with instant mashed potatoes and frozen corn. Kassie helped herself to tiny portions and pushed the food around on her plate, trying to make it look like she was eating more than she was. The conversation was painfully slow. Whenever someone spoke, Carter spelled into Jake's hand, interrupting his meal. Kassie noticed that the unspoken rule seemed to be to wait for Carter to finish before saying something else, so Jake could keep up with the conversation. Jake sat with his head bowed, dipping lower and lower as he concentrated on what Carter was transmitting to him, a thin line of white visible beneath his half closed eyelids. Every once in a while, his mother reached over and pinched his shoulder, and he would straighten up again.

Kassie tried her best, but she was not the kind of person who could strike up a conversation with just anyone, and she had nothing to say to Jake's parents. His father was a middle manager at Boeing, and his mother was a housewife. Mr. O'Malley told a few stories about his work, then asked Kassie about her work and her ASL classes, but from there the conversation ground to a halt.

She looked across the table at Jake, who was surreptitiously pushing corn onto his fork with his fingers. It felt wrong to talk to him through Carter; she longed to sign to him directly, but she would have to wait until after dinner.

"So Jake, do you want to come over again next weekend?" she asked, trying to look at him and not at Carter. "We could take a walk in Ravenna Park."

"I can't. We're going to visit my grandparents," Carter interpreted, as the signs flashed with a staccato rhythm between him and Jake.

"Oh right, I forgot," she apologized, blushing.

After dinner, Kassie helped Mrs. O'Malley clean up while Mr. O'Malley wandered off to the living room and turned on the television. Carter and Jake remained at the table, engaged in what appeared to be a heated conversation.

"Thanks very much for inviting me over," Kassie said nervously as she took the rinsed dishes from Mrs. O'Malley and loaded them in the dishwasher. "It's, um, nice to have a chance to get to know you." She felt like she was reciting lines from a script.

Mrs. O'Malley kept her gaze lowered toward the sink. "Bill and I want to get to know you too. It's not every day that Jake brings a girl home."

"I know," Kassie replied. "I'm the first, right?"

Mrs. O'Malley turned and gave her an unfriendly look, her mouth set in a grim line, but she didn't answer Kassie's question. "Sometimes people, I mean girls mostly, try to hang around Jake for the wrong reasons."

"I'm not..." Kassie gaped at her, unsure how to answer, or even what she meant exactly. It didn't seem like she was talking about sex.

"He doesn't need your pity," Mrs. O'Malley said, handing her a dripping plate.

"It's not like that," Kassie met her eyes briefly, then turned to put the plate in the dishwasher. "I, um, ah, I really like Jake a lot. He's a great guy. I'm not just hanging around out of pity." Kassie's voice quavered slightly, despite her effort to hold steady. Did they really think that no girl could truly be attracted to Jake? He was smart and funny and handsome, and more genuine than anyone else she knew. She wanted to say that, but it was hard to put into words to his mother, especially when she was giving that disbelieving stare.

Mrs. O'Malley looked like she wanted to say something more, but at that moment Carter called to her from the table, translating for Jake.

"If you're done over there, I'll show you around the upstairs."

"Well, I'm not sure..." Mrs. O'Malley trailed off. As soon as Carter spelled out her words, Jake stood up from the table, pushing his chair back noisily.

"Mom, no," he said in his own voice, loud and flat. He moved around the table, keeping the back of his hand against the edge until he was parallel with the doorway. He stopped abruptly and waved in Kassie's general direction. "Come on." His mother looked surprised but did not try to stop them. Kassie took his hand so he would know she was following him.

As they walked down the hall, Kassie noted again how easily Jake moved around in his own house. It wasn't just that he didn't use his cane; his whole manner was more relaxed, confident. He ran the back of one hand against the wall, his other hand holding hers as he led her up the stairs. The lights were all turned off, and Kassie followed him into the dark, feeling a bit as if she were stepping off a cliff.

At the landing, he turned slightly to the left and led her through a pitch black doorway.

M-Y R-O-O-M, he explained. D-O Y-O-U L-I-K-E I-T?

C-A-N I T-U-R-N O-N A L-I-G-H-T? she asked.

S-O-R-R-Y I F-O-R-G-O-T.

He felt along the wall by the door, and snapped on the light, revealing a Spartan room. A twin bed was shoved in one corner and a desk in another, with a dresser in between them, but there were no decorations on the walls or the kind of knick knacks, ironic toys, and pop culture detritus that Kassie and everyone she knew seemed to accumulate so quickly. On the desk was what she took to be his computer--as he said, just a keyboard and Braille display bar next to a hard drive, although she noticed a dust-covered monitor on the floor next to an old castiron Perkins Braillewriter. In the opposite corner was a waist-high stack of bulky Braille books.

Jake shut the door and sat down on the bed, pulling Kassie down beside him.

N-I-C-E R-O-O-M, she said.

Thanks. He smiled at her, that dazzling white grin, and she felt her heart melt within her. He put a hand on her cheek and pulled her in for a slow kiss, although Kassie still felt extremely self-conscious. She could hear his parents downstairs, talking to each other over the TV. Were they talking about her? She couldn't make out the words.

Jake stroked her cheek, then moved his hands to hers again. W-H-A-T Y-O-U S-A-I-D T-O M-O-M W-A-S N-I-C-E T-H-A-N-K Y-O-U.

Kassie felt her stomach seize up in embarrassment. She had assumed that was a private conversation. C-A-R-T-E-R T-O-L-D Y-O-U?

Y-E-S O-F C-O-U-R-S-E.

Kassie's embarrassment only deepened. Of course Carter had told him--that was his job. How often had Erik told her about interpreting everything he heard, and the oblivious hearing people who assumed their offhand comments wouldn't be passed along. She should have known, but she still felt irritated with Carter.

I'm embarrassed, she said.

D-O-N-T B-E. S-O-R-R-Y M-O-M W-A-S B-I-T-C-H-Y T-O Y-O-U.

Kassie laughed despite herself, and kissed his cheek. He found her chin with his fingers, and turned his face to kiss her properly. Kassie leaned into the kiss, running her hands over his solid shoulders. He did the same, then reached under her sweater. It was sweet, but even though she had been hoping for a moment alone with him all evening, Kassie could not relax with his parents and Carter right downstairs.

W-E S-H-O-U-L-D G-O B-A-C-K D-O-W-N, she suggested.

N-O-T Y-E-T, Jake replied.

Kassie gave him a playful little shove. C-O-M-E O-N, she insisted, standing up and tugging his hand, but Jake refused to stand up.

No, he signed, and a dark red flush crept up from his neck to his cheeks.

"Wha...? --oh!" Kassie blushed as well, and sat back down next to him on the bed, but not too close. She tried to sign *sorry* but realized too late she had once again brought his hand to her chest.

Y-O-U-R-E N-O-T H-E-L-P-I-N-G, Jake teased her, smiling.

S-O-R-R-Y, she spelled into his hand.

Y-O-U S-U-R-E L-I-K-E P-U-T-T-I-N-G M-Y H-A-N-D O-N Y-O-U-R B-O-O-B-S, he said, then added H-U-S-S-Y.

H-A-H-A, she spelled.

For a few minutes, they sat with their hands still.

Your mother, father don't like me, she signed sadly, breaking the mood.

I-T-S O-K T-H-E-Y W-I-L-L C-O-M-E A-R-O-U-N-D, he assured her. O-K L-E-T-S G-O.

Kassie followed Jake back downstairs, watching as he made a straight unerring line for his father's easy chair.

Mr. O'Malley stood up. "Jake tells me you need to get home."

"Yeah, sorry to keep you up so late. But thank you very much for having me over."

"You're welcome," he replied, shaking her hand. She noticed he didn't invite her to come back again. Mrs. O'Malley also shook her hand and gave her a quick smile that did not reach her eyes.

Kassie gave Jake a quick hug, feeling all eyes on her, and signed *goodnight*.

But still she couldn't breathe a sigh of relief; somehow she and Carter ended up walking outside to their cars at the same time. Kassie waved once more to Jake's parents, then turned to Carter as they shut the door. It was raining, a persistent drizzle that soaked the pavement.

At the end of the walkway Kassie gave Carter a little wave. "Okay, goodnight," she said. He just scowled at her, and her patience snapped. "What's your problem with me, anyway?"

Carter gave her a searching look, his eyes flicking over her face in a disconcerting manner, as if he were tallying all the ways in which she fell short.

"I've known Jake a lot longer than you," he said, his voice tinged with hostility.

"Yes, I know that." Kassie wasn't sure how to reply. "I'm not, like, trying to come between you or anything." If anything this felt even more awkward than trying to have the same conversation with Jake's mother. Rain was trickling onto her neck, into her collar. "So you agree with his mother? You think I'm only interested in Jake out of pity?"

Carter shook his head. "Bill and Irene are great parents, but sometimes they have trouble thinking of Jake as an adult. But she isn't totally wrong, you know. When Jake was in college, there were one or two girls who tried to get close to him to demonstrate their selflessness."

Kassie wondered how he could know that, but she really didn't want to hear the details. "So it's your job to scare away any potential girlfriends?"

"No, it's my job to explain to him social cues that he might have missed, so he doesn't mistake charity for love."

Kassie folded her arms, feeling defensive. "So you do agree with his mother."

"No, I never said that," Carter said, squinting at her irritably. "I'm just trying to explain why she said those things."

"So then what is the problem?" Kassie burst out.

"I don't think either of you realize what you are getting into, or how much he will be hurt when you decide you can't deal with his disability."

"I wouldn't...it's not...you don't know..." Kassie spluttered, stung. She tried to think of the perfect comeback, but she was too shocked. Did they really all think so little of her? Of Jake?

"I'm just looking out for Jake," Carter warned her before walking off to his car without a farewell.

Kassie felt her blood boiling, and a nasty reply rose to her lips, but somewhere deep within her, a voice whispered to stay calm, take the high road, for Jake. Erik was right, there was nothing to be gained by alienating Carter. It would only make things harder for all of them.

Before things could escalate any further, she turned and got into Erik's car, slamming the door and driving off without looking back. Her heart was pounding, and she had gone several blocks before she realized she was turned around. She hoped Carter hadn't noticed her driving off in the wrong direction.

CHAPTER TEN

The next day at work Kassie was deep into proofreading a report when she heard a rustle right behind her, and a snort. She jumped and turned around, to see Dave laughing right behind her chair.

"Jesus! What the hell?"

Dave just laughed. "You should have seen your face! You were all 'ah!'" He made an unflattering imitation of her. She had a strong feeling he had sneaked up on her to catch her IMing again, but he would never admit it.

"What do you want?" she demanded, turning back to her work.

"Come have lunch with me. There's this new food truck selling authentic Tibetan food nearby. I just got an alert." He flashed his phone at her.

"No, I brought lunch today."

"Come on, this will be a thousand times better than whatever leftover crap you brought. It'll blow your mind. I promise you won't regret it." He leaned over her chair, rocking it back and forth as she tried to concentrate on the report.

"Quit it. Okay, I'll go with you if you just shut up," she snapped.

In the elevator on the way down he commented, "You're awfully cranky today. What is it, boy trouble?"

"None of your business," she said, brushing past him and striding out into the lobby, the hard soles of her shoes clicking purposefully against the granite floor.

Dave loped along easily beside her as they walked out and down the street. "No, something is definitely up. You're seeing someone, aren't you?" Kassie didn't answer. "Come on, tell me! Tell me tell me tell me tell me." He tugged insistently on her hand, swinging her arm around playfully.

Kassie yanked her hand away then paused for a second and glared at him. "Okay, fine, I guess I am kinda seeing someone."

"No shit!" Dave marveled at her. "So who is he?"

"His name is Jake," Kassie replied, dodging a panhandler. "Where the hell is this truck anyway?"

"It's like four more blocks. What does he do?"

Kassie increased her pace. She only had thirty minutes for lunch, and this was starting to seem like a hike. Dave's question had irritated her, and she wasn't sure how to answer. What did Jake do? What should she say? They crossed a busy street, and Dave repeated his question, as if she hadn't heard him. Finally she simply said, "He's deafblind."

"He's whaaaaat?" Dave halted in the middle of the sidewalk, staring at her with wide eyes behind his black framed glasses.

"He's deaf and blind," Kassie repeated more slowly, staring back at him and trying to play it cool.

"What, like Helen Keller?" He was still staring at her in shocked disbelief.

"Yes, just like that," Kassie snapped impatiently.

"You're shitting me."

"Why would I make up something like that? You asked and I told you. Now can we please go find this truck already?"

Dave started moving again, although he was clearly still processing this new bit of information. "So does he talk laaaaaaiiig thiiiiiiis?" he drawled, imitating what he thought a deaf person might sound like.

Kassie's head whipped around, and she stopped dead. "You're a fucking asshole. I'm going back to the office." She started off in the opposite direction, but Dave grabbed her arm.

"No, wait, I'm sorry! Come on, it was just a joke. Jeez, don't take everything so personally."

Kassie shook his hand off her, but reluctantly agreed to continue on with him.

"So how do you talk to him?" Dave asked in a more serious tone, as they started walking again.

"We use sign language," she answered shortly, not wanting to go into more detail. Dave wouldn't care anyway.

"Oh, that's right! You're taking that class or whatever." He waved his fingers in a crude imitation of signing, which earned him another glare from Kassie. "What, was that rude?" He shoved his hands in his pockets, but did not look particularly apologetic.

They found the truck at last and ordered steamed momo, dumplings stuffed with organic potato and free range goat meat, with chili sauce on the side. It was good, Kassie conceded, as Dave rhapsodized about the special blend of chili sauce only available at this truck, but she had to bolt it down, and she was so annoyed with him, the food held little appeal for her. It was starting to rain again, a light mist that nevertheless gradually soaked into her hair.

"Look, I'm sorry I hasseled you about your new guy," Dave said around a huge bite of momo. "It's great that you're seeing someone. You should bring him out with us sometime. We're going to Angie's this weekend. You should come."

She said, "He's out of town this weekend."

Dave gave her a funny look, and she knew he was wondering how Jake could go out of town, how he did anything at all, but she didn't feel like elaborating. Tossing her paper plate into the trash, she started the long walk back to the office.

The weekend seemed strangely empty without Jake
around. His computer was too big to take with him, so Kassie
couldn't even message him. Saturday she found herself missing
him more than she expected, even as she tried to distract
herself by catching up on the laundry and housework she had
been neglecting lately. She called her mother, because it had
been a while. They chatted about the most mundane things:
work, gardening, the weather. As she hung up, Kassie felt a
stab of guilt for not mentioning anything about Jake, but she
just wasn't ready to tell her yet, expecially not after Dave's
reaction. She wondered if she would have told her dad.
Probably not, she conceded, but thinking about him depressed
her further.

Despite her earlier refusal, in the evening Kassie found
herself heading out to Angie's anyway. Lately she had been
wondering if it was even worth it to keep hanging out with
Dave, but she didn't really have anything else to do. Her
friends from yoga class were all older and married. It was
either go out with Dave and his friends or sit at home alone,
trying to drown out the sounds of Erik and Dillon going at it.
Suddenly Angie's didn't seem so bad.

Her friends were already there when Kassie arrived. In
the back corner of the dingy bar, Dave and Adam were
engaged in a heated game of Ms. Pac Man on an ancient
arcade machine, the kind that was like a table with a glass top.
Marty, Sandra, Tara and Jenny sat around a table nearby, with
a giant half-eaten plate of nachos in the middle. When Kassie
joined them they all shouted out her name, and the girls stood
up to hug her.

"Hey, Dave said you're seeing someone," Marty said as
she sat down. Kassie glanced over at Dave. He was half
jumping out of his chair, pounding the buttons, and swearing

at the game. She wondered what exactly he had said about Jake. "So where is he?" Marty asked.

"Uh, he's out of town this weekend," she answered.

"I think it's great that you met someone," Tara said, smiling. "You should bring him with you next time. We want to meet him."

Kassie nodded uncertainly, but already the conversation was moving on to movies they had seen recently. No one mentioned Jake again.

Kassie got up to get a drink from the bar, and as she stood she thought she saw Sandra put her hand on Marty's thigh, but she couldn't be sure. When she returned to the table, Dave had finished his game and squeezed himself in between Marty and Sandra, half sitting on both their chairs, gloating about his win over Adam.

To distract him from trash talking, Adam asked, "Hey, so what's up with Degrees of Doug? Are they ever going to get a gig?"

"Nah, the ukelele player moved to fucking LA. Can you believe that shit?"

They all stared at him blankly until Kassie asked, "So?"

"So they broke up!" He pounded on the table, making their drinks slosh. "Man, that dude was the shit. There's no band without him. But I still have t-shirts if you want one."

It was a tempting offer: t-shirts from a band so obscure they had never even played one paying gig. Adam definitely wanted a t-shirt.

"So much for your new career as a manager," Tara laughed.

They drank another round, then Jenny pulled out a battered old Trivial Pursuit box, and they played an entire game, making up the most ridiculous answers they could think of when they didn't know the real answer, which was often, and elaborate backstories for their fake facts.

Kassie looked around the table as they all laughed together, feeling glad she hadn't stayed home. It was nice to hang out and joke around. And Dave was always easier to take in a big group, with more people around to diffuse the more obnoxious aspects of his personality. The game didn't finish until after midnight. She got a ride home with Tara then went straight to bed, exhausted but happy.

Sunday morning, however, she was missing Jake again, wishing she could IM him and tell him about going out the night before. She killed some time by making bread, and while the dough was rising she did some internet research. Still, the day dragged on. This is silly, she told herself as she kneaded the dough on the kitchen counter. I have plenty of friends. There's no reason to feel so alone just because he's gone for a few days. Still, she was filled with the overwhelming sense that there was no one she wanted to be with more than him.

Her heart gave a little happy thrill when she saw him come online at last, late Sunday night.

>Hi Jake! How was the trip?

>Ugh. Don't even ask.

Kassie typed a sad face, then caught herself and erased it. A colon and open parenthesis would not come through in Braille as anything meaningful. Instead, she typed,

>Sorry to hear that. What happened?

> My grandparents are nice but they don't know how to sign well. Sometimes Carter comes along to interpret, but he couldn't come this time. My mom interpreted but she's not as fast, and I know I was missing most of the conversation.

>That sucks.

>Yes, I know they just skip telling me things because it's too much trouble, or they think it doesn't matter. It makes me so angry.

>Oh no! Did you lose your temper?

>Let's not talk about that.

>Ok, sorry. I wanted to tell you, I did some internet research and found some online classes you might be interested in.

>Thanks, that's really nice of you. But online classes are just videos of lectures, which is pretty useless to me.

>I know, but I found ones that are totally text-based. See, now you can keep studying for free.

She sent him the link, then went to brush her teeth and get ready for bed while he looked around the site.

>So what do you think? she asked, when she came back.

>Wow, that site is really good. How come I never found it before?

>I'm just that good, I guess.

>Haha. I think you're pretty awesome.

>Aw, I'm blushing. I'm sending you a great big smile and a kiss. I can't wait to see you again.

>Me too.

CHAPTER ELEVEN

The week passed slowly for Kassie, but Jake seemed excited about the online classes. She had been looking for astronomy and physics classes, but Jake surprised her by going for computer programming. He finished the first course by the end of the week.

>It's just another language, Jake told her over IM. Actually it's easier to learn a machine language because it's orderly and doesn't have useless distractions like facial expressions or intonation.

>I never thought of it like that.

>I already added some code to my screenreader that makes it easier to read the Seattle Post-Intelligencer website.

>Awesome! Hey, this could be your new career!

>I really don't think completing one free online class qualifies me for any kind of job.

>Oh sorry, I didn't mean to upset you. But it could be eventually, right?

>I suppose a deafblind IT guy is like .000001% more employable than a deafblind astronomer. Maybe.

Kassie let it drop and changed the topic to their plans for the weekend.

First thing Saturday morning she drove out to pick Jake up at home. She still worried what his parents thought of her, but Jake insisted it was fine.

"You don't have to keep coming over," Mrs. O'Malley said as Jake pushed past her out the front door.

"Okay, nice to see you again!" Kassie replied, pasting on a purposely obtuse smile. She waved as they walked toward the car, Jake's hand resting in the curve of her elbow.

On the ride from Bellevue, Jake again sat stiffly in the passenger seat while Kassie drove. She was frustrated at not being able to say more than a few words to him, but he seemed more relaxed, less fidgety than before. How many hours did he have to spend patiently waiting while he was shuttled around, she wondered. Maybe he was used to it.

Back in Ravenna at last they had the house to themselves, as Erik and Dillon had gone out for the day. Kassie pressed shuffle on the MP3 player Erik had left plugged into the stereo and turned the bass up. Jake seemed to like the heavy vibrations emanating from Erik's boxy speakers.

As Jake stood swaying to the beat in the middle of the living room, impulsively she grabbed his hands and began to dance, waving their arms around together and shaking her butt. At first he stiffened up in surprise, but once he realized what she was doing, he tried to match her. She twirled them both around, arms up over their heads, and he gave his strange, gasping laugh. She smiled up into his face, only a few inches higher than hers. He was smiling too, the color high in his cheeks. She put his hands on her swaying hips and pulled him closer to her, then leaned up and kissed him. He wrapped his arms around her, squeezing her tightly as the music pounded all around them. Fire coursed through her veins, and she kissed him even harder.

At last she came up for air. *Dinner now, kiss later,* she signed. Reluctantly he nodded and followed her into the kitchen. Kassie pulled the steaks, potatoes, and broccoli from the refrigerator and lined them up on the counter.

Y-O-U C-O-O-K E-V-E-R-Y-T-H-I-N-G she explained. They went slowly, with Kassie showing him the steaks wrapped in plastic and the cast iron pan before she put it on the stove. She taught him how to use the different parts of his palm as a guide for how the meat should feel for rare, medium, and well done. He was very reluctant to put his hands anywhere near the hot pan, so they compromised, using a timer, a fork, and aroma to tell when the steaks were done. Then she showed him how to chop up the broccoli and steam it, again using the smell and a fork to check that it was cooked just right. She gave him Erik's industrial strength oven mitts to pull the potatoes out of the oven, and they were done.

E-A-S-Y he said, smiling. As they ate at the kitchen table, Kassie watched him feeling for the food on his plate with his fork and carefully cutting up his steak. She tapped him on the shoulder, and he had to put his knife down so she could ask him, G-O-O-D? Y-O-U L-I-K-E?

Jake made the ASL sign for *like*, pinching his middle finger and thumb together near the top of his chest, then went back to eating. Kassie watched him, wishing they could talk over their meal. What was he thinking? Was he bored, or did he enjoy cooking with her? It was impossible to tell, but she didn't want to interrupt him again. She finished her dinner and waited for him to reach out for her.

D-E-S-S-E-R-T? he asked hopefully.

O-K she answered, *But first wash dishes.* R-U-L-E *here, if you cook, must also wash dishes.* She had expected him to complain, but instead he seemed happy to help her, rinsing the dishes carefully and handing them to her to stack in the dishwasher.

For dessert, she scooped up bowls of ice cream for each of them. Jake gulped his down, and was already reaching for her as he swallowed the last bite. He put his arm around her and pulled her close on the bench, then found her lips with his other hand and kissed her, his mouth still cold and sweet.

Without breaking the kiss, he put his hand in hers and spelled,
N-O M-O-R-E W-A-I-T-I-N-G K-I-S-S N-O-W.

Kassie smiled and leaned even closer to him as they
kissed. Suddenly the bench seemed so uncomfortable,
trapping them between the table and the wall. She gently
tugged his arm, and he slid out from behind the table and
followed her into her bedroom, seeming to understand what
she had in mind.

Kassie's bed was just a mattress and box spring on the
floor, but at least it was a double. She yanked his t-shirt up
over his head and pulled him down on the bed beside her,
pressing herself up tight against him, from her lips to her toes,
as she kissed him again and again. They rolled over and over,
grappling, trying to get even closer. He was not that tall, just a
few inches taller than she, but solid and well-muscled. She ran
her hands all over his bare chest, but when she reached down
to unzip his jeans, he stopped her.

Why stop? she asked.

Jake sighed fretfully. F-I-R-S-T T-I-M-E, he explained,
his hands moving nervously. I D-O-N-T K-N-O-W H-O-W
T-O D-O I-T R-I-G-H-T.

Right, wrong, doesn't matter, all the same, Kassie tried to
reassure him, but he only became more agitated, sitting up and
pulling away from her, except for his hands.

I-F I D-O I-T W-R-O-N-G, Y-O-U W-O-N-T L-I-K-E
I-T, he said.

Unsure what to say, Kassie just spelled O-K O-K
repeatedly. I L-I-K-E, she added.

Jake snapped his fingers together. *No no.* I-F I-T-S B-A-
D, Y-O-U W-O-N-T L-I-K-E M-E, he elaborated.

Kassie stared at him, feeling her heart ache for him. His
closed eyes twitched into a frown, and his jaw set anxiously.
She leaned closer and kissed him all over his face, wishing she

could transmit her thoughts directly to him, let him know he could trust her. I L-I-K-E Y-O-U A-L-R-E-A-D-Y, she said. D-O-N-T B-E S-C-A-R-E-D O-F S-E-X. *We practice together, get better each time.* Still his hands remained loose in hers, without attempting an answer, and she guessed he was not convinced. L-E-T-S G-O S-L-O-W, she suggested, unsure if he was really taking her meaning. She elaborated, W-E D-O-N-T H-A-V-E T-O G-O A-L-L T-H-E W-A-Y Y-E-T.

Kassie kissed him again, slowly, moving from his face to his neck, then down his chest, until she felt him relax, and his breathing became slower and deeper. His eyelids fluttered, showing white half-circles at the bottom. Again Kassie felt a strange lingering sense of guilt, as if she were doing something wrong. But that was ridiculous--he had as much right to have sex as anyone else. She thrust the thought aside.

She continued to kiss and caress him, working her way down to his waistband again. This time as she unzipped his jeans with one hand, she spelled to him with the other O-K O-K D-O-N-T W-O-R-R-Y. As she opened his pants, his penis sprang out, already fully hard, poking through the flap in his boxers. She put her hand around it gently, and he quivered all over with a loud, ragged groan. Slowly, she started stroking, but within moments he had gone rigid all over, then with a loud cry, he sprayed all over his bare chest. With a broad grin, Kassie reached over to the box of tissues she kept on the floor beside the bed and helped him clean off.

She kissed him again, trying to communicate her delight, but he still seemed nervous. T-O-O F-A-S-T? he asked.

J-U-S-T R-I-G-H-T, she spelled back.

W-H-A-T A-B-O-U-T Y-O-U?

I-T-S O-K W-E C-A-N D-O I-T N-E-X-T T-I-M-E. Not that she didn't want to, but she was serious about taking it slow, even if it meant waiting. Besides, they would have to leave soon. She lay next to him quietly until the late summer twilight turned the room dim then dark. She wanted to lay like that, next to him, all night. But Erik would be home soon, wanting the car probably. Kassie sighed, wishing they could be more impulsive.

As she drove Jake back home, Kassie thought about getting her own car, but she wasn't sure she had the money. Sharing Erik's car had never been a problem before.

Thank you, Jake said again, as they stood on the front step of his house.

Don't worry, I still like you, she teased.

I like you too, he replied, then found her lips with one hand and gave her a big wet kiss. His other hand strayed down towards her ass.

At that moment, Mrs. O'Malley opened the door.

Unaware of what was happening, Jake continued to kiss her, but Kassie broke away, hurriedly making the sign for *mother*. Mrs. O'Malley stood framed in the doorway, staring at them, her mouth in a perfect O of surprise. Instinctively, Kassie started to step away from Jake, but he pulled her close again and gave her a loud kiss on the side of her head.

O-K B-Y-E, she spelled to him quickly.

At the same time, Mrs. O'Malley recovered enough to offer woodenly, "Kassie, would you like to come in?"

"Sorry, I, ah, I have to get the car back to my housemate," Kassie mumbled, then fled down the walkway. Behind her, she heard Jake say something in his flat, strangled voice that sounded like, "Dammit, Mom!" Or maybe, "Stop it, Mom!" It was hard to tell.

As she drove off, Kassie wasn't sure whether to laugh or cry. Surely now they had proven to Jake's mother that their relationship was not asexual. Even so, Mrs. O'Malley hadn't gotten angry or threatened her, as Kassie was half expecting, but had invited her in. Kassie kicked herself, realizing she should have taken up the invitation, but she couldn't imagine what she would say. "Your son and I made a nice dinner together then I gave him a handjob in my bed"? The whole situation felt ludicrous. Why was everyone trying to keep them apart?

When they were alone together, it felt so right. She sighed, thinking back to earlier that day, and letting the warm, languid feeling of being in his arms wash over her. His sensitive touch and intense concentration was intoxicating. But as she wound her way through the stop-and-go traffic, red brake lights flashing on and off in front of her, doubts started to surface in her mind like wriggling little worms. Despite her calm in the moment, she was a little surprised at how nervous he was about sex. Did she really want the responsibility of being with him? And would he ever get a job and move out of his parents' house? Was it even possible? She didn't want to stop seeing him. It had to be possible. But the details remained fuzzy.

CHAPTER TWELVE

"Kassie, I just met the perfect guy for you. You have to let me introduce you," Cyndi said. Once a month Kassie's friends from yoga class liked to get together for brunch at Sunflowers, a vegan cafe in the Roosevelt neighborhood. Kassie was the youngest in the group; the others were all in their thirties or forties, and well past their first or even second marriages, but they never stopped trying to set Kassie up with any single young men who crossed their paths.

"Well?" Cyndi demanded, her wild, frizzy white curls bobbing.

"Um, thanks, but I think I'll pass this time," Kassie mumbled, toying self-consciously with her soy chai latte.

"Stop trying to set her up all the time," Abby scolded. Abby, who worked at a branch of the public library and always wore garish vintage dresses she bought for a dollar at the Goodwill, thought of herself as a free spirit and was the only one who regularly objected to the others' matchmaking.

"Maybe she's found someone on her own," Gail suggested in her high, reedy voice. She had been an RN for years but now was working on a degree in homeopathy.

"Look, she's blushing!" Lorna cried. "She has met someone!" Lorna's husband was a software engineer, leaving her free to self-publish her poetry and teach knitting.

"Oh my God! Tell me! Tell me! Tell me!" Cyndi brayed, as the waitress brought their seitan scramble and whole wheat cinnamon buns. "I'm sorry to shout," she apologized to the server, "It's just that our dear *dear* friend here has finally met someone special after years and years, and we are *so excited* for her."

Kassie waited quietly for the storm to die down. It was Cyndi who had first befriended her when she started with the

evening yoga class, and invited her to join them for their
monthly ladies' brunch. At first Kassie found them all a little
dingy, and it took her awhile to get used to Cyndi's hyperactive
enthusiasm. But as she got to know them all, Kassie found
their unquestioning encouragement and support for each
other refreshing, especially compared to Dave and his friends'
sarcastic, competitive ways.

"So what's his name?" Abby asked when the server had
left.

"Jake," Kassie said, looking down at her plate and
blushing. Thinking she might as well get it all out at once, she
added in a lower voice, "He's deafblind."

"Whaaaaat?" They all started talking at the same time.

"Like Helen Keller?" Lorna blurted out, her pale eyes
bugging out even more than usual.

"Yes, just like that," Kassie sighed, wondering if she was
going to have this same conversation every single time she told
anyone.

"Wait, so how do you even talk to him?" Cyndi
demanded.

"Did you teach him words like in *The Miracle Worker*?"
Lorna asked.

Kassie goggled at them, unable to even begin answering
such a question.

"He must know ASL," Abby stated authoritatively. She
had learned a few basic signs, part of her sense of civic duty as
a public servant, as she was often reminding them, although
Kassie knew she was disappointed that she had not had a
chance to use it with any library patrons yet.

"Yes, we use ASL and fingerspelling," Kassie said,
grateful for once for Abby's know-it-all attitude.

"Oh. My. God. That must be. So. *Hard*," Cyndi said,
punctuating every word. "I can't *even imagine*."

Their pitying looks made Kassie feel contrary. "Not at all," she replied breezily. "We communicate just fine. And we chat a lot online too," she added. "He's so smart, like you wouldn't believe. He reads classic novels all the time, and he's really into astronomy and computers too. And chess," she babbled on, but even as she spoke, they regarded her with a mixture of horror and sadness. Cyndi and Lorna continued to pepper her with questions. How did he use a computer? A phone? How did he get dressed in the morning?

"How do you, you know, have sex?" Lorna asked in the little girl lisp she affected when she wanted to appear especially earnest.

"What? In the normal way!" Kassie snapped back, not wanting to explain that they were taking it slow and had not gone all the way yet. She was losing patience with these moronic questions. Where was the unconditional support?

Abby sat back and crossed her arms over her chest. "Well I think it's wrong," she said.

"What? Why is it wrong?" Gail leapt to Kassie's defense. "She's helping him!" She laughed uncertainly in her high voice, always teetering on the edge of hysteria.

"So what happens when you break up and move on to someone else?" Abby demanded. "What happens to him then? Are you really prepared to commit to someone like that for the rest of your life? Because if you're not, then you're just messing with him, and it's not right," she concluded smugly.

"He's a consenting adult," Kassie replied defensively. "I'm not his caretaker." She wasn't about to admit she had entertained similar doubts herself, not when they were being so clueless.

"Well I think it's *just fabulous*," Cyndi blustered on. "Kassie, you are a *saint*. A real, living saint."

Kassie could not suppress the urge to roll her eyes, but no one seemed to notice. Gail changed the subject to her niece with Down syndrome, what a lovely and special girl she was, and wouldn't Jake like to meet her? Kassie murmured noncommittally, wondering how she could let them know they were making her crazy without being too rude.

"I don't think they'd have anything in common," she said at last, when Gail still seemed determined to set up a play-date. Gail stared back at her blankly, as if that was hardly a consideration.

"Well I just think its so wonderful what you're doing for that boy," Cyndi repeated as they were leaving, during the rounds of multiple goodbye hugs.

"I'd like for you all to meet him," Kassie offered hopefully.

Even Cyndi looked a bit shocked and wary at the suggestion. "Yes, yes, we'll see," she called out with false cheer as they went their separate ways.

Kassie caught the bus home, feeling exhausted and out of sorts. At home she found Erik sprawled on the couch watching *Law and Order* reruns and eating corn chips. She had intended to go out for a run, but within seconds she was drawn into the show. Before she knew what has happening she was on the couch with him. During the commercial breaks she gave a disjointed account of the conversation over brunch.

"I mean, what the hell!" she burst out, grabbing the remote to turn down the volume on an ad for fast food. "What makes them think I want to hear about every disabled person they ever met? And why would Jake want to meet Gail's niece?"

Erik laughed, but without much humor. "Welcome to the world of disability. People say all kinds of stupid things.

When I was a kid, one of the boys in my class was convinced my dad was a robot because of his hearing aids."

"Yeah, but these are adults," Kassie pointed out. Erik did not say anything, but only raised an eyebrow, making it clear that he doubted their intellectual maturity.

"I thought deafness wasn't a disability." Kassie couldn't help needling him.

"You know what I mean." Erik turned the volume on the TV back up. It wasn't that Kassie disagreed with that attitude, but Dillon's insult against Jake still rankled.

"So where is Dillon?" Kassie asked at the next commercial break.

Erik shrugged. "I dunno, he hasn't texted me." Kassie stared at him, and he shrugged again, self-consciously. "What? It's fine. We're not joined at the hip. I'm sure he'll text me later. It's no big deal." Kassie felt it was kind of a big deal. For all his bravado, Erik was not the casual, friends-with-benefits type. He wanted a boyfriend, not someone who would flake out and disappear randomly, especially not on the weekend. To her, this just seemed like more proof that Dillon was all wrong for him.

Erik deflected by turning to her. "How is Jake?"

"Oh my God, his mother caught us kissing on the front step of his house."

Erik snickered. "But this could be a good thing, right?"

"Yeah, I think so. He told me that he talked to her after, and she seems to be coming around on the idea of us having a real relationship."

"See, his parents aren't so bad." Erik crumpled the empty chip bag and tossed it on the coffee table.

"I dunno," Kassie said. "Get this! I offered to call him by TTY and he said he doesn't have one!" Erik had a TTY, or telecommunication device for the deaf, sitting on the kitchen counter, for calling his parents. It was basically a keyboard with digital text display for the telephone. Kassie was sure there had to be models with Braille display, like Jake used on his computer. But he had seemed completely uninterested when she brought it up over IM.

"Seriously! How can they keep him so isolated!" she ranted. "He just lets his parents relay all his phone calls for him."

"TTY is obsolete technology," Erik said calmly, refusing to get caught up in her outrage. "I think my parents are the last Deaf people in Seattle to still use it. Everyone else just texts on their cell phones, or uses video chat."

"Well, he can't use either of those," Kassie argued. "There has to be something with Braille, right?" But the episode, the third in a row they had watched, now reached the dramatic twist ending, and Erik had already tuned her out.

The next day at work Kassie looked online, trying to find a TTY with a Braille display. She couldn't make much progress, though, because every time Nancy approached her desk, Kassie hurriedly quit her browser, automatically deleting her search history. She had already been reprimanded once for inappropriate use of internet resources on company time, and had cut way back on IMing Jake during work. From her limited searching, though, it seemed clear that although there was once such a device, it was no longer being manufactured.

Kassie resisted the urge to IM Jake right away, forcing herself to wait until she got home. The bus ride from downtown seemed interminable. As soon as she got home she went straight to her computer.

>Sorry I didn't IM you at work today, she typed.

>It's ok. Did you get yelled at?

>Haha, not today. But I still have to be careful, sorry.

>Don't be sorry. Your work is important.

>No, it really isn't. But I need the money. Oh, hey, I looked for a Braille TTY but it seems they're not being made anymore. Sorry.

>It doesn't matter. I told you I don't need it.

>Why not? Don't you want to be able to take phone calls yourself?

>Carter or my parents can interpret for me. Besides, you're the only one who wants to call me.

Kassie didn't reply. Remembering what Erik said about obsolete technology, she decided to drop it. She still couldn't understand why he wouldn't want an assistive device even if he only used it once in a while, but she didn't want to force it on him.

>Guess what, Jake continued.

>What?

>I made steak for my parents last night. They were so surprised! They couldn't believe how good it turned out.

> Yay! That's so cool!! So it came out ok? Did you test it with your finger?

>No, I used a fork. And I remembered how it smelled when it was done. My dad said later they usually don't eat it that rare, but it was so good, he's going to insist I make it from now on instead of my mom.

>Oh no, now you're on the hook, haha.

>Well, Mom's cooking is terrible so it's about time someone else took over.

>But seriously, this is another reason for your parents to hate me.

>Oh please, they don't hate you. Mom wants to invite you over for dinner again next Saturday, but you don't have to come if you don't want to.

> I was just going to say, my friend Dave is having a party that night. Do you want to come with me?

>Are you sure? I'm not the best conversationalist. It might be awkward.

>Yes, I want you to meet my friends.

>Ok.

Kassie felt a happy little thrill.

>I'll ask Carter if he's free, Jake added. Kassie slumped in front of her keyboard. Of course, Carter.

CHAPTER THIRTEEN

Carter was not free the night of Dave's party; he had already booked time with another client. Kassie got the impression that when this happened, Jake would either try to reschedule his plans or resign himself to not going. It took some persuasion on her part to convince him that she could handle the interpreting herself. As for his parents, it seemed Jake was right that they were warming up to her. They didn't object, and Kassie was secretly relieved to postpone the dinner indefinitely.

Feeling like she was back in high school, Kassie borrowed Erik's car and picked Jake up on Saturday evening, waving to his parents as they stood in the doorway. She started the car, but before taking it out of park, she took a close look at Jake. Rather than his customary plain t-shirt, he was wearing a dress shirt buttoned all the way up to the top, and his thick black hair had been parted on the side and brushed down. Kassie didn't want to undermine his confidence, but she couldn't let him go to the party looking so obviously dressed by his mother.

You look different than normal, she signed.

Jake stiffened self-consciously. *No good?*

Normal look is better, she replied. She opened his top button--thankfully he was wearing a t-shirt underneath. *Open is better,* she suggested unbuttoning a few more, then fluffed his hair up so it looked more normal.

Y-O-U T-H-I-N-K I L-O-O-K B-A-D, he said with dismay, seeing right through her attempt to be tactful.

Now you look C-O-O-L, she said, trying to be reassuring.

Now, he repeated, with obvious emphasis, knowing she meant he had looked bad before.

You always look good, Kassie replied, her quick signs betraying her mounting impatience. She felt terrible for starting the evening off on a bad foot by ruining his confidence, but she didn't have time for an extended talk about it. If they didn't leave now, they would be really late. She put the car in gear, effectively terminating their conversation.

On the drive over the bridge Jake remained sitting bolt upright, fingering his cane which lay across his shoulder, projecting into the back seat. Kassie could tell he was nervous and she wanted to reassure him, but all she could do while driving was spell O-K and C-O-O-L to him again when they were stopped at red lights.

Dave's apartment was in Queen Anne, close enough to their office that he could ride his fixed-gear bicycle to work and brag about never owning a car ever again. A year ago Kassie had wholeheartedly agreed with him, a conversation that came back to her as she had to circle the steep hills again and again in ever wider concentric circles, looking for parking. At last she was able to wedge the Acura into a tiny spot, going forward and back about twenty times.

"Good enough," she said to herself, even though as she stepped out of the car she noticed she was still over a foot away from the curb.

Walking around to the other side of the car, she took Jake's hands.

Don't be nervous, she signed, shaking her hands in imitation of someone feeling jittery.

I-M T-O-T-A-L-L-Y C-A-L-M, he lied, pushing at her hand playfully so she knew he was joking. *You're the nervous one.*

She had finally told her friends about Jake, and about him being deafblind, a week before when they were all out running together. No one really said anything; they just stared at her as they were stretching before the run. Actually she was a little surprised Dave hadn't told them himself. But at least their reaction was not like Dave's or her crazy yoga friends' had been, so she decided to be thankful for that. It will be fine, she reassured herself as they walked up the street together through the steady rain, Kassie balancing a plate of cookies in one hand and an umbrella in the other, Jake clinging to her elbow.

Over the previous few days Kassie had listed for Jake the people in the running group, hoping it might make things less confusing, and they agreed she would refer to each of them by the first letter of their names in ASL fingerspelling, as a kind of quick name sign. Despite having spent much of her free time with them, running or hanging out in bars afterward, Kassie found herself hard pressed to give any meaningful description of her friends to Jake. He wasn't interested in their appearances, hair color, or fashion sense. She told him anyway about Dave's tattoos, and that Marty had even more tattoos and had stretched his earlobes with plugs the size of quarters. But as for their personalities, she couldn't say much more than things like Jenny is really good at Trivial Pursuit, or Tara doesn't like to drink beer, or Adam collects vinyl records of old educational albums for kids. Jake gamely commented along with her marathon messages, but Kassie was left feeling like she had done nothing more than list a series of fashion choices and personal quirks.

After a long slog uphill, and up two sets of stairs, they finally reached Dave's apartment. The door was open, so Kassie wandered in with Jake trailing behind her, holding his cane straight upright. Sandra, Jenny, Tara, Marty and Adam were lounging in the living room, Snow Patrol playing on the vintage hi-fi, outfitted with an iPod jack.

"Hey," Kassie said weakly, waving. "Sorry we're late. This is Jake." She quickly fingerspelled everyone's initials, hoping Jake remembered them and understood what she meant.

Dave emerged from the kitchen, a towel over his shoulder. "Kassie!" he thundered, and crushed her in a rough embrace, then with a big show of camaraderie did the same to a startled Jake.

D-A-V-E, Kassie spelled in his hand, just to be sure, when Dave released him.

"Hi my name is Jake," Jake said in his slow, thick, flat voice. The consonants were almost completely rounded off.

Everyone stared at him for a full minute, with more or less undisguised looks of embarrassment. Kassie started to wonder if maybe they simply hadn't understood. Should she repeat it? Sign something to him? Or what?

But then Dave suddenly burst out laughing, and clapped Jake hard on the shoulder, making him jump again. "Hey dude, welcome!" he shouted. "Let me get you some beers."

"Hey," Kassie hissed to Dave as they followed him into the kitchen. "Don't shout, okay? He can't hear you no matter how loud you talk." Dave only laughed as he handed them each a Pabst Blue Ribbon, then turned back to the refrigerator and started pulling out packs of ground beef.

Oh God, he hasn't even started cooking yet, Kassie thought with dismay. It was already past eight o'clock, and she was starving. Their only contribution to dinner was a plate of cookies, which she left in the kitchen. She led Jake back out to the living room. Jenny and Tara, who had been talking quietly but urgently together, glanced up at them, then retreated to a corner of the room. Marty, Sandra and Adam clustered around the stereo, looking through Dave's playlist. Kassie and Jake took up a position perched at the far corner of the hard Ikea sofa. She put their beers on the coffee table so it would be easier to sign; Jake didn't seem interested in drinking his anyway.

Y-U-C-K, he said, handing it to her. Then he added, I-M H-U-N-G-R-Y.

M-E T-O-O, Kassie said. On the coffee table was a bowl of corn chips, which they ate in large quantity; after awhile Kassie felt kind of gross, but still hungry.

Meanwhile Sandra, Adam, and Marty left the stereo to sit at the opposite end of the coffee table and quickly fell into conversation, with Dave interjecting comments from the kitchen. The topics veered widely from work to TV to movies to sports, peppered with lines from favorite comedies quoted with only the most tangential referent. Kassie found herself torn between trying to make a comment that would get her included in the conversation, while also translating for Jake and letting him know who was talking and what they were doing, all while unthinkingly gorging herself on chips.

As the minutes ticked by Kassie realized, somewhat frantically, that she was failing on every level. The physical gulf between her and her friends widened as they shifted or got up to get another drink and came back. Even Jenny and Tara gave up their private discussion to join the others again. Soon they were all clustered at one end of the living room, with her and Jake at the other. The conversation meandered on. Kassie had barely managed to say more than a few words, and was feeling increasingly invisible. She could feel Jake's frustration mounting as she relayed snippets of the conversation. She had gotten faster at spelling, but it was starting to feel like their first attempts at conversing again, as he kept pulling his hands back: *I don't understand.*

All jokes, repeating movies, T-V, she signed. N-O-T-H-I-N-G T-O U-N-D-E-R-S-T-A-N-D, J-U-S-T J-O-K-E-S.

I-S I-T F-U-N-N-Y? Jake asked, poking her hand with some insistence. Kassie noticed the color starting to rise in his cheeks.

I D-O-N-T K-N-O-W K-I-N-D O-F, Kassie replied. She felt terrible for not being able to convey more of what was going on, but there honestly wasn't much to translate. They had moved on to rehashing some in-jokes.

A-R-E T-H-E-Y L-A-U-G-H-I-N-G? Jake asked. Kassie nodded with her fist. He gave a sigh, and for a moment she was worried he might start yelling, but luckily just then Dave announced the burgers were ready. She passed along the message, and they stood along with everyone else to get some dinner.

Dave's original idea for the party had been to have a cookout in Gasworks Park, but it had rained steadily all day, so in the end he shifted the location to his apartment. Kassie was secretly relieved: the park, while scenic, was so contaminated that signs warned visitors not to let their dogs dig in the dirt, and she didn't like the idea of eating there. But since Dave had already bought the food they had burgers fried in the pan, along with whatever paltry salads the others had thrown together at the last minute and brought along.

Once everyone resettled around the coffee table with dinner plates, the divide between them was less stark, and Kassie made a determined effort to draw her friends into the conversation with Jake. Turning to Jenny, who sat down next to her on the sofa, she said, "So, um, are you going to train with us for the full marathon next month?"

Jenny flipped her long brown hair to her right shoulder and turned to Kassie. "Yeah, I guess so."

Jake was still eating, but Kassie tapped his hand anyway and passed along what Jenny had said, then added, "Jake likes running too."

Jenny nodded. "That's nice," she said blandly.

"Maybe he could come with us sometime," Kassie suggested.

"Mm hmm," Jenny answered, looking purposely noncommittal.

"How...?" Sandra asked, her whispery voice barely carrying from where she was squeezed in at the end of the sofa on the other side of Jenny. "I mean, how does he...?" She trailed off, her eyes wide with concern.

Ask him yourself, Kassie wanted to say. She was painfully aware that she was doing the whole interpreter thing wrong. They should be addressing Jake directly, and she should be translating rather than talking for him, saying "I" instead of "he." She'd seen Erik do it dozens of times, heard him gripe about bad interpreters who distanced their clients from the conversation. But she couldn't bring herself to scold her friends, and she couldn't figure out how to turn the situation around.

"He holds a rope, with someone leading," she explained quickly. She tried to sign as she spoke, but she couldn't do two things at once, and her hands kept stopping.

Sandra leaned forward curiously, watching Kassie signing, with Jake's hands resting on top of hers. "Are you really making words?" she asked breathlessly. "Does he really understand all that?"

"No, I'm just making it all up as I go along," Kassie snapped sarcastically. She'd had it with Sandra's stupid questions and her affected little baby voice. "Of course he understands me. ASL is a language, you know. Anyone can learn it."

Sandra pulled back, looking hurt. "I was just curious," she whispered. Jenny snorted with laughter, not out of any allegiance to Kassie, but because she openly disliked Sandra and was on a campaign to get Dave to dump her.

Kassie had ceased signing to Jake during this exchange, but evidently he could tell that she was saying something, because now he was signing *What? Tell me!* insistently. Their burgers were going cold on their plates.

N-O-T-H-I-N-G she replied.

Jake snapped his fingers together in sharp, angry movements. *No, not nothing.* Kassie felt as if she could see the anger boiling up within him from his belly up to his face, which turned red as he opened his mouth and gave a strangled, incoherent shout. Instantly everyone else in the room stopped talking and turned to stare at him.

T-O-O L-O-U-D Kassie spelled frantically, and to her relief he stopped.

"There a problem, girlie?" Dave's smirking voice rang out in the appalled silence.

Instead of answering him, Kassie asked Jake, *You want to leave now?*

No.

Kassie breathed out, only now realizing she had been holding it. *Ok, I'm sorry. I'll try harder,* she signed. Turning to Dave, she said, "It's just hard to translate when the conversation goes by so fast."

Dave shrugged and rolled his eyes, then got up to get another beer, but no one else dared to speak. Kassie realized they were all waiting for her to say something, to give a cue for how to proceed. She cast about desperately for some easy conversation topic that didn't revolve around movies or TV.

"So, um, Tara? You know, Jake grew up in Bellevue too." Tara was sitting on the floor in front of the coffee table, across from them. She was the kind of tall rawboned athletic girl who bought all her clothes at REI, a girl whom Kassie had come to think of as the quintessential Seattleite. The rest of them had all moved to Seattle from somewhere else; only Tara was a native.

"Oh really?" Tara had been looking distracted all night, but when Kassie spoke to her, she seemed at least seemed slightly more engaged than Jenny or Sandra. "What street?"

Kassie duly translated, and as they exchanged small talk, the other girls drifted off to the kitchen, while Adam and Marty went back to discussing the latest Sigur Rós album.

"So your parents are still in Bellevue?" Tara asked. "Where do you live now?"

Fighting her instinct to answer for him, Kassie passed along the question, then Jake's reply: "He lives with them." She still could not bring herself to say "I" instead of "he." If she changed pronouns now, it would be even more weird and confusing, she thought.

"Oh." Tara looked embarrassed.

After a few more banal exchanges Tara announced she was going to get more food, and disappeared into the kitchen.

You O-K? Kassie asked Jake. *Want more food?*

No, I-M O-K, he replied. Kassie took his plate and placed it on the coffee table. He had hardly eaten anything. She rolled her shoulders, which had become unbearably tight, and looked closely at Jake, trying to see him as her friends might. He was perched stiffly at the end of the sofa, his back straight, but his head drifted off to the side and down. His eyes, as always, were closed, but his eyelids and eyebrows tended to jump and jerk as he was thinking, and he sometimes moved his mouth as well. She had become so accustomed to these tics that she never noticed them anymore. How long until her friends could see past it?

Jake rubbed his hands along his jeans, sighing as his head dipped even lower. He did not usually show emotions in his face, but Kassie had learned to read his other cues, and she knew what this meant: he was bored.

Still she hung on stubbornly for a little while longer. They ate some of the cookies she had brought for dessert, and Kassie again tried in vain to get the group interested in including Jake in their runs. Finally she asked Jake again if he wanted to go. He would not answer directly, only asking what she wanted to do.

O-K L-E-T-S G-O, she said, feeling defeated. They said their goodbyes, but when Jake stuck his hand out to shake, no one took it.

Kassie heaved a sigh of relief the moment they stepped out the door. The rain had slowed to a drizzle. As they hurried back to the car she started to feel anxious again. Once they were seated inside she took Jake's hand. *I'm sorry you were bored. Why not say you want to go?*

I-T W-A-S I-M-P-O-R-T-A-N-T T-O Y-O-U, he answered simply.

Kassie felt her heart break just a little. W-E C-O-U-L-D H-A-V-E L-E-F-T E-A-R-L-I-E-R, she clarified.

I W-A-N-T Y-O-U T-O B-E H-A-P-P-Y, he said.

Kassie threw her arms around his shoulders, pulling as close to him as she could with the gear shifter between them and kissed him on the cheek. She took his hands again. *Together with you, I'm always happy*, she signed, trying to put all the emotion she felt into her hand movements. *I'm sorry my interpretation is no good.*

Yes, I-T-S E-A-S-I-E-R W-I-T-H C-A-R-T-E-R.

Kassie sat back in the driver's seat, stung. All the warm, affectionate feeling from a moment ago dissipated, she started the car and slowly edged out of the spot. Like before, she had to pull forward and back at least ten times before she was confident that she was clear.

When she got home from dropping off Jake it was close to midnight, but Erik was out, as she had expected. Nor did she see him at breakfast the next morning, but by noon he dragged himself out of bed to sit vacantly over a cup of coffee, looking hung over and tired. He stared at Kassie as she kneaded and slapped a fragrant round of bread dough on the kitchen counter.

"So how was the party last night?" he asked.

Kassie rolled her eyes, smacking the dough down angrily. "It was a total disaster. Can I just say, I fucking suck as an interpreter."

Erik grimaced at her. "I could have told you that you were setting yourself up for failure. You were trying to do two separate things, interpret and be part of the conversation."

"I've seen you do that all the time with your parents," Kassie said defensively, her curls bobbing as she kneaded more vigorously.

"That's different. I am the Jedi Master of the 'terps," he said, adding a few flamboyant signs as he spoke. "Besides, I've been interpreting for them since I was three years old. You guys are still getting used to communicating with each other. It takes time. If you're going to interpret, you have to let the conversation flow through you."

Kassie made a little moue of frustration as she shaped the dough into a round loaf and slid it back into a bowl to rest. "But it wasn't just me," she said defensively. "They were all being jerks and refusing to talk to him."

Erik shrugged as he slid his lanky frame out from the built-in bench. "I can't help you there."

CHAPTER FOURTEEN

Kassie found herself increasingly frustrated with the routines of her life. Up every morning, try to look professional, or at least presentable, for a long boring day at work. Nancy, her boss, had threatened, only half jokingly, to send Kassie back to Dyanne if she didn't start getting her work done more efficiently, so she didn't dare IM with Jake at the office anymore. Monday and Wednesday evenings she had ASL class, Thursday nights were yoga class, and Tuesdays she met Dave and the others to train for their next run. She felt less and less like running lately, but since they had agreed to meet on Tuesdays to fit her schedule, she couldn't easily blow them off. All that activity meant she rarely got online before ten pm, and then it took all her willpower to sign off and go to bed by one am, leaving her tired and cranky the next day.

By the weekends she was exhausted, but it was her only time to see Jake, that is, if Erik let her have the car. He usually did, but if he had a client, that was that, they had to wait for the next week. Kassie could not bring herself to ask Jake's parents to drive him to her house and pick him up again, like they were children. She had looked at some used car listings in the paper, but anything even halfway decent was far more than she could afford, and she would not ask her mother for help, not with the huge debts left after her father's illness. She still had not brought herself to mention Jake to her mother.

Riding the bus back and forth from work each day, Kassie found her thoughts drifting toward Jake, reliving the moments when they were together: his sensitive fingers on her skin, the look of his mouth split in a rare grin, his intense concentration when they signed together. Just reliving those moments gave her a warm rush, but soon after doubts would come creeping in. When they were together, there was no one else she wanted to be with more. But there was no denying that it was hard. Communication had gotten easier--he was learning more ASL from her, and she had gotten faster at fingerspelling. But the logistics of meeting up wore her out. And she felt depressed and annoyed whenever she thought back on the disastrous party. Would they ever have a normal relationship, she wondered. Was it even possible?

Kassie knew Ms. Hansen would tell her that thinking in terms of "normal" was ableist. Kassie should meet Jake where he was, not expect him to adapt to her. But doing that all the time was exhausting. She hoped it would get easier the longer they were together, but what if, like Carter said, she just got more and more tired until she couldn't take it any more?

Whenever Ms. Hansen brought up disability rights in ASL class, Kassie couldn't help talking about deafblind issues. She had been a little hesitant at first, after the lecture she had gotten about the deafblind alphabet. But she soon realized that Ms. Hansen actually liked it when her students challenged her, and sometimes even made outrageous statements just to provoke them into debate. Deaf culture is very direct, she was always reminding them. People just say what they think, no wasting time with empty formality.

One week Ms. Hansen assigned them to research an assistive communication device and prepare a speech explaining how it worked. It was clear the point wasn't so much to research something new as to have a topic to practice signing. But Kassie was still wondering about the Braille TTY. A more thorough internet search confirmed that it was no longer being manufactured. But there was something else instead, called a deafblind communicator. As far as she could tell, it was a cell phone paired with a Braille notebook computer, kind of like a big laptop with a Braille bar display below the keys. The seeing hearing person could use the cell phone to type a message, and the deafblind person could read the message in Braille, then type back, and the message would be displayed as text on the cell phone.

Kassie jumped up, her heart beating hard. How amazing would that be! She brought up her IM account immediately and pasted in the URL.

>Hey! Check it out! she typed excitedly. Jake took a few mintues to read through the page.

>Yes, I've heard about that, he replied at last. Kassie was disappointed by his lack of enthusiasm.

>Just think, you could use this to talk to anyone. Like at Dave's party, you wouldn't need me to interpret. You could talk to everyone there directly.

Jake had seemed to shrug off the experience of the party more easily than Kassie. She got the impression that experiences like that were not so uncommon for him, especially when Carter wasn't around. But it didn't have to be that way! An image of him red, shaking, shouting, as his anger and frustration boiled over flashed before her eyes.

>Come on, she typed, why aren't you more excited about this?

>Did you see the price? It's $6000. I don't have that kind of money lying around.

>Oh, I didn't see that.

>You sighted people, always jumping ahead before finding out all the details.

>Sorry.

>It's ok. I've thought about it before. It would be a great thing to have, but I can't ask

my parents to pay that much when I'm not even
working.

>But you do want to find a job, right?

>Of course I do! You think I like sitting
around feeling useless all the time? But who's
going to hire me? It's not like I have potential
employers beating down my door. And even if
there were, I wouldn't know they were there.

Kassie let it drop, feeling bad that she had upset him.
She wished she had an answer for him about how to find a
job. It seemed to her the device would make it easier for him
to get a job, but he said he couldn't afford it until he started
working. He had accomplished so much just getting through
high school, but then it was like he got stuck. She didn't know
what to say to him.

They said their goodnights and logged off. It was past
midnight, but Kassie felt keyed up. Wondering if Erik was still
up, she peeked out her door. She noticed the light was on in
the kitchen. Erik was sitting at the kitchen table with a bottle
of vodka.

"Hey" she said, helping herself to a glass of water. "Still
up?"

Erik just shrugged. "How's Jake?"

Still standing by the sink, Kassie told him about the
deafblind communicator. "Seriously!" she ranted. "How can he
not want one right away? And his parents! Oh my God, how
can they not care?"

"I'm sure they care," Erik said wearily. "Six thousand
dollars is a lot of money."

"He said he wants to wait until he gets a job, but who
knows when that would be."

"You know how hard it is for someone with a disability
to find a job," he pointed out. She did know. Dillon didn't
have a job, he just lived off his SSI and his parents, but she

secretly thought he was the kind of slacker who would do something like that even if he were hearing. "For a deafblind person, it's really, really hard to find an employer willing to take a chance."

"I know. But come on! It's like since Helen Keller went to Harvard, that's it, deafblindness is solved. That was a hundred years ago!"

Erik laughed, but his voice had a strangely flat, humorless tone. Kassie looked at him more closely. His eyes were ringed with red, and his face was ashen.

"Hey, are you ok? What's going on?" she asked, sitting down on the bench beside him.

"Dillon broke up with me," he said, pouring himself another shot.

"Oh God, I'm so sorry! Jeez! And here I was babbling on about my own shit instead of asking about you." She slid over next to him and put an awkward arm around his shoulders, but even sitting down, he was so much taller, she had to reach up. Her touch did not seem to comfort him. She drew her arm back after a moment. "I'm so sorry," she said again. "What happened?"

Erik gave an exaggerated moan. "I don't even know. One minute we're all happy and the next he's sending me a text saying it's over."

Kassie had noticed that Dillon hadn't been over in quite some time, and that Erik seemed to be going out less. "Did he seriously break up with you by text message?" Kassie was outraged. "That fucking asshole. He could have at least told you in person."

"Ah, it doesn't matter. He has a hard time dealing with shit like that face to face."

"I can't believe you're making excuses for him," Kassie fumed. "Did he even say why?"

Erik shrugged. "Nah, but I know. It's because I got too serious with him too fast and scared him off. He's not good with the heavy emotional shit, you know?"

"I'm sorry he hurt you, but you know it's better this way, right?"

Erik's glazed eyes suddenly narrowed and slid over to focus a bit unsteadily on her. "Fuck you."

"Oh come on! He's an asshole! You deserve so much better!"

"You don't know anything about him. He's had a really hard life. You know, his parents are hearing and never bothered to learn ASL properly. They can barely sign. He's like, invisible to his whole family."

"So that gives him the right to be a dick all the time?" Kassie knew she was being unkind, but she couldn't help it. Erik ignored her and tossed back another shot.

"It's my fault," he moaned, his words starting to slur. "I should have taken things slower, given him space to work out his issues. Why do I always do this? Stupid! Stupid!" He pounded his head with his fists.

"Ok, that's enough," Kassie declared, grabbing the bottle as he started to pour another shot. "Let's get you to bed."

"Noooooo!" Erik groaned and clung to the bottle, but eventually she managed to herd him into his bedroom, where she pushed him down on the bed fully clothed and turned out the light. By the time she was done brushing her teeth she could hear him snoring loudly.

The next morning Kassie stumbled into the kitchen to find Erik already there, standing by the sink with a cup of coffee, staring out the window at the backyard, a vacant expression on his face. He looked haggard and gray.

"You're up early," she commented. "Are you feeling okay?"

"Client," he muttered, setting down his cup and disappearing into the bathroom. Kassie heard him turn the shower on. She felt sorry for whoever had hired him to interpret that morning. She finished her breakfast but he was still in the shower, so she used the time while waiting her turn to make a lunch to bring to work. At last Erik reappeared, still pale, but at least looking clean and professional.

Impulsively Kassie gave him a quick hug. "I'm sorry about what happened," she said. He just stared at her blankly, not speaking. "Oh hey, you know the deafblind meetup is next week." Kassie and Jake still met there every month; despite his complaints about the meetup, Kassie found that once Jake was set in a routine he was reluctant to change it. Erik had stopped attending while he was seeing Dillon. "You should come along," Kassie said. "Everyone there is always asking for you. It'll be fun."

"Okay," he said flatly, but she couldn't tell if he was agreeing to go or just indicating that he had heard her. He nodded vaguely, then left.

Later that day as she was eating her lunch in the break room at work, Kassie found herself across the table from Dave.

"'Sup, girlie!" he greeted her. "How's the pinball wizard?"

"Fuck you," she replied. "I am truly not in the mood today, okay?"

Dave leaned back in his plastic chair, making a great show of hurt and outrage. "Okay! Jeez! It was just a little joke." He leaned forward again, letting the legs of the chair slam down. "You used to be cool. What happened to your sense of humor?"

Kassie just scowled at him, at a loss for what to say. She wanted to ignore him, but it stung just a little bit. It was true--

back in the Dyanne days his wisecracks had saved her sanity, but lately she had less and less patience for him. Was being with Jake making her lose her sense of humor?

When he realized he was not going to get a rise out of her, Dave rambled on to other topics. He was thinking of starting a blog about his fixed-gear bike. Or maybe that plus reviewing downtown food trucks. But he didn't want to use a premade webpage design, that was like, totally fake, but he was having trouble convincing one of his coworkers to create a kickass design for him for free. Eventually he got around to mentioning that Marty had just asked them all to go for drinks at Angie's that Saturday night.

"I have plans with Jake on Saturday," Kassie said.

Dave looked uncomfortable. "Oh. Um, maybe..."

"Don't say maybe he could come along, because last time at your house it was a total fail," she cut in before he could finish the thought. "You all treated him like some kind of freak."

"Hey, hey, ease up there! That's not true!" He held his hands up in front of him, as if warding off her attack.

Kassie folded her arms over her chest. "It's true. You all refused to talk to him."

"Well, it's not my fault we don't have anything in common. What was I supposed to say? 'Felt any good books lately?'" He snickered and repeated it while pretending to feel an imaginary book, enjoying his own joke.

"Oh my God, what is wrong with you?" Kassie burst out. The other people in the break room suddenly stopped talking and stared at her. She balled up the plastic wrap from her sandwich and tossed it in the trash. "I have to get back to my desk," she muttered.

"See, no sense of humor," Dave called after her as she stormed out.

CHAPTER FIFTEEN

To Kassie's surprise, Erik did accompany her to the deafblind meetup. He had stopped mentioning Dillon's name, although he still was uncharacteristically subdued. They drove over to the Center in silence.

Once inside, however, they were greeted with noisy enthusiasm by both the interpreters and their clients, many of whom tended to vocalize while they signed. Erik perked up a bit at this outpouring of affection.

"Erik! So good to see you again! Where've you been hiding?" Mandy, a heavy-set woman with streaky blond hair, greeted him with a hug. They had often worked together.

"Hey, there's someone here I want you to meet," she continued, gesturing toward a bearded man with close-cropped dark brown hair, full sleeve tattoos, and fang-shaped plugs in both ears, dangling just below prominent hearing aids. He was engaged in what looked like an intense conversation with an older woman. "Kevin here is with Work Seattle, you know, the employment agency."

Making a mental note to talk to Kevin later, Kassie wandered away to look for Jake but found Carter instead.

"Mike just called to say there's a huge backup on the floating bridge," Carter said by way of greeting. "Jake will be late."

"Oh, um, okay," Kassie said, shuffling her feet. Carter still had a way of making her feel an inch tall. She reached for a slice of pizza to avoid having to make small talk with him. But they were slightly separated from the rest of the group, and everyone else was signing animatedly in pairs, standing or sitting close together. Erik had started signing with Kevin the employment counselor on the other side of the room. Kassie felt stranded. She could feel Carter's eyes boring into her as she gulped down the already-cold pizza. She instantly regretted taking it, because now her hands would be greasy for talking to Jake. There didn't seem to be napkins anywhere.

"You need to be nicer to Jake's parents," Carter informed her in an accusatory tone, again without preamble.

"I...what?" Kassie mumbled, wondering how she could escape from this conversation.

"Mike and Irene," Carter elaborated irritably. "They're good people. Don't be so judgmental about them just because they're not cool like your hipster friends."

"I'm not judgmental!" Kassie flared, but with a touch of guilt, because she did feel impatient with their suburban blandness, with Mrs. O'Malley's terrible cooking and polyester outfits. And they way they let Jake be so isolated, yes, that was the main thing.

Carter merely stared at her coolly. "You have no right to judge them for how they raised Jake," he said. "They've done an amazing job with him."

That hit more closely home. "Oh no?" Don't pick a fight, don't pick a fight, she told herself. "So why do they just let him sit around the house and do nothing all day?" The words slipped out before she could stop herself.

"Let me tell you something, Kassie," Carter said, taking a step closer to her and folding his arms over his chest. "Do you realize how hard it is to raise a deafblind child? It was a full time job for both of them when Jake was growing up. It doesn't matter how great the therapists and interveners are if the parents aren't on board too. Do you realize how rare that is? For the parents to even keep the kid at home? They had specialists urging them to put him in an institution, saying that he could never go to school. Everything Jake has achieved has been because his parents fought for him, every step of the way."

Kassie shifted from foot to foot, feeling like she was about to cry, unsure if it was because of Carter shaming her, or hearing this about Jake's childhood. "I didn't know," she whispered.

"I thought you didn't," he replied. "All these people here," he waved at the rest of the group, "they grew up Deaf but they could see until they were teens, most of them. They went to regular schools or Deaf schools. It was a different experience."

"Okay yes, I did know that," Kassie said, her irritation rising again. "But if they can have jobs and live independently, why can't Jake? I get that even graduating from high school was a huge deal for him, but it's like he got to that point and just stopped." She felt ashamed of the tinge of desperation that was creeping into her voice. This wasn't her fight, wasn't that what Carter was trying to tell her?

Ignoring everything she had just said, Carter only replied, "If you really want what's best for Jake, then don't be so rude to his parents."

"But I haven't--"

"I know you only had dinner there the once. You go to pick him up but never go in. Would it kill you to be a little friendlier?"

Luckily for her, before she could formulate a response, Jake showed up on the arm of Mr. O'Malley. As Jake's father bemoaned the state of traffic on the bridges, Kassie fumed silently to herself. And another thing, she thought, I know Jake could find his way in from the parking lot on his own if you only let him. You don't need to ferry him in every single time.

"Well, you kids have fun," Mr. O'Malley said in the self-deprecatingly corny tone he used every time.

"Oh wait, before you go, I wanted to ask you," Kassie said suddenly, just as he was turning to leave. "Maybe we could all go running on Saturday? If you're free?"

She made the invitation fully expecting him to blow her off, as he had the first time they met, so she could prove to Carter that the unfriendliness was not on her side. But to her astonishment, Mr. O'Malley smiled and said, "Sure, that sounds like a great idea."

They paused while Jake and Carter exchanged rapid-fire signs, then Carter said, "Jake wants me to come along also."

"Okay, sounds great. I'll see you at six AM on Saturday, then," Mr. O'Malley said. He signed something quickly to Jake and left. Carter led Jake to a chair, then sat back to let Kassie take his hand.

W-O-W I D-I-D-N-T T-H-I-N-K H-E W-O-U-L-D S-A-Y Y-E-S, she said.

S-U-R-E W-H-Y N-O-T? Jake seemed unsurprised.
I thought your father, mother don't like me.

Jake gave an impatient sigh and shifted in his chair. *Father, mother like you*, he signed back to her emphatically.

Kassie realized with a pang that she was annoying him with this question. She tried to ignore Carter smirking at her in the chair beside her as she signed back to Jake, *Running on Saturday will be fun. I'm excited.*

Not too early? he teased her, his fingers moving lightly, playfully.

Yes too early! So tired, she replied, with deliberately slow movements, reflecting how tired she would be. *But I will do my best!* He smiled at her, a flash of white teeth opening his normally closed face. She felt a warm glow in her chest, and suppressed a strong urge to lean forward and kiss him.

Y-O-U A-R-E S-O H-A-N-D-S-O-M-E W-H-E-N Y-O-U S-M-I-L-E, she spelled to him, moving her fingers as quickly and discreetly as she could, although she knew Carter almost certainly had picked up her meaning anyway.

Jake flushed dark red. *No no no*, he said. N-O-T H-A-N-D-S-O-M-E.

I think you are very handsome. Why say no?

Deafblind make bad sounds, bad face, seeing hearing don't like, he answered quickly. Once again Kassie felt like she had stumbled into a difficult discussion, one she would rather have in private, but she didn't want to just dismiss what he had told her.

No, she signed vehemently. *Doesn't matter.* Y-O-U A-R-E G-O-O-D-L-O-O-K-I-N-G Y-O-U J-U-S-T H-A-V-E T-O T-R-U-S-T M-E O-N T-H-A-T. *Trust me*, she added in ASL, ending by giving his hand a little shake for emphasis. When he didn't respond, she asked, *You don't trust me?*

Finally he smiled again. O-K O-K *I trust you.* P-U-S-H-Y. *Can't say no to you.*

H-A-H-A-HA, she spelled back to him, at last feeling more at ease. From there they moved on to chat about other things and the time flew by. Erik came over and said hello to Jake, then indicated it was time for them to leave. They all stood up together.

O-K B-Y-E, Kassie spelled to Jake, feeling awkward again. She wanted so much to kiss him, a real kiss, like a real girlfriend, but the vaguely official, institutional atmosphere of the Center, with Carter and all the other interpreters watching, made it feel wrong somehow. She settled instead for a quick hug and a kiss on the cheek, which made him stiffen and turn pink.

Y-O-U-R-E S-O C-U-T-E W-H-E-N Y-O-U B-L-U-S-H, she said.

He swatted at her playfully. S-T-O-P. But he didn't seem to really mind, and it felt so good to joke around. She poked him in the ribs, and he reached for her to do the same, until Erik stepped between them.

"Okay, enough, you guys. Plenty of time for that later. Let's go." She signed good night to Jake, and gave him a discreet kiss on the cheek. As she waved goodbye, Kassie couldn't be sure, but she thought she saw the hint of a smile on Carter's sour face. And she realized he hadn't interrupted their conversation once, but just sat back and let them carry on however they liked.

"Hey, where is that guy from the employment agency?" she asked as she and Erik walked out.

"Kevin? He left already."

"Oh no, I was hoping he'd come over and talk to Jake."

"That's okay, he'll be back next month." Erik paused as they were getting in the car. "He, um, didn't get around to talking to everyone before he had to leave, so he's going to come back next time." Kassie squinted at him in the orange glow of the street lights. Was he embarrassed?

"What? You monopolized him the whole evening?" she demanded. Erik slid into the driver's seat, ignoring her question. "Wait, is he gay?" He turned started the car, still not speaking, his eyes trained carefully ahead. "Oh my God! You dog! I can't believe you prevented him from doing his job just to flirt with him. You know this is a meetup, not a dating service."

Erik slammed the car in gear and slid his eyes over to her. "You're one to talk," he said, and they both laughed.

As they drove home Kassie told Erik about her plans for the weekend. She had already planned to pick up Jake on Friday afternoon and bring him over for dinner. But that meant she would have to drive him back home the same night, then be back in Bellevue early Saturday morning to go running. All that driving back and forth was such a pain in the ass. If they were a normal couple he could just sleep over, or she could sleep at his place. But there was no way she was going to ask to sleep at his parents' house. Having him sleep at her place was a whole other battle, but since it would not really solve this particular problem it didn't seem worth bringing up.

"It's not fair," she complained to Erik. "Normal couples don't have these problems."

"Enough with the 'normal' bullshit," he scolded her. "It doesn't matter anyway, I have a client on Saturday so I can't let you have the car."

"Shit! I'm sorry." Kassie felt genuinely bad. She was presuming too much lately, and it really was his car.

"Just take the bus," he suggested.

"Oh God, I hate the fucking bus," she groaned. But there was no other way, besides asking Mr. O'Malley or Carter to pick her up, and that she would not do. Back at home she checked the schedule online, and it seemed that if she got up at five AM and took the first bus, with a transfer downtown, she could make it there by six thirty. Hopefully Jake's dad wouldn't mind starting just half an hour later. She set the alarm both on her clock and her cell phone just to make sure she wouldn't oversleep.

Chapter Sixteen

The first half of the trip to Bellevue, Kassie spent the bus ride from Ravenna to downtown staring out the window at the dark and deserted streets, daydreaming about the night before. She and Jake had made dinner together, roast chicken and potatoes. He was very hesitant to touch the raw chicken, but for dessert she showed him how to mix together a simple chocolate cake. She pulled an old kitchen timer out of the back of a drawer, the kind with a dial and a buzzer, and gave it to him to time the cake. When it rang, he could feel the vibration as it sat on the table. She told him to keep it, in case he wanted to try making the cake at home.

Erik came back from dinner at his parents' house to find Jake filling the dishwasher while Kassie put the leftover food away.

"Wow," Erik said, watching Jake carefully rinse each dish, feeling along its surface to be sure there were no bits of food left. "How much do we have to pay him for this?"

Kassie laughed. "You know, I think he really likes doing housework. It makes him feel useful, I guess."

Erik shook his head. "Yeah, well tell him he's welcome to move in here anytime."

He meant it as a joke, but once he'd planted the seed, she couldn't get the idea out of her head. Why not? Isn't that what couples did? Move in together? Later that evening as they lay half-naked in bed together, she was strongly tempted to mention the idea to him, but held back. It had been about half a year since they got together--maybe it was still too soon to start talking about living together. After all, they hadn't gone all the way with sex yet either.

He was still hesitant despite her reassurances, still worried that he wasn't good enough. After the first time he didn't have such a hair trigger, and she showed him how to get her off, placing his fingers in her most sensitive spot and moving in a circle, first slowly then quickly. With his delicate touch it felt amazing, and as he learned to read her cues he got better each time.

That night as they lay facing each other, he started almost agonizingly slow, then built to a crescendo of nearly impossible intensity. She clung to his shoulder and yelled right in his ear as he brought her to a shuddering climax, thinking surely he could feel her breath against his skin, could tell from the way she writhed around, how good it felt.

She really didn't care that they hadn't had intercourse yet. It was his lack of confidence that was the problem. He still could not believe that he was objectively good-looking. They went around and around on that point. Did he think she was just with him out of pity, she demanded.

No, he replied, Y-O-U-V-E G-O-T-T-E-N U-S-E-D T-O M-E.

She couldn't change his mind, convince him that he did not look ugly, or make strange noises. Well, he did sometimes make strange noises, especially when he was excited or angry about something. And during sex, but that wasn't bad, in fact she kind of liked it. His voice was all him, like no one else's. She tried to explain it, but in the end she worried that she had just made him feel worse. She thought about how Dave and her other friends had reacted to him at the party. If people always recoiled from him, and avoided touching him, it was no wonder he felt hideous.

Later that night she drove him home with all these thoughts swirling around in her head, and in the end forgot to say anything about taking the bus rather than driving.

It was pleasant at first to ride the bus so early in the morning when everything was quiet, to be alone with her thoughts of lying in bed with Jake, of how he touched her so intently, reading every part of her with his fingertips.

The bus pulled into the tunnel at Westlake. Kassie filed off with the few other bleary-eyed passengers and walked over to the stop for the outbound bus to Bellevue. She waited, playing Tetris on her phone to pass the time, still thinking warm thoughts about Jake. It was an old flip phone that everyone teased her for hanging on to, but it still worked. She hadn't seen a reason to upgrade to a smart phone. Minutes ticked by, and still no bus. The tunnel was nearly empty.

At a quarter past six, with still no bus in sight, Kassie got up and checked the schedule. There, in stark letters, she saw the first bus on Saturday would not come until 6:45 AM. She felt all the blood drain from her face. How was this possible? She had checked online so carefully! Frantically, she scanned the schedule again and again, hoping she had misread it. But no, the Saturday buses came later. The first weekday bus was at six AM. She must have looked at the weekday schedule online by mistake.

There was nothing she could do--she was going to be late. Even worse, since Jake didn't have a TTY, and she didn't have internet or email on her cell phone, she couldn't contact him directly. She was going to have to call his parents and talk to them rather than to him. At six thirty she called Mr. O'Malley to let him know and to ask if he could pick her up at the Transit Center. He agreed readily, but just having to ask made her feel like dying inside. That's it, I am getting a new phone, she thought.

The bus arrived at last, pulling up sedately, then taking off at a glacial speed that made Kassie want to scream with frustration. What a fucking disaster, she thought, leaning her head against the window as the bus slowly chugged over the floating bridge. So much for making a good impression on Jake's parents.

It was past seven o'clock by the time she finally arrived. Off the bus at last, she ran out to the curb and jumped in the car, apologizing profusely. Jake and Carter were in the back, forcing Kassie to sit in front. She reached back and flashed him the ILY sign as a greeting. He gave her hand a little shake and spelled H-I back to her, but after that she had to face forward and let Carter do the talking.

"Do you need to change?" Mr. O'Malley asked as he pulled away from the curb.

"No, I'm good," she said, pointing to her running shoes. "I'm really, really sorry I kept you all waiting."

"I knew you'd be late," Carter said, and it took Kassie a minute to realize he was talking for Jake. When Kassie didn't respond, he added, "I'm just teasing you." Kassie rolled her eyes. Would it kill Carter to put some emotion in his voice? He repeated the message like he was reading off a teleprompter.

"Haha, very funny," she said. "But I do really feel bad."

"Don't worry about it," Carter-as-Jake said. "I overslept too. We weren't ready at six either." Kassie reached back and patted Jake's knee. She wasn't sure if that was really true or if he just said it to make her feel better, but it worked.

Mr. O'Malley drove to the same part of Chism Park where Kassie had come with Jake on what she now thought of as their first date. It seemed Jake came here with his father to run at least once a week; no wonder he knew the area so well.

They all piled out of the car to stretch in the parking lot. Jake left his cane angled across the back seat of the car. Despite the cool weather, he was wearing running shorts and a thin gray t-shirt that showed off his well-muscled if somewhat stocky frame. She greeted him again, but restrained herself from kissing him. She just couldn't in front of his father. Or in front of Carter, in his incongruously sporty shorts, which showed off his spindly legs.

"I'm sorry, I don't know if you're here on the clock or just as a friend," she said to him. "Do you mind if I talk to you directly?"

"Uh, okay," Carter said, shooting her a look that said: it never stopped you before. Nonetheless, he took Jake's hand and translated their conversation anyway.

"I mean, are you here in a professional capacity as an intervener, or as a friend?" She tried to make her voice sound casual, not judgmental.

"I'm here because Jake asked me to come," Carter replied coldly.

"Yeah, but...isn't it expensive?" she blurted out. "I know interpreter services cost a lot. And it's not like this is the kind of activity where there'll be a lot of talking..." she trailed off.

"Since you asked, no, I'm not on the clock. If I'm not busy with another client, sometimes we do things as friends. I've been trying to get in better shape too." Carter gave a small, twisted smile. "Don't worry, they're not exploiting me," he said, although he knew that was not her primary concern.

"Carter is like a member of the family," Mr. O'Malley added, clapping him on the shoulder. Then, in a more business-like way, "Come on, let's hit the trail."

Jake wrapped a length of rope around his left hand, and Carter looped the other half around his right hand. Mr. O'Malley took off along the trail, with Kassie falling into place beside him, and Jake and Carter behind them. He set a slow, steady pace, much slower than what Kassie was accustomed to with Dave and the others, but after getting up so early, she was happy to take it easy. For a long time, the only sounds were the gentle slaps of their sneakers on the paved trail, a few lonely birds, and the tiny waves of the bay rushing to the shore. The morning was chilly and heavily overcast, but it was pleasant to be out in the quiet, away from the noise of the city.

The longer they ran, the more Kassie unintentionally edged toward her usual pace. Mr. O'Malley kept up with her, until they had drawn several yards ahead of Jake and Carter.

"Thanks for coming out with us," Mr. O'Malley said, panting slightly between words.

"Uh, sure. Thank you for including me," Kassie said slowly. "I, ah, didn't want to intrude on family time."

"No, not at all. It's just, you know, it's all new for us. Jake having someone in his life," he elaborated, then paused for a long time, never taking his eyes off the trail in front of him. "We didn't think it would ever happen."

"I know, Jake's mom said something like that."

He glanced at her briefly from the corner of his eye. "I'm sorry if she was rude to you. She was just being protective. You have no idea what it was like when he was growing up. How hard it was to teach him anything. We just accepted he would never have a normal life."

Kassie nodded. With great effort, she restrained herself from turning around to see if Carter was close enough to hear them, if he was interpreting for Jake. Could he even do that while running? Just assume he is, she told herself, pinning her eyes to the trail ahead.

Mr. O'Malley continued, "Some people, doctors even, told us to just put him in an institution, that he couldn't be taught."

"You're kidding!" Kassie burst out.

"Yes, or to send him to a residential school. But Irene was determined to keep him at home. She quit her job to concentrate on teaching him before he was old enough to start school, to make sure he had the best specialists. She was a teacher herself, you know, elementary school, and I know she really loved it, but she gave it up for him. She felt horribly guilty, you know."

"For what?"

"For getting sick while she was pregnant with him. She thought she'd been vaccinated against rubella, but it turned out the shot was too long ago, and it had worn off. She didn't even know that's what she had until after he was born, and he failed the hearing test in the hospital. She'd had such a mild case, she thought it was just the flu. It tore her up inside, thinking that if she only hadn't gotten sick, he would have been fine."

Kassie was stunned. Of course, this wasn't exactly news, but still, she had never thought about it quite that way before. She tried to imagine a seeing, hearing Jake, with eyes open, and a clear voice. What would he have been like?

They jogged on awhile longer without speaking.

"Maybe you think we should have taught him ASL," Mr. O'Malley said after a time. Kassie shook her head, but she wasn't sure just what to say, and it was hard to have a normal conversation while they were running. Before she could formulate a response, he continued, "There are no set rules for how to raise a deafblind kid, you know? It's so rare." He paused between phrases as he caught his breath. "We tried ASL fingerspelling first, but he just wasn't getting it. His hands were so tiny, he couldn't feel the whole shape. One of his therapists suggested switching to the deafblind manual alphabet. We tried it, and it was like the light bulb went on in his head. He picked it up immediately. I don't regret that decision."

"It's amazing how much he has accomplished," Kassie said carefully. "You've done so much for him." She paused for a while, then added, "But I think he could do so much more. There's this new device, like a cell phone--"

"Yes, I've heard about it. It sounds great, but it's just, it's so expensive..."

They had reached a little open area on the trail, with benches and a drinking fountain. Evidently this was their turnaround, because Mr. O'Malley stopped at one of the benches and stretched his legs, then splashed some water onto his face.

"I know, but it could make him so much more independent!" Kassie insisted, with a bit more emotion than she intended. As she spoke, Jake and Carter caught up to them and stopped as well.

"Are you talking about me?" Carter interpreted for Jake.

Kassie felt a twinge of guilt, even though she had been careful not to say anything she wouldn't want him to know. "We were just talking about the deafblind communicator," she said, trying to look at Jake and not at Carter, even though she could feel the intervener's eyes boring into her. How would he feel about being replaced by a machine?

"I don't need it. It's too expensive."

"How much do you spend each year on interpreters or interveners?" she asked, then immediately regretted it. No one said anything. "I'm sorry, it's none of my business," she muttered.

"It's okay." She could see Jake make the sign in ASL a moment before Carter spoke the words, and she thought on what Mr. O'Malley had just said. Was Jake using ASL more now, even with Carter, because of her? She rubbed her hands through her short hair and paced nervously in a circle, unsure what to say or where to look. Mr. O'Malley finished his stretching routine, and Carter guided Jake to the fountain to take a drink of water, placing his hands on the rim. His cheeks were flushed and mottled, and his damp hair stuck out stiffly from the sides of his head.

When he had finished drinking, Kassie took Jake's hand. *Sorry sorry sorry.* I D-I-D-N-T M-E-A-N T-O B-E R-U-D-E.

I-M J-U-S-T T-H-A-T P-O-P-U-LA-R, he answered. *Everyone talks about me all the time.*

C-A-N I R-U-N W-I-T-H Y-O-U O-N T-H-E W-A-Y B-A-C-K? she asked.

He smiled as he spelled I-D L-I-K-E T-H-A-T.

Y-O-U R-U-N F-A-S-T, he added.

Sorry, is it too fast? she asked.

No, it's good, let's go.

Kassie looked hesitantly at Mr. O'Malley as she wound the rope Jake preferred around her hand. "Do you mind?" she asked, gesturing at the rope. He just shook his head and smiled, waving them on.

They jogged along the path together, Kassie holding the rope to guide him, and Jake half a pace behind her. Trying to sign to him caused her to break stride, so she just enjoyed the quiet morning, storing up her impressions of the scenery to share with him later: the distant rush of the waves, the birds in the trees, the way the gray sky and the gray sea met at the horizon. Once they fell into rhythm together, it was easy and peaceful.

Back at the house, Mrs. O'Malley had Bisquick pancakes with bacon and eggs waiting for them. As they ate, Kassie explained again how she'd taken the bus because Erik had the car, and apologized for making them all wait.

"Do you ride the bus often?" Mrs. O'Malley asked blandly, clearly just making small talk.

"Everyday to work," Kassie replied, pushing the chalky pancakes around her plate. The intense sugar rush from the imitation maple syrup was making her vaguely nauseated and light-headed. "I'm not usually that bad at reading the schedules, sorry," she added ruefully.

"I've never ridden the bus," Jake said through Carter.

"What? Not at all?" Kassie asked.

"I rode the school bus when I was a kid, but never the city bus."

"There was never a reason to," Mr. O'Malley said.

"Would you like to try it?" Kassie asked. Before he could answer, she added in a rush, "I was going to say something later, but the truth is, Erik needs the car again next Saturday, so if we're going to get together, it has to be by bus again. It won't be so hard. Just get on here and ride to the last stop. Maybe your dad or someone could help you get on at the Transit Center in Bellevue, then I'll meet you at Westlake. What do you think?" She looked entreatingly at Mr. O'Malley.

Jake did not reply immediately. His parents exchanged a significant look. His mother looked as if she were about to refuse, but his father shifted uncomfortably on his chair, staring at Kassie.

"Maybe..." he said slowly. "Carter, what do you think?"

Carter only shrugged noncommittally. "Whatever Jake wants," he said flatly.

"It sounds pretty straightforward. I'll take you to the bus, and Kassie can meet you downtown," Mr. O'Malley said, sounding as if he were convincing himself. "What do you think? "

"Sure, sounds like fun," Carter interpreted.

CHAPTER SEVENTEEN

Saturday morning was gray and drizzling, a fine blowing mist. Kassie woke early, even before her alarm. The plan was simple: Mr. O'Malley would call her to let her know when Jake got on the bus, then she would meet him at the transfer point downtown. It was the last stop, so there was no way he could miss it. All he had to do was stay on the bus until he felt the engine turn off, and she would meet him as he got off. As an extra treat, she decided that rather than coming straight home, they would take another bus to the International District and have Chinese food for lunch. If Jake was apprehensive about the plan, he didn't say anything to her about it.

Kassie caught the bus downtown even before she got the phone call from Jake's father, just to be certain she wouldn't be late. As it was, she ended up waiting around the bus tunnel at Westlake for over thirty minutes, anxiously peering into every arriving bus.

At last the bus from Bellevue pulled up, and she could see Jake sitting in the first seat behind the driver, dressed in a blue windbreaker, with his white cane sticking up beside him. She waited impatiently, dancing from foot to foot, as the other passengers got off, then rushed in.

"Hey there, last stop!" the driver yelled at her, but she ignored him, and went straight to Jake, grabbing his hand and making her name sign.

He greeted her without expression, only commenting that the bus was still running.

"LAST STOP!" the driver repeated.

Doesn't matter, must get off B-U-S *now*, Kassie explained, tugging him to his feet impatiently.

He followed her off the bus, moving slowly and stiffly. She gave him a quick hug, then took his hand.

Y-O-U D-I-D I-T, she spelled eagerly, trying somehow to convey encouragement through her fingers. *Easy, right?*

Jake didn't really answer, but just sort of nodded vaguely. For a second Kassie wondered why he was acting so standoffish, but as quickly as the thought occurred to her, she shoved it aside, intent on getting them to the restaurant she had picked out. She dragged him across the way to the stop for the buses heading south. A knot of people milled about, waiting for the next bus.

Kassie cursed inwardly as they joined the crowd. She had forgotten there was a Mariners game that day. All the buses were going to be packed. She started to explain to Jake, but before she could be sure he understood her, the bus pulled up and the crowd surged toward the opening doors.

O-K, she spelled with one hand, as Jake kept hold of her other arm at the elbow. S-T-E-P U-P. She pulled him up behind her into the back of the bus. Jake stumbled a bit over the steep steps. All the seats were already taken, and the aisle was full of people standing, but the crowd behind them pushed them further in, and they found themselves propelled forward, bodies pressed up against them on all sides.

The bus started with a lurch, and Jake fell against her, looking panic-stricken. Kassie guided his hand to a metal bar, but with one hand on her elbow and the other holding his rigid cane, he had a hard time holding on. The bus lurched again as it emerged from the tunnel and rounded a corner, the whole crowd moving as one solid mass. Jake tightened his grip on her elbow, squeezing so hard she started to feel pins and needles. She pried his fingers loose to spell into his hand O-K O-K. She anxiously watched the gray downtown buildings slide away as the bus wound its way south.

They had gotten into the back of an articulated bus, the kind that had two sections joined in the middle like an accordion, but they were going to have to exit through the front so they could pay the fare. Because everyone was going to the stadium, no one was getting off yet, and the driver was speeding past all the bus stops, waving to the frustrated people waiting, to indicate that the bus was already full. Kassie realized they were going to reach their stop soon, and if they didn't push to the front, they were never going to be able to get off.

W-E M-O-V-E T-O F-R-O-N-T she explained, her hand jerking around uncontrollably as the bus swayed from side to side. F-O-L-L-O-W M-E.

She placed his hand on her elbow again and squeezed through the solid mass of people until they reached the jointed middle of the bus, which was also completely filled. Jake was trailing behind her, their arms stretched out as they pushed sideways through the crowd. But just as they were crossing the middle, the bus turned a sharp corner, and the floor shifted beneath their feet. Kassie pushed forward but the movement of the bus made the crowd shift against them. Before she realized what was happening, Jake's hand slipped away, and a hefty man in a Mariners baseball cap and his Spandex-clad girlfriend interposed themselves between them, pushing Kassie forward and Jake backward.

She paused for a second, expecting Jake to continue moving forward toward her, but instead, she heard the most horrible, strangled scream. Kassie shoved aside the man in the baseball cap, who had turned to stare at Jake, now red-faced and howling.

She grabbed his hand, trying to sign *stop stop stop* but it was awkward to make the sign with only one hand, and she couldn't seem to get him to pay attention anyway. The din of the chattering crowd fell away as people stared at them with a mixture of horror and annoyance. Kassie yanked him forward, the people in the aisles now parting before them as Jake continued to wail. As they reached the front, the bus driver glared at them in the mirror.

Kassie paused by the till as the driver, cursing them under his breath, brought the bus to a shuddering halt at a deserted stop. As soon as the bus stopped moving, Jake mercifully quieted.

O-K? Kassie spelled out as quick as she could.

O-F-F, he insisted.

N-O-T O-U-R S-T-O-P.

Off now now now, he signed, his hand stiff and fast, as he started yelling again.

"You getting off or what?" the driver demanded.

"It's not our stop," Kassie explained, as Jake continued to batter her with *off off off*.

"I ain't having that noise on my bus," the driver drawled, his voice dripping with hostility. "You either shut him up or get off."

"Okay, okay," Kassie conceded, fumbling through her purse one-handed for her pass and fare for Jake. She didn't dare let go of Jake with the other.

"Never mind that, just get the hell off," the driver barked. Kassie stomped down the steps with Jake behind her, wondering if she could lodge a formal complaint with Sound Transit against the driver for swearing at a disabled person.

The bus pulled away with a rumble and whoosh of exhaust, leaving them stranded on the sidewalk. Jake's face was pale, and he was standing as rigid as the cane he clutched in a white-knuckle grip. Kassie stared at him.

"Now what are we going to do!" she burst out uncontrollably, then instantly felt guilty for yelling at him. She took his free hand, which was sweaty and trembling.

Restaurant nearby, she signed. W-E C-A-N W-A-L-K O-K?

N-O, Jake replied with angry strokes. I W-A-N-T T-O G-O H-O-M-E.

Kassie stared at him. Go home? All the way back to Bellevue? How? She made him repeat it just in case she had misunderstood, but he was insistent: *home now*.

She looked around despairingly. They were in the desolate nowhere in between I-5 and the Alaskan Way Viaduct. All she could see was blank sidewalk, chain link fences, and huge faceless buildings, probably warehouses, some clearly derelict. Even the bus stop they were at was no more than a signpost, with no shelter from the persistent drizzle. There were never any taxis outside downtown, and besides she didn't have enough cash for the fare all the way to Bellevue, or the phone number of a cab company. The only way back would be on the bus again.

When Kassie tried to explain this to Jake, he flew into a rage again, punctuating his gestures with angry, inarticulate cries that made Kassie feel as if she were being stabbed in the heart. No, he would not get on another bus, or walk anywhere else, or do anything unless she promised to take him straight back home.

O-K I-L-L C-A-L-L E-R-I-K, she spelled, feeling defeated.

With shaking hands, she pulled out her phone and dialed, but after four rings it went to voicemail. Shit! she thought, he must still be with that client. She closed her eyes and counted to ten, then tried again. Still no answer. A homeless man staggered down the sidewalk, coming toward them. Please don't say anything, please don't say anything, she prayed as she watched him draw nearer. She dialed a third time.

"Spare change?" the homeless man called out, as Erik's phone started ringing. Kassie shook her head, avoiding eye contact, mentally willing Jake not to start yelling again.

"Bitch!" the man yelled as he passed by them, just as she finally heard Erik pick up.

"Hey," she said weakly.

"Kassie? What the hell?"

She explained what had happened, and he gave a grim laugh. "Okay, you're in luck. I just got done with my client. I'll come get you. Where are you exactly?"

Kassie craned around, trying to see a street sign. "Uh, I'm not sure. Somewhere on First and something, maybe Jackson? Just south of Yesler."

"Jesus. Okay, I'll try to get there as soon as I can, but I'm all the way up at Northgate."

"Thank you so much. I'm really sorry," she said as he hung up.

Kassie passed the message along to Jake. He indicated that he understood her but wouldn't say anything else, even when she explained it would take Erik at least twenty minutes to drive across town, if there was no traffic. And so they just stood there, side by side, locked away in miserable silence. There was no place to sit down; the sidewalk was wet and dirty, covered in bits of broken glass. The drizzle increased to a light rain. After a few minutes, Kassie could feel the water penetrate her curls to drip down her scalp and into her collar. She had a strong desire to pace around in a circle, but she didn't want to let go of Jake's hand and make him feel abandoned. That was how all this had started.

As they stood there, she swung back and forth between guilt and anger. She would start to compose an apology in her mind for pushing him too far too fast, for breaking his trust and making him feel unsafe, but as soon as she thought back to those moments on the bus, she felt the thread of her patience snap. The yelling, the insistence on running home, it was all so childish. His disability didn't give him the right to carry on like that. Then a more sobering thought: maybe it meant he really couldn't have an adult relationship. If he even still wanted to be with her after all this. Kassie felt her mood grow blacker and blacker. As for what Jake was thinking, it was impossible for her to tell.

Finally, after what felt like the longest thirty minutes of her life, she saw the little green Acura turn the corner and head toward them. She waved frantically with one hand while making Erik's name sign to Jake with the other. Erik pulled up and they piled in the back seat together, wet, tired, and sore. Erik reached back to sign a greeting to Jake before putting the car in gear, but Jake didn't respond to him any more than he had to her.

"You're sure you want to go straight back to Bellevue?" Kassie relayed Erik's question, but Jake was emphatic.

"Yeah," she said. "I'm really sorry to make you do this."

"It's okay," Erik replied, but Kassie still felt bad. This could not be how Erik had intended to spend the remainder of his Saturday.

They drove in silence back past downtown then over the floating bridge.

O-K, Kassie signed to Jake as Erik pulled up in front of his house. H-O-M-E. B-Y-E.

C-O-M-E I-N W-I-T-H M-E, Jake suggested, but Kassie had had enough.

No. You decided to go home yourself. You explain to your parents why, not me, she said, her hands shaking. Still Jake seemed reluctant to get out of the car. *Straight line from car to house*, Kassie explained, exasperated. *You know the way. Go.* She gave him a little push on the back, then watched as he climbed out of the car, tapped his way up the walk to the front door and pulled out his key. She looked away before she could see his parents looking for her.

As Erik pulled away, she scrambled over the gear shifter into the front seat.

"I'm sorry," she said again, leaning her head against the window.

Erik glanced at her. "Don't be."

Tears stung her eyes. "Why does it have to be so fucking hard?" she whispered. Erik just patted her knee and didn't say anything.

CHAPTER EIGHTEEN

That night, Erik made homemade pasta and a thick tomato sauce, with plenty of red wine. Kassie knew he had made it for her, to help her feel better, but she could only pick at it.

"You know, I've been thinking," he said, tossing back another glass of wine then helping himself to more pasta, "If you're going to keep seeing Jake, you really need your own car."

Kassie felt the tears starting up again. "Forget it. I don't think he wants to see me again."

"Whatever." Erik waved his fork dismissively. "He'll get over it. Look, I was going to say something later, but we might as well talk about it now. Do you want the Acura?"

"What?" Kassie looked up at him in surprise. "You'll just give it to me? Just like that?"

"Yeah. My dad's been talking about getting a new car and giving me his old one. You can have the Acura, if you pay for the title transfer."

"That's really generous of you," Kassie said slowly. "But I can't just take it from you. You have to let me pay you something."

"Sure, if you insist, we can work that out later. But I can't let you have it yet. I'm meeting Kevin for lunch tomorrow."

"Kevin who?" Kassie lifted out of her own obsessive thoughts for a moment to look at him curiously.

"You know, the dude from Work Seattle."

Kassie's eyes widened. "No way! Is it a date? He seems really cool."

"Eh, we'll see." Erik shrugged in a self-conscious show of indifference.

"I can't believe there's a gay guy in the Seattle Deaf community who you haven't f--, I mean, haven't met yet," Kassie teased him.

"I know, right?" Erik laughed. "He just moved here from New York a few months ago to take the job with Work Seattle. He's hard of hearing, and I don't think he hires interpreters that often. But he's super involved with the Deaf community, and his ASL is amazing. He went to Gallaudet," he concluded in awed tones.

Ordinarily Kassie would have given him a hard time for so obviously falling for this guy already, but she just smiled at him. Maybe at least one of them could have a relationship that wasn't a total disaster.

After the way they had left things, Kassie didn't expect to hear from Jake, and sure enough, when she went online after dinner, his icon was grayed out. It was the first time that had ever happened, except for when he went to Oregon. Even though she didn't feel like talking to him yet either, it still stung a little.

While Erik went out on his maybe-date on Sunday, she loafed around the house, feeling a little like she was home sick from school. The thought of food turned her stomach, and she couldn't concentrate on anything. Finally, annoyed with herself for moping around like a stupid teenager, she decided to take advantage of the break in the rain to do some yard work. Pulling weeds and trimming back the hedges at least gave her a savage sense of satisfaction, and it wore her out.

Later that evening after she had showered and scrubbed most of the dirt from under her fingernails, she slumped wearily in front of her computer. Even while telling herself she was being ridiculous, her heart still raced as she brought up her browser. To her surprise, the minute she came online, Jake messaged her.

>Hey.

>Hey.

>Kassie, I'm sorry about what happened yesterday.

>No, I'm sorry. I pushed you too hard and made you mad at me.

>What? I'm not mad at you.

>Yes, you are.

>No! I'm sorry I wouldn't talk to you at the bus stop or in the car. I was so ashamed and angry at myself I couldn't say anything. I was terrified to ride that stupid bus. The whole way over I kept thinking I had missed the stop, that I was going to get stranded and lost somewhere. Then by the time I met you, I was already worked up, and you just dragged us onto the next bus and I couldn't take it anymore. I'm really sorry I let you down.

>No! Don't say that. You didn't let me down. Next time we'll go more slowly, no rushing around.

>So there will be a next time? You're not breaking up with me?

>I thought you wanted to break up with me.

There was a long pause. Kassie stared at the blinking cursor, waiting for Jake to respond, her heart thudding. She didn't want to break up. The thought of not having him in her life was too big to fully grasp. But she wanted him to be different than he was, more independent. Maybe it was too much to ask.

At last he wrote,

>Everyone is always saying how pretty you
are. You could be with any guy you want. You
don't have to be stuck with someone like me.

>I'm not stuck with you. Jake, I love you.
I want to be with YOU, not some other guy.

>...

>I thought you were going to break up with
me because you're mad that I fucked everything
up, that I'm not good enough at signing and
interpreting and that I make you do things you
don't want to.

>No! It's not that at all. I'm so tired of
always being a problem, of always being tied
down and scared all the time.

>So...it seems pretty stupid to me to break
up just because we are both feeling guilty and
embarrassed. I spent the whole day feeling like
shit, thinking I would never see you again. I
really don't want to break up. Do you?

>No. I want to be better for you, but I'm
not sure I can do it.

> I promise not to make you ride the bus
again.

>No, it's not that. You were right. I
realized when you made me walk from the car to
the house--when I was a kid I used to always try
to do things on my own. I don't know when I
stopped doing that. I guess it's just easier to
slip into a rut and let other people do things
for me.

>Ok, but I never know when I'm being too
pushy. You have to say when you don't want to do
something.

>I just wanted to impress you. Why would
you want to be with someone who can't even do
the simplest things on his own?

>Please, you have to stop saying that. You
already impress me. You don't have to do

anything special just for me. Don't you believe
that I love you?

>I do. I love you too.

>So can we accept each other's apologies
and move on?

>I'd like that. I shouldn't have freaked
out like that. I promise it won't happen again.

Kassie felt gut-wrenched and exhausted by the time she
finally logged off and got into bed. Still wound up, she lay in
the dark, staring at the moonlit outline of the trees against the
window. She hated it when Jake started talking about how he
wasn't good enough for her, or how he was just a burden to
her. Why didn't he get it? Helping him, interpreting, guiding--
she didn't mind doing any of those things, because she loved
him. It was the self-doubt, the constant need for reassurance
that made the relationship sometimes feel like slogging
through heavy mud, like they were never going to move
forward. Then something occurred to her: they had just said "I
love you" for the first time. Sure, they flashed the ILY sign to
each other all the time, but that was so casual, in her mind it
didn't carry the same weight as typing it all out, and really
meaning it. She rolled over with a little smile. Maybe they were
making progress after all. And she was definitely going to buy
Erik's car.

A few days later Kassie found herself with a rare
unscheduled evening. Just as she was gazing into the
refrigerator and pondering what to make for dinner, she heard
someone banging on the front door. That was odd, usually
people rang the bell, and besides, she wasn't expecting anyone.
Shutting the refrigerator, she hurried across the living room to
open the door. It was Jake, and he was dressed up. Instead of
his usual t-shirt and jeans, he had on a crisp white button-

down shirt, dark pants, and leather shoes instead of sneakers. The effect was stunningly sexy.

Kassie's jaw dropped. She took his hand. H-O-W? she spelled slowly.

C-A-R-T-E-R, Jake explained, tucking his cane under one arm and gesturing behind him with the other, without turning around. Kassie craned around him; at the curb she could see Carter's aged Civic idling. *I want to take you out to dinner, to a nice restaurant.*

Erik is out interpreting, Kassie replied, still a bit dazed. N-O C-A-R.

O-K, C-A-R-T-E-R W-I-L-L D-R-I-V-E, Jake assured her, smiling. I M-A-D-E R-E-S-E-R-V-A-T-I-O-N-S A-T R-U-B-Y-S. O-K? *You like?*

Yes, yes! I like! she signed back enthusiastically. *Just a minute, I'll get ready to go.* She raced back to her bedroom to grab her purse, regretting that she was still wearing her boring work clothes. After a moment's hesitation, she pulled off her shirt and switched to a more form-fitting, lower cut one. If Jake was taking her on a real date, she wanted to look nice.

Grabbing her purse, Kassie clattered down the steps to the car, with Jake holding on to her arm.

"So, um, thanks for helping out..." Kassie said hesitantly to Carter as she slid into the back seat behind Jake.

"Don't worry, I'm not coming with you to dinner," Carter said, glancing at her in the rearview mirror. And was that the ghost of a smile? "I'm just the driver tonight. I have a client later."

"Wow, okay, well it's really nice of you to drive us. Thank you," Kassie said.

"No problem."

"So you're really okay with all this, even after...?" Kassie felt bad having a conversation with Carter when Jake couldn't take part, but she had to know.

"I know, Jake told me what happened. But honestly, you've stuck around longer than I thought you would. You two deserve a chance to work things out."

"Um, thanks, I guess?"

"Just so you know, this is all Jake's idea. I only made a few phone calls for him. Sorry I can't drive you home too, but here's the number of a cab company. Just call when you're ready to go." He handed her a business card.

At the restaurant, the staff was clearly expecting them. They were seated in one of the curved booths so they could sit next to each other on the same side of the table. As Kassie translated, the waiter explained that all their food had been ordered in advance over the phone.

I-S I-T O-K? Jake asked anxiously.

Yes, yes good! Kassie assured him. R-U-B-Y-S *is my favorite.*

I know. You told me and I remembered, he said.

Even the food I like?

I pay attention when you tell me things. Not just talk, talk, talk, no listen. His ASL was still a little shaky but she understood what he meant.

H-A-H-A *I'm smiling,* she replied, so he would know.

I want to go out with you more, not just sit at home, wait for you to think of everything first, he continued more seriously. *I'm sorry about the* B-U-S. I W-A-N-T T-O D-O S-O-M-E-T-H-I-N-G N-I-C-E F-O-R Y-O-U.

Thank you, this is very nice. She gave him a kiss on the cheek. I A-P-P-R-E-C-I-A-T-E I-T T-H-A-N-K Y-O-U.

The dinner was delicious, but more than the food, she was happy just being with him, trading little jokes. She didn't have to interpret, only relax and enjoy his company. After dinner they took a cab back to her house. It was late, and she had to get up early for work the next day, but there was still time for a few passionate moments on the couch before she called another cab to take him back home.

Later as Kassie lay in bed, the sensation of his lips still lingering on hers, for the first time all week she felt hopeful. No one had ever made her feel so loved. Maybe there was some way for this relationship to work.

CHAPTER NINETEEN

After completing the half-marathon with a personal best time, Dave decided the group needed to up their training. Half-marathons were for wimps, he declared--they needed to go full marathon. To level-up their routine, he badgered them all into meeting early one morning before work to run along the Gilman Trail. Kassie hated getting up so early, but at least Tara promised to give them all a ride to work afterwards. Marty rode up front, the privilege of being Tara's boyfriend, but the others had to go in the back. As the smallest person Kassie got the middle, squashed in between Dave and Adam who were loudly making plans for the weekend over her.

"So Kassie, when are you going to start coming out with us again?" Dave asked, even though their talk had not progressed beyond a vague plan to go drinking at Angie's.

"I already have plans to see Jake," Kassie said.

"Oh please," Dave retorted dismissively, blowing air between his taut lips. "How much longer are you going to keep this up?"

"Keep what up?" Kassie asked, an edge in her voice. In the front seat, Tara and Marty stopped talking.

"Oh come on, we all know you're just seeing him to feel better about yourself."

Kassie turned to him furiously, only the close confines of the car preventing her from shouting.

"Fuck you," she spat. "Not everyone is an image-obsessed poseur like you. Jake and I love each other, and if you can't deal, that's your fucking problem."

"Whatever." Dave rolled his eyes, ignoring her insult. "The sign language, the volunteering, we get it, you're a *good person*," he said with sing-song mockery. "You don't have to also be doing the handicapped guy."

"You really don't get it, do you?" Despite herself, Kassie's voice was rising too loud for the tiny car. "Not everything in life is about showing off your perfectly curated taste. Ordering other people to make things for you doesn't make you a creative person. I'm so fucking sick of your advice and opinions. You've disappeared so far up your own ass, you can't even tell something real when you see it. I love him, and it has nothing to do with my image or what other people think of me. But that's it, I am done with you. If you're asking me to choose between you and Jake, I choose him, no question."

There was a shocked silence for a moment, then Dave muttered, "That's not what I meant."

"I don't fucking care!" Kassie exploded. "I've had it with you! No more!"

Tara pulled up in front of their office building, and as soon as she reached the curb, Dave and Adam both leapt out as fast as they could. Kassie took a second longer, struggling to slide out from the middle seat. Tara glanced at her in the rearview mirror.

"Dave's just being a dick," she said apologetically. "You can still keep running with us if you want."

"No, I don't think so. Thanks for the ride." Kassie slid out, and tried not to slam the door too loudly behind her. Her arms and legs were shaking as she hit the sidewalk, but she ignored it, and strode inside as fast as she could. For a moment, as they stood around waiting for the elevator, Dave looked like he might say something more to her, but she glared at him, and he just shrugged and turned away.

All the rest of the day Kassie dreaded running into Dave again, but it was surprisingly easy to avoid him. She took her lunch half an hour later than usual, and he didn't come by her desk. Adam and Marty never crossed her path at work anyway. It didn't stop her from stewing over even nastier things to say to all of them, but by the afternoon some of the sting had faded. In the evening she went to ASL class, and by the time she got home it felt like a distant memory.

The only question was what to tell Jake. She had to tell him she'd decided to stop training for the marathon, but she didn't want to get into the details of her fight with Dave. He didn't need to know that the hurtful things he imagined people said about him were sometimes true, or that Dave accused her of only being with Jake to pose as a saintly martyr. In the end she only told Jake that he was right, she was doing too many things and needed to slow down. Which she had to admit might be true.

The following weekend Kassie dropped Erik off at his parents' house in Ballard to pick up his dad's old car, then drove straight to Bellevue to get Jake. She had explained the car swap to him, and driving back over the floating bridge, they were both in high spirits.

Y-O-U-R C-A-R, he reminded her, whenever she paused in traffic and put a hand on his knee. She responded by tapping his hand for *yes*. Maybe it's silly to be so excited over something so minor, she thought, after all, it was still the same old beater she had been using for months, but it did seem like now things would be just a tiny bit easier.

Back at the house, they decided to take a walk in Ravenna Park. The weather had turned chilly but it was a rare sunny day, and as they crunched through the fallen leaves they commented to each other on the clear cool air--somehow it always smelled different in autumn, clearer but sharper. Someone had lit a fire; the faint tang of wood smoke only added to the feeling that the seasons were changing.

Inside the park the smell of the air changed again, purer under the trees, with the undercurrent of water from the river, moss, and decaying leaves. Kassie always marveled at how removed the park felt from the rest of the city. Because it was in a gorge the sights and sounds of the traffic were hidden, and walking the springy trails under the trees, she could feel almost as if she were in a densely overgrown forest, far from civilization. They walked slowly, not only because the ground was uneven with tree roots, but because Jake seemed to be soaking in the forest through his skin. She knew he was exquisitely attuned to the slightest vibration or change in wind direction or quality of air, and now she could tell by the look of concentration on his face that he was feeling the shifting breezes all around them. As they walked, whenever they passed a particularly large or oddly-shaped tree, she paused to let him run his hands over it. With the largest tree, he wrapped his arms all the way around the trunk and leaned his face up against the bark.

She tapped his hand. W-E-L-L?

S-M-E-L-L-S N-I-C-E, he answered.

Not for the first time, Kassie wondered what it was like for him, how he really experienced the world. She had asked many times, but his answers always tended toward explaining how he did things. He knew when someone approached him by the vibrations in the floor, or he could tell the mood of a person signing to him by the feel of the hand, the position or shifting of the body. That was all quite remarkable, but not exactly what she was asking. She knew he didn't really think in terms of light or darkness, silence or noise. *The world is always coming at me*, he had said once, the closest he had gotten to a satisfactory explanation. She watched him now, leaning into the tree with his whole body, and wondered how it would be to only know of things as they collided into you without warning, to be always dragged forward into the void. It was little wonder he was so easily frustrated or spooked.

When he had finished with the tree, he reached out for her hand and she took it, drawing him closer to her. They walked side by side further along the trail until they came to the creek. Kassie guided him to one of the rough-hewn wooden benches beside the creek, then sat close to him, her head on his shoulder. Jake carefully laid his cane on the ground beneath the bench, then straightening up, threw his head back and breathed in deeply.

Water smell, he signed to her.

Yes, small river here, she replied. *Sound of water, birds, very pretty*. She held his hand, running her fingers over his palm without saying anything for a while, then finally said, *Sorry I let go your hand on the B-U-S.*

He made a brushing motion across her palm, a gesture he usually used when he had made a mistake, wiping away the words. She took it to mean she didn't need to apologize again. Y-O-U-R-E A-LW-A-Y-S R-U-S-H-I-N-G F-O-R-W-A-R-D, he said, I-M T-R-Y-I-N-G T-O K-E-E-P U-P.

I-L-L G-O S-L-O-W-E-R she replied, P-R-O-M-I-S-E. I W-A-N-T T-O B-E W-I-T-H Y-O-U.

Back at the house Kassie was not surprised to find that Erik still had not returned from visiting his parents. They had the house to themselves, probably until after dinner. Erik had left his mp3 player on the stereo, so she turned it on. The first song that came up was by Stereolab. She turned up the bass. Jake leaned his cane in a corner by the door, then kicked off his shoes and stretched out lengthwise on the sofa, relaxing into the vibrations coming up through the floor.

Kassie lay down next to Jake, snuggling up against him on the narrow sofa. He responded to her immediately, rolling onto his side and wrapping his arms around her in a crushing embrace, his face buried against her neck. With his nose right against her skin, he took a long, deep breath of her, then slid his hands down her back to her butt, his motions confident, trusting her to respond. She could feel his sudden erection swelling against her thigh. He found her hand and spelled S-E-X-Y, signing a bit awkwardly with their arms pinned together against the sofa. Rather than attempting an answer, she only laughed and kissed him.

The kiss turned into another, then another, longer and deeper. Jake kept one hand along the side of her face, as he often did, as if he wanted to always ascertain her position. But when he started to tug at the bottom of her shirt with the other hand, suddenly the sofa seemed far too cramped and confining. Kassie sat up, then took Jake's hand and pulled him to his feet. She didn't have to explain to him what she had in mind or where she was leading him--by the wide grin on his face, he clearly understood.

Kassie flipped the light on in her bedroom and they sat on the edge of her bed, facing each other, knees touching. Their conversation in the park was still echoing in her mind. There was so much she wanted to say to him, but instead, without signing anything at all, she placed her hands on either side of his face. Slowly, she ran her fingers over every contour, from his high forehead and flat cheeks, down to his pointed chin, then again over his closed eyes, straight nose and red, soft lips. He didn't ask what she was doing, but just sat still, enjoying her touch.

She leaned forward and kissed him, at the same time taking one of his hands and guiding it toward her breast. He stiffened and gave a sharp intake of breath, then kissed her harder, squeezing, wrapping his other arm around her, reaching under her t-shirt. Suddenly it was as if they couldn't move fast enough. He pulled her shirt over her head and she did the same to him, their hands moving faster as they continued kissing. With one hand, Jake yanked open the fly of her jeans and tugged them down. They rolled over onto the bed, rolling around and around. His breath was coming ragged and faster.

They had been together long enough to have developed a rhythm and habits. Now that he had pulled off all her clothes, Kassie put her hand on his cock, springing insistently in her direction and began rubbing slowly. But to her surprise, he stopped her.

N-O-T L-I-K-E T-H-A-T, he explained.

A-R-E Y-O-U S-U-R-E? she asked. She didn't have to ask what he meant.

Jake nodded, tapped her hand firmly, then added I W-A-N-T T-O, shaping each letter clearly and emphatically.

Rather than answering in words, Kassie kissed him again, pressing her body against his all the way down to the tips of her toes. Then she spelled, C-O-N-D-O-M and slid from the bed.

Kassie cracked the bedroom door open and peered into the hall. The late fall afternoon had waned, leaving the rest of the house shrouded in twilit silence. Erik wasn't back yet. Tiptoeing over the cold hardwood floor, Kassie slipped naked from the bedroom into the bathroom. From the bottom drawer next to the sink, she snagged a strip of plastic-wrapped condoms and a little tube of lube.

Back in the bedroom, Jake sat up and reached for her as he felt her sit back down on the bed. She detached one of the wrapped condoms from the strip and placed it in his hand. He turned it over and over gingerly, looking slightly puzzled.

You want me to....she mimed putting it on. Instantly Jake's face was aflame, all the way to the tips of his ears. *Sorry*, Kassie signed, kicking herself for killing the mood. *Never mind.*

She plucked the condom from his fingers and tossed it aside, kissing and caressing him, trying to get back to the place they were a moment ago. It didn't take long. They lay back down on the bed, with Kassie on top. She gently fingered his sack, smiling to herself as his cock throbbed and pulsed insistently. His breathing was becoming deeper and hoarser again.

O-K she said. L-U-B-E. She ripped open the little packet of lube and rubbed it on his cock. For a second he jerked at the chill of it, but after a moment he was groaning and arching his back as her slick hand rubbed over him.

O-K, N-O-W C-O-N-D-O-M she explained, then took both hands away to open the wrapper. Then instantly cursed herself aloud for not opening it first, as the tiny square wrapper slid through her lubed-up fingers. After what felt like a lengthy struggle, at last she resorted to ripping it with her teeth. The wrapper burst open and the condom flew out, landing on Jake's belly.

He picked it up and fingered it seriously. Rather than taking it from him and putting it on herself as she had planned, Kassie put her hands over his, showing him how to turn it right side up, pinch the top to keep out the air, and then slide it on. How strange, she thought, that something so ordinary could feel so profoundly intimate, heightening the anticipation of what they were about to do.

Jake's breath caught in his throat as she glided her hand over his cock again, applying more lube. With the other hand, she spelled out R-E-A-D-Y? He tapped her hand, and she added R-E-L-A-X O-K, as she slid herself down on him slowly, until he was all the way inside her. He groaned loudly as she began to grind her hips against him, and delicately ran his fingers over her shoulders, her breasts, her belly, taking in all of her as she moved against him. She started slow, wanting to take her time and savor the moment, but soon the steady rhythm was carrying them both away. She took one of his hands and guided it between her legs, pressing his thumb firmly against her clit. The sight of him writhing in ecstasy under her, his pale cheeks flushed and mouth open, his primal groans were all too much for her, and although she had intended to hold back, she came before him, in rippling hot waves. She increased her rhythm, faster and faster, until he finally joined her, bucking and twisting underneath her hips.

With a little cry of pleasure, she pulled up and collapsed against him, hugging him tightly and burying her face against his neck, still feeling like she was soaring. But almost immediately his fingers found her hand. G-O-O-D, R-I-G-H-T?

She nodded her head vigorously against his shoulder, and replied Y-E-S V-E-R-Y V-E-R-Y G-O-O-D as firmly as she could with shaking fingers.

He grinned and nodded, then wrapped his arms tightly around her and squeezed as hard as he could, and gave her a wet kiss on the cheek. She laughed, and feeling the movement of her ribs and her breath on his face, he laughed too, his strange, low, gravelly laughter.

I-M G-O-O-D, R-I-G-H-T? he asked again.

Big head, she signed teasingly, then added more seriously, Y-O-U A-R-E T-H-E B-E-S-T. He squeezed her again, and the look of pleasure and satisfaction on his face made her feel like she might bust with happiness.

Kassie wanted nothing more than to lie in that bed with Jake forever, or at least to drift off to sleep with him and not have to get up until the morning. But it was getting late, and they hadn't even eaten dinner. It was hunger that drove them from the bed, forced them reluctantly to dress and head into the kitchen to scrounge up something easy. It seemed Jake's thoughts were running in the same direction, because when they sat down side by side on the bench to eat their cold sandwiches, he said, *I wish I could sleep here every night.*

But the sign for wish and the sign for hungry are the same, and with his looping, uncertain signs, at first Kassie wasn't sure she understood him properly.

You want to live here with me? she asked.

Yes. No good?

Yes, good, I want too, she replied. *If you want, you can live here with me and Erik. You sure? Your mother, father say what?*

Instead of answering, he gave a noncommittal sort of wave and started eating his sandwich. Kassie let it drop, not wanting to spoil the mood. The idea of living with him, being able to cuddle up next to him in bed at night and wake up next to him in the morning, was almost unbearably sweet.

Chapter Twenty

As the autumn deepened, Kassie found a new rhythm to her days. It was just the smallest change, but cutting out running with Dave left her with more time to spend with Jake, and yes, even his parents. She joined Jake and his father for jogging on the weekends, and drove over for dinner even on weeknights. Erik was right, having her own car made spending time together so much easier.

But the question of Jake moving in hung in the air between them. The idea filled her with a warm glow, but thinking it over in the cold light of day, Kassie had to admit to herself that she had some doubts. How independent could he really be? Could they ever have anything approaching an equal partnership, or would his disability overwhelm everything else? The more she thought about it, the more she realized that before he could move in, he had to have a job, something to do so he wasn't just sitting around the house all day reading the internet. Besides, she couldn't ask Erik to let him move in rent-free.

>Is there space in your house for a desk for my computer? Jake asked one evening over IM, bringing a new topic up out of nowhere, as he often did.

>Yes, there's a finished room in the basement. If you don't mind, there's plenty of space down there, she replied.

>Is it dark down there? Because I only want a room with a lots of light, and a huge window with a view of Puget Sound.

>Haha, very funny.

>Of course it's ok. I don't mind the basement.

>But you know, I was thinking, if you're
really serious about moving in, maybe it's time
to really look for a job? Don't you want to do
something?

>Kassie, of course I want to do something.
Do you think I like being a useless drain on
society?

Kassie stared at the words on the screen, stung. She felt
terrible--this was exactly what she had been avoiding, and now
she had hurt his feelings.

>I'm sorry, she typed quickly. You're not
useless. I didn't mean it that way.

>No, I'm sorry, but I don't know what to
say. I've told you, I want to work, but I don't
know what I could do. The truth is I've been
thinking about it a lot lately but I'm kind of
scared to even ask. Who would hire a deafblind
guy who doesn't even have a college degree?

>There has to be something. How about if
you talk to Kevin?

>Ok, I guess. But I'm not going to work in
some sheltered workshop with a bunch of re,
excuse me, developmentally delayed people
sorting trash or some other mindless menial
task.

>Come on, you haven't even talked to him
yet. You don't know.

>Ok, you're right. I'll talk to him.

It was not exactly the response she was hoping for, but
it was at least a start.

It wasn't hard to find a chance to talk to Kevin, because
he was at their house all the time. She thought it was adorable
how head over heels Erik was for him. He was completely
unlike the kind of skinny, slick club kid that was Erik's usual

type. Kevin's thick beard was trimmed carefully away from his mouth but otherwise he was a bushy, hairy, burly kind of guy. He had a piercing intensity that Kassie found intimidating at first, although she admired his passion for disability advocacy. But there was no question in her mind about his feelings for Erik, as she noticed the tender expression on his face as his eyes followed Erik, bouncing and beatboxing around the kitchen as he put the finishing touches on dinner.

More importantly, Kevin had taken to Jake immediately. Kassie was deeply touched that Kevin had even learned the deafblind alphabet for him, picking it up in a day. When the four of them were together in the house on weekends, over dinner or even just passing through, Kevin made a point of signing directly to Jake rather than expecting Kassie to interpret.

One weekday evening over dinner when it was just the three of them, Kassie asked Kevin, *Can you help Jake find a job?*

She gathered that Kevin could speak and lipread pretty well, but whenever he and Erik were together, they used ASL most of the time. Kassie did her best to keep up, and since Kevin found out she was taking classes, he continually prodded her to do better.

Kevin fixed his dark, intense gaze on her and shrugged elaborately. *If Jake wants to work, he must talk to me himself.* As always, his signs were fluid and lightening fast, but he paused at the end to make sure she had followed him.

I understand, she signed, flicking her finger up by her temple, as if a light had just turned on in her head.

Jake wants to work? Erik asked, his eyebrows high, as if he didn't quite believe her. *What does he want to do?*

He doesn't know, Kassie replied, feeling exposed, unprepared. *That's the problem.*

Kevin nodded seriously. *Ok. I can advise him but desire to work must come from Jake himself, or it's no good.*

Later that night as she was chatting with Jake online, Kassie tentatively broached the subject.

>Kevin had dinner with us again tonight, she typed carefully.
>Oh?
>Yeah, I asked him about you.
>What did he say?
>Nothing really, just that you have to talk to him yourself, not me.
>...
>Come on, don't get mad at me. You said you would talk to him.
>I'm not mad at you. I'll think about it.

Feeling a bit like they were going in circles, Kassie let it drop. As they signed off for the night, she remembered Jake's words from when they first started dating: You have to be more patient with me. Deafblind people have to do things slowly. She sighed as she powered down her computer. Maybe he was right: she was too impatient, always rushing, rushing on to the next thing. He wanted to work, she was sure of it, but she had to let him figure it out at his own pace.

CHAPTER TWENTY-ONE

As the autumn drew to a close, Jake's parents invited Kassie to spend Thanksgiving with them. She was touched that they were being so welcoming, but politely turned them down. Since her father died, she didn't like to leave her mother on her own over the holidays. The truth was, she still found it hard to go back, and she really hated to fly. So she put off visiting as long as possible, until the holidays came around again. Her mother never said anything, but Kassie knew it would upset her if she didn't go.

Jake was unhappy, since this meant he would have to endure another trip to Bend on his own.

>If you came over, then my grandparents would drive up here for Thanksgiving. But if you don't, we have to go down to their place, and my aunt and uncle and horrible cousins from Eugene will come too. I won't have anyone to talk to, he complained over IM.

>What about Carter?

>It's Thanksgiving. He's going to visit his own family.

>So your cousins don't know sign? Not even the alphabet?

>No, only my parents really know it, and they are terrible interpreters. They keep getting caught up in the conversation. The more people are there, the worse it is.

>But the others could at least print the letters on your hand, right?

>I don't know, they just don't.

>I'm sorry, I really don't want to leave you but I kind of promised my mom I would visit.

I haven't been home since last Christmas. The
holidays are hard on her with Dad gone.

>You're right. You should see your mom.

>Sorry.

>I'll be ok. I've endured countless trips
there before, I can do it again. But I will miss
you.

>I'll miss you too, but we can talk online
every day.

>No, I won't have my computer at my
grandparents' house.

>Dammit! I forgot! Maybe I should stay.

>No, you're right, go be with your mom.
It's only a few days.

In the end, she took the trip, and Jake let her go with
good grace.

H-A-V-E A G-O-O-D T-I-M-E W-I-T-H Y-O-U-R M-
O-T-H-E-R, he told her as they were saying goodbye on the
front step of his house. Y-O-U-R-E A G-O-O-D D-A-U-G-
H-T-E-R. She knew he meant to tease her gently, but Kassie
felt a sharp twinge of guilt as his words spooled out on her
hand. She didn't feel like a good daughter. She hadn't gone
home for a visit in the summer, even though she could have
taken time off work. And despite talking to her mother on the
phone regularly, their conversations were never that in depth.
She still had not told her mother about Jake. Or rather, she
had not told her about Jake specifically, but only hinted in a
vague way that she was seeing someone.

The flights from Seattle to Chicago then from Chicago
to Fort Wayne were relatively smooth, but Kassie still found
herself reflexively gripping the armrests at every bump and
rattle. The minute the plane landed, she heaved a sigh of relief.

Knowing how much her mother liked to meet her at the airport, Kassie had tried to book a flight that got in when her mother was off work, but it wasn't possible. She arrived late in the evening, took a taxi through the dark streets, and let herself into the empty house with the key her mother insisted she keep.

The tiny house was dark and cold. Kassie switched on the lights and turned up the heat, dropped her suitcase in the extra bedroom, then went down to the kitchen to wait for her mother to return from her shift at the hospital.

This was not her childhood home. She and her mother had both agreed after her father's death that it was better to sell the house, a comfortable, rambling prewar bungalow, and find something more economical for one person, less freighted with memories. Kassie had already left for college when her father suffered the first stroke, so for her, the old house only held happy memories, but she could appreciate that for her mother, it was where she had first found him on the bathroom floor, then tried in vain for months to help him recover before the second and third stroke that finally killed him. But coming back to Fort Wayne, even to a different part of town, always reminded Kassie of the other house, now lost to her.

Her mother didn't return home until close to midnight. As always, her mother made a big deal over hugging and kissing her, but Kassie was struck more by how her mother seemed to shrink just a bit every time she saw her. Although it was late, they were both too keyed up to sleep, so they sat together at the round kitchen table over mugs of peppermint tea.

"You look fantastic!" her normally businesslike mother exclaimed repeatedly. "You're practically glowing. Tell me, who is this mysterious person you've been seeing?"

Kassie shifted in her chair, terrified that what she was about to say would ruin the whole weekend. But she knew that if she didn't bring it all up right away, the right moment would never come around again.

"Um..." she hesitated, toying with her cup.

"What's his name?" her mother cried, before she could say anything more. "Or is it a she? Because that's perfectly all right. You can tell me."

"Jeez! Mom!" Kassie felt her face go red. "His name is Jake. We've been together for like eight or nine months now, I guess. I'm really sorry I didn't say anything sooner."

Her mother waved a hand, sweeping away the apology. "It doesn't matter. You're an adult, you can do what you like. So tell me more about Jake. What does he do?"

Unreasonably, Kassie felt herself go even redder. "He, um, he doesn't have a job yet." She emphasized *yet* ever so slightly. "Because he has a disability. He's deaf and blind."

"Really?" Her mother's eyebrows shot up. She clearly wasn't expecting that. "So how did you meet?"

"You know I've been taking ASL classes for a while now," Kassie babbled nervously. "And I've been going to some Deaf and deafblind community events. I mean, Erik introduced me, and I've been going, mainly just to practice, and everyone there is really nice...anyway I met him at one of those events." She paused, but when her mother didn't say anything, she continued on a bit desperately, "Please, please don't say anything bad about him. Mom, I really love him. He's a great guy, really smart and kind. I'm sorry I didn't tell you sooner. Maybe I'm just tired from traveling all day, but if you say anything against him I don't think I could stand it." She was shocked to find herself blinking back tears.

"Oh, sweetie!" Her mother put a hand on hers. "Why would I say anything against him? He treats you right, doesn't he?"

"Yes, yes, of course! I don't know...some of my friends don't understand how I could be with someone who's so disabled. They've said some really mean things like you wouldn't believe."

Her mother's mouth settled into a grim line. "Anyone who says mean things and makes you feel bad isn't a real friend."

Kassie burst out laughing through exhausted tears at that bit of trite, motherly advice. "I know."

"People say stupid things all the time, just out of ignorance. But you know I see people with all kinds of disabilities and conditions at work every day. They're just people like everyone else." Kassie burst out crying even harder. "Kassie, sweetheart, what's wrong?"

Kassie pulled her chair closer and threw her arms around her mother's narrow shoulders. "Nothing, I'm just so happy," she sobbed.

Her mother patted her messy curls. "I can't believe you thought something like that would bother me. Come on, have a little more faith in your old mom." Kassie nodded, wiping her eyes and feeling a little foolish. "I just want to get to know him," her mother continued. "Although I guess talking on the phone is out of the question, right? How do you communicate?"

Kassie launched into a detailed explanation. By they time they finally decided to turn in, Kassie still hadn't finished. The next day, they followed what had become their new yearly ritual and spent the whole day cooking the traditional Thanksgiving feast: turkey, stuffing, gravy, cranberry sauce, apple pie, all from scratch. When Kassie was younger, her mother's cooking was more of the frozen or boxed dinner variety, but her daughter's discovery of cooking had inspired her as well.

"You've made me such a gourmet, I can't stand to eat in the hospital cafeteria anymore," she joked.

"Don't worry, after today you'll have enough leftovers to take to work for a month," Kassie assured her.

All through their day of cooking, then even as they at last sat downto a massive meal, exhausted but happy, Kassie couldn't stop talking about Jake. Ordinarily she couldn't stand the kind of girl who wouldn't shut up about her boyfriend, but she figured her mother was the one person who would indulge her.

"I can't wait to meet him," her mother said as she served out steaming slices of apple pie. "You should bring him along next time you visit."

"Are you sure? There's only one guest bed. Where would he sleep, on the couch?"

"Oh please, you're an adult. I don't mind if he sleeps in the guest bed with you."

"Really?"

"Yes, really! Come on, I want to meet him."

Kassie hesitated. "I want you to meet him too, but I have to warn you, it's hard for him to communicate with someone who doesn't sign. I'm not very good at interpreting." She didn't add the story of how Jake had freaked out on the bus. She couldn't imagine him flying in an airplane.

"Well, show me this alphabet you use, and maybe I can try to learn a little."

"Wow Mom, you're the best!"

"Ha! I said I would try, not that I would be good at it. But every little bit helps, right?"

Kassie felt herself tearing up again. "You don't know how much this means to me. Even people in his own family haven't bothered to learn."

"Well, I can't say anything about that. But if he makes you happy, that's all that matters to me."

The rest of the weekend passed slowly. Kassie had not kept in touch with any of her high school friends, and her mother had to work. She spent the days watching endless reruns of *Law and Order* on TV and checking her email every few hours, hoping that Jake might be back, but it seemed his parents were determined to stay in Oregon for the whole four day weekend.

At last, late on Saturday night, she refreshed the page and saw the smiley face icon next to Jake's name. She opened a chat window right away.

>Hey handsome, she wrote.

>Hi! He answered immediately.

>Wanna chat?

>You must be psychic. I just got home and came online a few minutes ago.

>Haha, do not doubt my power, hahaha.

>So how is Indiana?

>Bleah, ok. Boring. My mom says hi. She wants to meet you. How was Oregon?

>I don't want to talk about it.

>That good, huh.

>A disaster of epic proportions. I hate not being able to talk to people.

>I know. Was there yelling?

>There might have been some yelling.

>Maybe?

>I don't know, I'm deaf. I didn't hear any yelling.

>Hahaha. I miss you so much!

>I miss you too.

On Sunday morning Kassie's mother drove her to the airport. Kassie hugged her tightly beside the idling car at the departures gate. A light dusting of snow had fallen in the night, and the air was sharp and cold. She felt a twinge of guilt for wanting to leave so badly. She couldn't get back to Seattle fast enough.

"I'll come back for Christmas, too," she promised, partly to assuage her guilt for not visiting more, although the thought of flying more made her slightly nauseated.

"Bring Jake with you," her mother replied, kissing her forehead.

CHAPTER TWENTY-TWO

The next Saturday morning Kassie was up and out of the house before Erik even stirred. She had returned late the previous Sunday and had go to work and classes all week. This would be the first time seeing Jake since getting back. As she drove over the floating bridge, she once again offered up a silent thanks to Erik for the car. It was all she could do to keep from speeding.

When she knocked on the door to his house, for the first time ever Jake opened the door himself. She threw her arms around him and they stood in the doorway for almost a minute, kissing and embracing until he finally closed the door. Despite the distraction, a part of her mind still wondered, had he been waiting by the door all morning? How did he know when she arrived?

Miss me lots? she asked, gesturing expansively.

Yes, he answered. *Also, I have a surprise. Come see.* He tucked her arm into his elbow as if he were guiding her, and led her down the hall to the kitchen.

As she passed the living room, she could see his parents sitting in front of the TV, and called out a greeting to them.

"Welcome back!" Mr. O'Malley called out without getting up. "Jake has something to show you."

Jake tugged her impatiently into the kitchen, then gestured in the general direction of the table, repeatedly swiveling his hand towards his own face then at the table, with his fingers in a v shape. *Look look look.*

On the table were two black electronic devices, one the size and shape of a small laptop, and the other a cell phone. Kassie recognized it instantly, and gave a whoop as she embraced Jake again, shaking him in her excitement. He grinned broadly.

W-O-W D-E-A-F-B-L-I-N-D C-O-M-M-U-N-I-C-A-T-O-R, she spelled out laboriously, her fingers stumbling in a rush.

D-B-C he corrected, acceding to at least one useful abbreviation.

So expensive! she signed. *How?*

Rather than answering, he groped toward the table until he found the cell phone, then shoved it in her hands and sat down in front of the larger device, a Braille note taker. Instead of the QWERTY keyboard, it had the eight large keys and space bar of a Perkins Braillewriter, and below that a thin metal strip with holes for the pins to pop out: a Braille display.

Kassie slid open the cell phone to reveal a full keyboard under a horizontal display. A message popped up on the screen, and at the same time a machine voice spoke from the note taker.

Hi, I'm deaf and blind. To communicate with me, type a message and press return.

Hi Jake, **Kassie typed.** This is so cool.

The machine voice spoke her message as well.

Jake ran his fingers along the Braille display, reading her message, then typed back, Yes! It's great. It has TTY, internet and email too. And I can use the cell phone to get text messages.

But how could you afford it? I thought it was too expensive? **Kassie typed.**

After the trip to Bend, Dad said he couldn't stand it anymore, and I needed a better way to communicate no matter how much it cost.

The flat, robotic voice of the machine echoed loudly in the kitchen, and Kassie glanced uncomfortably toward the living room. Then she realized it was the first time it was possible for someone to overhear a conversation with Jake. Impulsively, she hugged him again, and planted a kiss on his forehead, then climbed onto his lap. With her arms around him, she typed, I'm so happy for you.

I can go anywhere, and talk to anyone, even talk on the phone. I finally feel like a real person.

When the text appeared on the screen, Kassie wasn't sure what to say. Typing was easier than signing, but it still lacked emotional depth, the extra meaning imparted with the flick of a wrist, pressure of the fingers, or added flourish. She looked into his face, and saw his normally inexpressive, stiff features were still split by a wide grin. She kissed his cheek, deciding a teasing rather than serious answer was called for.

So if you can get internet on that thing, does that mean you will be reading websites and texting other people while I'm trying to talk to you?

As he read her message, he gave a wheezing laugh.

Because that's what real people do with their devices, she added, and he laughed harder.

Haha, no one can stop me now, he replied.

Emboldened by DBC, Jake agreed to meet Kassie's yoga friends, Cyndi, Lorna, Abby, and Gail, over brunch at Sunflowers. This was normally a strictly women-only event, but after much serious discussion they decided to make a one-time exception mainly, Kassie suspected, because they were curious about Jake.

This time Kassie was determined that things would be different than at Dave's party.

"You have to talk directly to him, not to me," she instructed them after yoga class in the changing room, as they were finalizing their plans for brunch. She explained about the communicator, and how to use it. "Please, just talk to him like any other person. It really means a lot to both of us." They nodded seriously, except for Abby, who still looked skeptical. She had not repeated her earlier objections to their relationship, but she hadn't really warmed up to the idea either. Kassie pointedly ignored her, reminding herself that she didn't need Abby's permission for anything. At least Cyndi had stopped calling her a saint.

Kassie also prepared Jake, telling him about each of them. They worked out quick name signs for each one based on the first letters of their names. She also found the menu for Sunflowers online and sent it to him to read, so they wouldn't have to waste time having her sign or type the whole menu to him in the restaurant. He wasn't so pleased with the idea of a vegan restaurant.

>It's not breakfast without bacon and eggs, he groused to her over IM.

>Whatever, one meal without meat won't kill you.

>You don't know that. It might. I don't know what half the things on this menu are. What is seitan?

>It's like a kind of fake meat.

>???? How can something be like fake meat? Does that mean it's circled back around and become real meat? And why would someone who chooses not to eat meat want to eat a meat approximation?

>Maybe you should stick to the cinnamon buns, those are always good.

>What is wheatgrass juice? Is it really juice made from grass?

>A kind of grass. Not the kind that grows in your yard, a special kind. It's supposed to be good for you.

>I want to try that. I want to be able to say I tried grass juice.

>Wheatgrass juice. Get whatever you want, but promise no yelling.

>I don't have to yell now. I can just turn up the volume on the DBC.

>Very funny, hahaha.

They arrived at Sunflowers late, the result of a tie-up on the floating bridge. As they ducked in from the chilly street to the warm, close air of the restaurant, Kassie noted with dismay that it was packed with people. She pulled Jake closer to her, hoping he wouldn't get jostled too much.

Her friends were huddled by the door, waiting for a table. Kassie squeezed in next to them, with Jake right beside her, and waved hello.

"Hi everyone, sorry we're late. This is Jake." She pulled him forward as much as possible in the tight space. They all stared at him nervously.

"So how does this work? Will you introduce us to him?" Abby demanded.

"It feels wrong not to introduce ourselves," Cyndi fretted. "Can I, like, touch him?"

"Oh my God, Cyndi!" Lorna cried, blushing in embarrassment on her friend's behalf.

"Why don't you each shake his hand and I'll sign your names," Kassie suggested, so that was what they did.

As he shook each hand seriously, Jake said, "Hi" to each of them using his voice, just one syllable to be certain he got it right, for once speaking reasonably clearly and not too loud. It worked--they seemed impressed. For his part, the introductions seemed to help him get oriented, and he relaxed visibly, even smiling.

"Wow Kassie, he's super hot!" Gail declared in a stage whisper as the hostess led them to their table.

Once they were seated, Jake pulled the DBC out of his backpack, and Kassie helped him clear a place for the note taker on the table. She offered the cell phone to Cyndi.

"Is this that communication device you were talking about?" Cyndi asked as she took it hesitantly.

"Yeah, you can talk directly to him. It's a lot easier than having me translate everything," Kassie explained.

Cyndi slid the cell phone open.

Hi, I'm deaf and blind. To communicate with me, type a message and press return.

"Whoa!" They all jumped as the machine voice thundered out. People at other tables turned around to stare.

T-O-O L-O-U-D T-U-R-N I-T D-O-W-N, Kassie scrambled to spell to him.

"I didn't think it would talk too!" Lorna exclaimed.

"It makes it easier for everyone to take part in the conversation," Kassie said. "Go ahead, just type something."

Hi Jake this is Cyndi, the machine spoke in a more reasonable volume, as Jake read the Braille message.

Hi Cyndi, nice to meet you. I'm Jake, he replied.

"Oooooh! So cool!" Cyndi wriggled like an excited child as she read the message, the machine speaking at the same time.

So nice to meet you too, she typed back. I've heard so much about you! Jake's cheeks flushed red as he read her message. All good! she added. Kassie can't stop talking about you. But she didn't tell us you're such a cutie! Jake turned even redder.

"Let me try!" Abby demanded. Kassie nearly fainted as Cyndi tossed the phone across the table.

"Jesus! That cost six thousand dollars!" Kassie exclaimed, as Abby clumsily caught the device.

"Seriously? Then you better not let Cyndi touch it again. You know she dropped her cell phone in the toilet again last week," Gail laughed.

"It's true!" Cyndi laughed even harder.

Ignoring them, Abby, in full librarian mode, had already introduced herself to Jake and was quizzing him on how often he used his local public library.

"Hey guys, the waitress is here," Kassie said.

Abby stopped typing and glared at her over the top of the cell phone. "Server," she corrected.

A tall woman with a labret and abundant blond dreadlocks tied up in a towering multicolored headscarf sauntered over to their table and thrust her hip out, brandishing a pen and order pad. "Hi, I'm Maggie," she said. "What can I get for you today?"

Kassie tapped Jake's hand, and spelled out W-A-I-T-R-E-S-S I-S H-E-R-E T-E-L-L M-E Y-O-U-R O-R-D-E-R.

"No!" Jake said, his voice loud and toneless. Typing on the note taker, he added, I want to order myself. Give her the DBC.

With some trepidation, Kassie reached across the table, plucked the cell phone from Abby's limp fingers, reset it, and handed it to the waitress. "Uh, do you mind?" she asked apologetically.

Without even blinking, as if this were something that happened every day, the waitress tucked the order pad under her arm and slid open the cell phone.

`Hi, I'm deaf and blind. To communicate with me, type a message and press return,` the machine said. She raised an eyebrow and glanced at Jake.

`Hi I'm Maggie,` she typed.

`Hi Maggie I'm Jake,` he replied. Kassie had a strong urge to grab his hand and tell him to hurry it up already--the restaurant was crowded and the waitress wasn't interested in chatting with him.

Maggie, however, did not seem hurried. She smiled and typed back, `Hi Jake nice to meet you. What can I get for you today?` Kassie made a mental note to leave her a huge tip.

`I want the potato and black bean scramble, a cinnamon roll, and grass juice.`

`Anything else? Do you want coffee or tea?`

`Yes, coffee please.`

`Ok, that's a potato and black bean scramble, a cinnamon roll, wheatgrass juice, and coffee. Correct?`

`Yes.`

`Thank you Jake.`

`Thank you Maggie.`

"Thank you," Kassie said fervently as she took the cell phone back. The rest of them all placed their orders without incident. Jake was positively glowing.

I T-A-L-K-E-D T-O H-E-R, he spelled into Kassie's hand, his fingers dancing with excitement. S-O E-A-S-Y I-T-S A-M-A-Z-I-N-G.

Kassie leaned over impulsively and kissed him on the cheek.

"Oh my God! You two are so adorable!" Cyndi crowed. "Here, give me that thing! I have to tell him too!" She held out her hand.

"Ok, but be careful," Kassie pleaded as she handed over the phone. "And let him know who's typing."

This is Cyndi, she typed dutifully. You two are the cutest couple I have ever seen.

I don't know what any other couples look like but thank you, he replied. Cyndi hooted with laughter.

You're too funny!

The waitress returned with their drinks.

W-H-E-A-T-G-R-A-S-S J-U-I-C-E, Kassie reminded him, and placed the glass in his hand. He took a deep swallow, then choked, wrinkling up his face.

"Ah!" he gurgled. "Yuck!"

They all laughed. "I'm so glad you took the time to learn to say that word," Kassie remarked sarcastically to no one in particular.

I agree, that stuff is gross, Lorna typed to him.

They passed the phone around the table, even after the food arrived, asking him all sorts of questions about himself. The conversation proceeded much more slowly than if they had only been speaking, but no one seemed to mind. Jake gamely responded to each question patiently and unselfconsciously, even when Lorna asked him how he used the toilet.

"Lorna!" Gail scolded. Kassie was about to tell Jake he didn't have to answer, but he was already typing back a response.

`I didn't know there was more than one way to use the toilet.`

"Ha! He got you there!" Cyndi laughed.

"Yes there is," Lorna said primly, and typed, `Standing up or sitting down?`

`Sitting down,` Jake replied expressionlessly. Cyndi and Gail were shaking uncontrollably with laughter. Abby snatched the phone away from Lorna.

"Give me that," she snapped. `This is Abby,` she typed. `Are you satisfied with your life?`

Instantly the table went quiet. Kassie rolled her eyes, but still found herself strangely relieved when Jake typed back `Yes,` without reflecting for even a second. `Are you?`

Abby scrunched up her nose. `Of course not. No one is ever fully satisfied. Things could always be better.`

"Oh honey, that's just sad!" Cyndi declared. "At my age, you learn to enjoy what you can."

`Are you really satisfied?` Abby pressed. `Even though you can't see or hear?`

Jake stiffened, and Kassie braced herself for an outburst, but instead he just typed furiously. `You think I can't be happy because I am deafblind?` he demanded. `Is happiness in life only allowed to people who are not disabled? My life is great, and it's getting better all the time. If you are unhappy or dissatisfied, it's only because you have a limited definition of happiness.`

"Ha, he told you," Cyndi said, and took the phone from her. `This is Cyndi, and I agree with you 100%.`

They all relaxed again as Cyndi proceeded to pepper him with more questions: did he dream in pictures? (no) did he know what people's faces look like? (not really) did he know she has crazy curly hair? (no). To Kassie's horror, Cyndi then reached across the table, grabbed his hand, and stuck it in her mass of wiry white frizz.

"Okay, I think it's time to go," Kassie interceded.

They paid the bill and walked outside where they all exchanged farewell hugs.

"Bye! See you again soon!" Lorna called out, waving.

"Don't say 'see'," Abby scolded, poking her in the ribs.

"It's alright," Kassie said, back to interpreting now that they were standing and Jake had returned the DBC to the backpack. "Jake says it was nice to meet you all, and see you soon too."

Back in the car, Kassie turned to Jake before starting the engine.

I'm sorry they were R-U-D-E, she signed.

What? No no no. I H-A-D S-O M-U-C-H F-U-N, he said, his fingers moving energetically. Y-O-U-R F-R-I-E-N-D-S A-R-E A-M-A-Z-I-N-G.

Kassie shook her head. She wouldn't go that far, but for once she was grateful for their eccentric ways; at least they had made an honest effort to reach out to Jake. It helped that Cyndi was pretty much impervious to any kind of shame or self-consciousness. Kassie still couldn't believe Cyndi had just grabbed his hand like that. She remembered Carter's stern lecture to her about respecting his hands. She would have to tell them not to do that in the future. But Jake seemed to take it in stride as just part of Cyndi's natural exuberance.

CHAPTER TWENTY-THREE

The change in Jake was beyond anything Kassie had dared to hope for. He went from withdrawn to chatty and smiling almost overnight. He was eager to go out, to be with people, and everywhere he went, he pulled out the DBC. Kassie worried at first that random strangers might find this annoying or off-putting, but to the contrary most people, like Maggie at Sunflowers, were kind and patient. Even more startling was the change in his relationship with his parents. Just knowing they could call or text him whenever he was out put them at ease.

The next Saturday Jake announced after dinner at her place that he intended to stay overnight. Kassie was nervous, and asked him over and over if he was sure, but he sent his father a text and that was that.

Ok, have fun. See you tomorrow, his father replied.

Kassie did a silent happy dance, and Erik winked at her as they cleaned up the kitchen together.

"Looks like your boy's coming along," Erik remarked. Kassie glanced at Jake, who was still sitting at the table with the DBC, probably checking his email. "Kevin tells me Jake asked him about a job finally."

"No way!" Kassie exclaimed. "Why didn't he tell me?"

Erik shrugged. "Maybe he wants to figure it out on his own. Don't tell him I told you. I'm sure he'll tell you himself when he's ready."

"I suppose."

"Oh hey, there's a pizza night tomorrow. Want to come?" Kassie had not been to pizza night at the Deaf Community Center in months, even though she knew it was good ASL practice. Ms. Hansen was always urging everyone in her class to go, but somehow Kassie hadn't found the time lately. As she hesitated, Erik added, "I already asked Jake and he said he wants to go."

Kassie looked at Jake, still pounding on the keys of the DBC, then slid her gaze back to Erik, her eyes narrowed. "You're sneaky," she said, laughing. Erik only shrugged.

"Hey, you wanted him to be less isolated, right?"

The concept of pizza night was the same as at the Deafblind Center--meet friends, relax while chatting in ASL. But in practice, it was quite different. While the meetup where Kassie had first met Jake was usually low-key and sparsely attended, the event Erik invited them to was raucous and crowded. Within moments of arriving, Erik was bopping around the room, greeting friends. Kassie led Jake to a table so he could set up the DBC, then went to get him a slice of pizza. When she returned, she found that Kevin had already introduced him to someone, an older man in a windbreaker, and they were deep in conversation using the DBC. Kassie waved to Kevin, gave the pizza to Jake, then stood back, not wanting to interfere with the conversation, which seemed to be about computer programming.

Kassie wandered back to get some pizza for herself, looking for any familiar faces. To her surprise, she noticed Carter helping himself to a greasy slice.

"Hey Carter, I didn't expect to see you here," she said, pulling out a piece with extra cheese.

"I've been interpreting for Luann, and she wanted me to come along," he said, indicating a middle aged woman sitting nearby. Kassie recognized her from the Deafblind Center.

"You should come say hi to Jake," Kassie suggested, pointing across the room to where Jake sat.

"Yeah, I will." Carter nodded seriously. "Sorry, I didn't see you guys come in."

"It's okay, we just got here."

Carter craned around to get a better view. "Looks like the DBC is working out well."

"Yeah, it's been great." Kassie nibbled nervously at her pizza. "But, um, you're not upset that he's hiring you less?"

Carter swung his owlish gaze around to glare at her. "Of course not. I'm happy that he has a new way to communicate."

Kassie dropped her gaze, unable to look him in the eye. "I just thought... I don't know..." she couldn't finish the thought.

"Look, it's clearly a good thing for him, right?" Carter said harshly. "And you seem to be good for him too."

Kassie looked up at him sharply, hardly believing her ears.

"What? It's true." Carter shrugged. "So when are you going to get your certification as an interpreter?"

"Oh! I don't know, I really don't think I could."

"Yes, you can. You have a knack for it, I can see. But you need to study more. Just do it, okay? You'd be good at it." With a terse, not quite friendly smile, he tossed his paper plate in the trash and set off to say hello to Jake. Kassie watched him go, stunned. Had she finally earned the Carter stamp of approval? And what was all that about her becoming an interpreter? It was true she had been thinking about it more lately. Her grades in ASL class had gotten better, and Ms. Hansen was encouraging her to keep going. Kassie had never before felt like she had a special talent for anything in particular. It was a nice feeling. But the thought of committing to years of training was daunting. She wasn't sure she was ready to take that on.

Kassie wandered through the room, greeting people she knew slightly from previous meetups. Every once in a while she glanced over at Jake, still seated at one of the tables. He seemed to be doing fine on his own. The man in the windbreaker had brought over a friend, and now all three were engaged in an earnest discussion, passing the DBC cell phone back and forth. She thought again about living together, about her mother's invitation to bring Jake to visit over Christmas. Both ideas still made her a little nervous. How would he react? Were they really ready for these next steps? But she wanted to try.

Several days later Kassie was just leaving work on her way to the bus stop when she saw a familiar tall, athletic figure crossing Westlake Center just ahead of her. Her first instinct was to say nothing, pretend she hadn't seen. But then chiding herself for cowardice, she called out, "Hey, Tara!"

Tara stopped and turned around. "Oh hey, Kassie! I haven't seen you in forever." She was wearing a lumpy knitted winter cap, a parka, and hiking boots, but somehow still looked effortlessly cool. "I guess since you, uh, decided to stop running...?" she trailed off uncomfortably.

"Yeah, I'm really sorry I yelled in your car. I shouldn't have subjected you to that. I haven't talked to Dave since then." Kassie fiddled with the oversized buttons on her pea coat, looking at the pavement.

"But you still see him at work, right?" Tara said slowly.

Kassie shook her head. "We're in different divisions. I just changed the time I take lunch and I never run into him anymore."

Tara's eyes widened in surprise. "So you didn't hear?"

Kassie shook her head. Tara hesitated for a moment, glancing past her. It was starting to snow, big fat flakes slanting down and melting as they hit the pavement. "Do you have a minute?" she asked. "Want to get a coffee?"

"Sure." In the middle of the plaza was a Peet's Coffee, crowded with office workers and students. Kassie followed after her, waiting impatiently to ask more questions until they ordered and squeezed themselves into the last empty table. Once they sat down Tara seemed a bit unsure how to begin. She pulled off her cap and ran a hand through her thin straight hair, pulling it back out of her face.

"So, um, Marty and I broke up," she said flatly.

"Oh! I didn't know. I'm so sorry! That's terrible!" Kassie blurted out, unsure how Tara expected her to react.

"He slept with Sandra," Tara continued in the same emotionless voice. She was making a careful study of her coffee cup, rolling it around in her hands. "Or I guess, according to Marty, Sandra slept with him."

Slowly, the whole story came out. Kassie made sympathetic noises, but she wasn't really that surprised. Sandra had been eyeing Marty for months; everyone assumed it was nothing. But one drunken evening, not long after Kassie's falling out with Dave, Sandra made her move. When he found out, Dave was furious and called her a whore. She cried. Marty said she was delicate and needed his protection.

"So I decided the hell with him," Tara said forcefully, looking Kassie straight in the eye. "If he would rather be with some little baby doll rather than an adult woman, if he likes being the protective daddy, the hell with him! I don't need that in my life. I never spoke to any of them again. I just assumed you had taken their side or something."

"What? No!" Kassie insisted. "Dave couldn't stop saying stupid shit about Jake. I told him if he couldn't respect my boyfriend, we were through as friends. You were there!"

"Huh." Tara stared at her as if she were seeing her for the first time. "You know, I just assumed you made up after that. I just thought of you as Dave's friend, and I always thought he was a hipster douchebag. I only hung out with those guys because of Marty."

Kassie smiled. "Yeah, Dave's an asshole. I don't know why I put up with him for so long. I guess I felt like I didn't have any other friends. But I realized that's not true."

"We're both better off without those guys," Tara agreed. "So are you and Jake still together?"

"Yeah, we've been talking about moving in together." Kassie tried to say it casually, but she couldn't help looking down shyly as she felt her cheeks flush.

"No kidding! Look at you. My God, you're so cute. It must be love," Tara teased her. "He seems like a great guy."

"Really? You think so?" Kassie was genuinely surprised.

"Yeah. Totally hot too. Look, I'm sorry I was kind of rude to you guys at the party, but I was in a bad place. That was the night I found out about Sandra."

"No way! It happened that night?"

"No, it was a few weeks later. But just before you got there, Jenny told me Sandra was serious about Marty. She said the two of them had been meeting for drinks on the sly, and Sandra was convinced Marty was really in love with her."

"Oh man, what assholes. Both of them. Tara, I'm so sorry."

Tara shrugged. "I'm over it. Maybe not totally, but I'm getting there. Anyway, I'm sorry I was kind of rude to both of you that night."

"It's okay, really. You weren't rude. So, um, maybe we could hang out sometime? Get dinner or something?"

"Yeah, I'd like that," Tara said, smiling.

Chapter Twenty-four

Even with the end of December fast approaching, Kassie kept putting off making plans for Christmas. First, she told herself, she had to finish the final project for her ASL class before she could think about anything else. Ms. Hansen had assigned each of them to make a speech about an issue they cared about, record themselves, add English subtitles, and upload the video to YouTube. Kassie knew immediately what she wanted her topic to be. It was just a matter of putting it all together, but creating even a simple video took a surprising amount of work.

The days ticked by, and still she hadn't made travel plans. She had basically promised her mother that she would bring Jake to visit. The more she thought about it, the more she wanted him to come with her, but still she was afraid to ask him. It seemed impossible that he would actually make the trip. For one thing, his parents had only just gotten used to the idea of him sleeping over at her house. How would they react to him flying halfway across the country with her? And for another thing, if he freaked out on the bus, how would he react to the many discomforts and indignities of air travel?

Instead, she only mentioned in an oblique way that her mother wanted to meet him. When she brought it up over IM, he didn't really respond, and she let it drop.

A few days later, he wrote,

>Tell your mother I'm coming.

Kassie almost fell out of her chair.

>Seriously? Your parents said ok?

>Carter told them it would be good for me. To expand my horizons or something.

>Really????

>I told you Carter likes you. I don't know why you're convinced he doesn't.

She knew that Carter still made time to visit Jake regularly and sometimes joined the O'Malleys for dinner. Kassie felt badly that she had once told Jake he wasn't really a friend.

>So your parents don't mind if you go with me and skip Christmas in Oregon?

>No, it's ok. Dad said that after Thanksgiving we all need a break. I think they're going Florida to see Mom's sister.

>Wow, cool. And you'll be ok on the plane?

>Yes, why not?

Kassie chewed her lip as she considered an answer. She didn't want to make things worse, or imply that she didn't think he could do it.

>Have you ever flown before?

>Yes, a few times when I was a kid. We went to Florida to visit my other grandmother before she died.

>But not recently?

>Why are you asking me all this?

>I just don't want you to get upset or freaked out like on the bus.

>That was different.

>Maybe, but there may still be times when I can't be right next to you, or when we'll have to get through big crowds.

>I know. Don't you think I can do it?

>I know you can.

They were lucky; Kassie was able to get off work a few days early so they could leave on a weekday morning when the airport was less crowded. Despite their planning, Kassie still felt a moment of panic as they went through security. They knew Jake would have to leave his cane on the x-ray belt and walk through the gate alone. Kassie stood behind him and squared his shoulders straight ahead. When she saw the guard wave, she signed to him as fast as she could, *Five steps, go!*

He marched forward confidently, lifting his feet high so he wouldn't trip, but just as he stepped through the metal detector, the guard unexpectedly took a step forward. Kassie watched helplessly as they collided in slow motion.

"Sir!" the guard said, "Sir! What's the matter, you blind or what?" He looked straight at Jake, and a look of embarrassment spread across his face as he noticed Jake's permanently closed eyes. He mumbled an apology as he manhandled Jake off to the side.

On the other side of the gate, Kassie was dancing with impatience and frustration, trying to get his attention. Finally realizing they were together, the guard waved her through.

Kassie grabbed Jake's hand, asking O-K? To her immense relief his hand was relaxed as he replied *yes*.

She turned to the guard. "I'm sorry, he can't see or hear."

"Zat so?" the guard said, clearly already losing interest in them. "You his caretaker?"

"I'm his girlfriend," she answered loftily as Jake signed into her hand. "He says sorry for bumping into you."

"You know, if you had asked you could've gotten priority screening and gone through together," the guard said.

Kassie grabbed at their backpacks and shoes, abashed. "Sorry, I didn't know," she mumbled, making a mental note to ask about that on the way home.

They retrieved their things and found the gate without further incident. Once they were sitting down, Jake pulled out the DBC to talk to her but also, Kassie suspected, because he was hoping to chat with other people too.

`I'm really glad you were ok when the guard bumped into you,` **she typed**. She had turned the volume down, but people seated on the benches nearby still stared at them.

`Why not?` he answered, and she thought she caught the shadow of a grin. `I bump into people and things all the time.`

`Yeah, but I was afraid you might panic.`

`No, I could tell by the way he grabbed me he wasn't angry, just trying to help. And I knew you were right behind me, there wasn't anywhere else you could go.`

`Haha, you're right, they wouldn't let me go anywhere else.`

`I told you, what happened on the bus was a one time thing. It won't happen again.`

`I know, sorry I doubted you.`

Kassie looked up to see a girl, probably around three or four, standing directly in front of them, staring at Jake with round blue eyes, the fingers of one hand shoved in her mouth. Kassie was debating whether to explain to the girl about the DBC when the child's mother strode over and yanked her by the arm.

"Don't stare!" the mother hissed.

The girl looked up at her. "Mommy, what's wrong with that man?" The mother's face went white and she smacked the child's bottom. "Mommyyyyy!" the girl wailed, as her mother picked her up and carried her off. Kassie wanted to tell her not to get mad at the kid for asking questions, but it was all over before she could say anything.

Unaware of the child's howling, which continued on the other side of the waiting area, Jake typed another message.

`So when do we board?` **he asked.**

`Oh, right, if I ask I think they'll let us board first. Let's go.`

The flight was full and the agents seemed brusque and preoccupied, but by hanging around the counter, Kassie managed to catch the eye of the senior flight attendant. A motherly, older woman with tall brassy hair frozen in a dramatic French twist, she took to Jake and the DBC immediately. It was a bit awkward to use the DBC standing up, his cane tucked under one arm, the heavy Braille note taker hung on a strap around his shoulders that allowed him to have both hands free to type and read.

`Since it's still early, do you want to meet the pilots?` the flight attendant asked him, after they had introduced themselves.

`Sure, why not,` he typed. She handed the cell phone back to Kassie and went to make a few calls. A few minutes later she returned to take their tickets and lead them down the walkway into the plane.

The pilot, a tall square-jawed, gray-haired man, greeted them kindly, blue eyes twinkling. With so many people in such a tight space Kassie was stuck outside the door, but she reset the cell phone and leaned forward to hand it to the pilot.

"Just slide it open," she explained.

`Hi, I'm deaf and blind. To communicate with me, type a message and press return,` the machine said.

"Nifty device you got there," the pilot remarked as he typed, `Hi I'm Steve.`

`Hi Steve I'm Jake. Nice to meet you,` Jake wrote back, then stuck out his hand. They shook hands seriously.

`My co-pilot is Don, but he's busy. He says hi,` Steve typed. The co-pilot, a younger, fatter man who had not risen from his seat, only grunted and waved without turning around and the machine voice spoke the typed words.

The pilot was deeply impressed when Jake identified the plane as a Boeing 737.

`My father works for Boeing,` Jake explained.

`Ah, no wonder,` the pilot replied, then invited Jake to sit in the pilot's seat. Jake held out his hand, and the pilot led him in a stiff-armed waltz to the seat. Jake ran his right hand over all the controls, but carefully, so as not to move any switches, while with his left he read the descriptions the pilot provided for him over the DBC. More discussion about the specs of the plane, and Kassie was totally lost.

The flight attendant glanced over at her with a grin. "Your guy's pretty smart," she commented. "I fly on these things every day and I don't know half of what they're talking about." She gave a hoarse, braying laugh. "Oh hey, I think we're going to start boarding in a minute. Let me help you find your seats before it gets too crowded."

They thanked the pilots profusely, and the flight attendant helped them stow their bags and get settled. Once they were seated, the DBC had to be turned off and put away.

`T-H-A-T W-A-S S-O C-O-O-L.` Jake was nearly glowing with excitement, oblivious to the hordes of people crowding onto the plane. Kassie kept him updated about their progress, until they were airborne and leveled out.

Feels strange, Jake said. *I feel vibrations, but I don't feel forward motion.*

That's always how it is, Kassie replied. At that moment they hit some turbulence, and she grabbed his hand instinctively, squeezing her eyes shut for a moment.

Don't be scared, he told her. *Wind never hurts the plane.* F-O-R-W-A-R-D T-H-R-U-S-T K-E-E-P-S T-H-E P-L-A-N-E U-P. T-U-R-B-U-L-E-N-C-E I-S N-O-T-H-I-N-G.

Your father told you that? she asked.

Yes. There was another sharp jolt, and in spite of herself, she squeezed his hand again.

He put one protective arm around her, and with the other hand said, N-O R-E-A-S-O-N T-O B-E S-C-A-R-E-D.

I know, she answered. *Sometimes just nervous for no reason.*

I-T-S O-K, he said, and kissed her on the forehead.

The rest of the flight was rough, but Kassie forced herself to relax. The flight attendant came by every so often, slipping them extra snacks or bringing messages from the pilot, seeing how they were doing. Once they landed they thanked both of them again as they walked out. The DBC was still put away, but Jake shook the pilot's hand and received a clap on the shoulder.

The next flight from Chicago to Fort Wayne was much the same as the first. There was only one flight attendant, a young black woman, but she too seemed happy to chat with Jake on the DBC. Kassie asked him if he wanted to check out the cockpit here as well, but he wasn't interested. It was only an Embraer RJ145, he explained. Just a puddle-jumper, nothing to get excited over.

Kassie hated flying in those buzzy little planes even more than in the big jets. As soon as they took off, she was once again gripping the armrests. Instantly sensing her change in mood, Jake took her hand.

Are you always scared to fly? he asked.

Yes. Then she added sheepishly, *I've never told anyone before.*

Why not?

Kassie thought for a moment. The fear always disappeared the moment she landed, and she realized how irrational she was being. The thought of the next flight was unpleasant, but each time she assumed it wouldn't really be that bad. After all, flying is safer than driving. It wasn't until she was in the air again that the unreasoning fear returned.

I'm embarrassed, she signed. *I understand it's safe but I feel scared anyway.*

I know, he replied. *Sometimes I'm scared too. Like on the bus. But I'm trying to be stronger. For you.*

Kassie hugged him fiercely, tears pricking at her eyes, then pulled away to reply, *Thank you. I feel stronger already. I want to be strong for you too.*

The flight was fairly smooth. They sat with their arms entwined, chatting idly. Kassie found for the first time the bumps and jolts didn't bother her so much. As they began the descent, however, Jake seemed to get nervous.

What do I call your mother? he asked, his signs stiff and jerky. M-R-S B-L-O-C-H?

Yes, O-K, Kassie said. *Don't be nervous. She's very nice.*

For once they had matched up their schedules, and Kassie's mother was there to meet them at the airport.

I S-E-E H-E-R, Kassie told him as they stumbled out from the gate to arrivals. Her mother rushed over and gave Kassie a big hug, then shook hands rather formally with Jake.

"Hi, I'm Jake, nice to meet you," he said loudly, sounding very much as if he had rehearsed that sentence, although he still missed most of the consonants.

"Nice to meet you too," her mother replied automatically, then glanced nervously at Kassie.

"It's OK," she said. "You can take his hand if you want to."

Kassie tapped the back of his hand, and he held it out. Her mother took it and spelled out very slowly and deliberately, H-E-L-L-O J-A-K-E. I-M T-I-N-A. N-I-C-E T-O M-E-E-T Y-O-U. She had tried to learn the deafblind alphabet but found it too hard to remember; instead she wrote out each letter on his palm with her index finger.

Jake stiffened instinctively as he felt the unexpected letters, but as she reached the end of her message, he smiled.

"Nice to meet you," he repeated, this time slightly more clearly, and they shook hands more warmly, each trying to communicate much more with the pressure of the hands alone. Kassie let out a huge breath she hadn't realized she'd been holding.

Back at the house Kassie showed Jake all around. The house was tiny, so it didn't take long. He settled at the kitchen table with the DBC to send an email to his parents letting them know he had arrived safely, while Kassie helped her mother prepare dinner.

"Jake was really pleased that you said hi to him yourself," Kassie told her mother as she rinsed lettuce for a salad. Her mother only shrugged. "No really," Kassie said, turning around to look at her intently. "You don't realize what a big deal it is to him. Hardly anyone does that."

"I don't see why not. It's so easy."

"That's what I said!" Kassie exclaimed, shaking the lettuce vigorously to dry it.

Her mother laughed and put her arms around her. "That's my girl. I'm so glad you're here, and that you brought Jake with you." She gave Kassie a sly look. "He's so handsome! Now I see why you chased after him."

"Mom!" Blushing, Kassie wriggled out of her arms and turned back to the sink, but inside she was glowing.

Over dinner Jake chatted with Kassie's mother, his food going cold as he typed on the DBC. He further endeared himself to her by helping to wash up afterwards.

They went upstairs after dinner, and Kassie showed Jake where everything was in the bathroom. Feeling exhausted from the long trip, they fell into bed early. Kassie snuggled up next to him, feeling strange to be with him here in the guest bed. But at the same time, it felt so natural. She sighed deeply, releasing a hard day's worth of tension. Within seconds she was asleep.

CHAPTER TWENTY-FIVE

Between the time change and the stress of travel, Kassie slept late the next morning. She awakened to find Jake already seated at the kitchen table, still in his pajamas and with his hair sticking up, drinking coffee and chatting with her mother on the DBC. Kassie put a hand on his shoulder then kissed him on the cheek, smoothing his hair down.

"Good morning," she said, then typed it again when her mother handed her the cell phone.

I didn't want to wake you, he replied. Sometimes I make a lot of noise without realizing it, he explained, presumably for her mother's benefit.

"Jake was just telling me about your video for ASL class," her mother said, taking the cell phone back and typing what she had just said, as Kassie poured herself some cereal.

You should show it to her, Jake wrote.

"Yes, I'd like to see it."

"Maybe later," Kassie demurred, suddenly embarrassed. "It's really nothing. Don't you have to go to work?"

"You're right," her mother said, draining her coffee and giving Kassie a kiss on the cheek. "But promise you'll show me when I get home tonight."

Kassie and Jake dropped her mother off at the hospital so they could use the car for the day. Their first stop was the supermarket to get food for the week and for Christmas dinner. Not surprisingly, the store was jammed with shoppers, but Jake stuck close by her, holding on to the shopping cart, and he didn't seem to mind the crowd. They had plenty of time, so Kassie guided him through the store slowly, letting him pick out the produce, discussing each purchase, describing all the items to him.

As she watched him select a bag full of shiny green apples, feeling each one carefully with his sensitive fingers, bringing each apple to his nose and sniffing before placing it in the plastic bag, Kassie again recalled his words about deafblind people doing things more slowly. Watching him standing over the bin of apples, she felt like he was one still island in a sea of frantic, rushing people, and it calmed her to be near him. Ordinarily when shopping with another person she would split up to find more items, but she didn't want Jake to turn around and discover her not there, with no way of finding her. He was always teasing her for rushing around, doing so many things at once, but now she found it relaxing to slow down and go at his pace. He was right, she realized. There is no reason to rush through life, to be busy just for the sake of being busy.

In the afternoon they drove to a tree farm at the edge of town and picked out a small tree. Her mother had waited for Kassie's arrival to put up any decorations. When they got home he helped her carry the tree inside and set it in the stand. Kassie pulled out the box of ornaments from the back of the guest room closet and sat in the living room with Jake, going through the box. Most of the ornaments were relics of her childhood, school art projects made of string and macaroni, or decorated with images of cartoon characters she had once loved. It was amazing they had lasted so long. At the bottom of the box was a small plastic frame in the shape of a wreath, with a hook at the top.

It's a photo of my father, my mother and me when I was ten years old, Kassie explained. Jake ran his fingers over the flat surface.

Your mother told me about your father, he said. *She said he was nice.*

Yes. I wish you had met him. Although she thought she had
long ago cried out all the tears she possibly could, he seemed
to sense the sorrow in her hands as she signed to him, because
he put his arms around her and squeezed her tight.

He took one hand away and rubbed it in a circle over his
chest. *I'm sorry*, he signed.

I-T-S O-K she spelled back to him. I-M J-U-S-T G-L-A-
D Y-O-U-R-E -H-E-R-E N-O-W.

M-E T-O-O.

When her mother came home they ate dinner then
decorated the tree, placing the photo ornament in a prominent
spot in the middle. Kassie thought Jake might find the tree
decorating boring, but he seemed happy to join in, carefully
unwinding the garlands of tinsel and laying them on the
branches.

After they had finished with the decorations, at Jake's
insistence, Kassie showed her mother the video she had made
for her ASL class final project. For her topic, Kassie had
chosen to give a speech on deafblind communication. She
wasn't sure what Ms. Hansen would say, but remembering
how her teacher was always encouraging her students to
challenge her, Kassie went ahead with it anyway.

In the video, she urged people in the Deaf community
to be more aware of different methods of signing, why it
might be difficult for some deafblind people to become fluent
in ASL, and how important it was to be inclusive of all kinds
of communication. Then she introduced Jake, pulling him into
the frame. He waved, smiling. The two of them slowly
demonstrated the deafblind manual alphabet, and ended with a
request for more people to use it.

It was a simple video, shot on the built-in camera on her
computer in her bedroom. According to the guidelines of the
assignment, she had attached English subtitles, and uploaded it

to YouTube. To her relief, Ms. Hansen gave her an A for the project, and for the semester. Her teacher still felt ASL was best, but she was willing to admit that Kassie had made an important point. And she was impressed that Kassie had taken a stand on a real issue in the disabled community. Most of the other students had chosen topics like parking on campus or the latest tuition hike.

She didn't expect anyone apart from her teacher to view it, since she didn't have a channel or a blog or any other means of promoting her video. The last she had checked, she only had a dozen or so views, and a few comments from Ms. Hansen and her classmates. But when she showed the video for her mother, she suddenly realized that she had over a hundred hits, and a bunch of comments saying her ASL was good for a beginner. Even more startling, there were comments from both Deaf and hearing people saying they had never thought about this issue before, but now they wanted to learn the deafblind alphabet.

"No way!" Kassie exclaimed. She turned to Jake, who was sitting behind her.

T-O-N-S O-F H-I-T-S A-N-D C-O-M-M-E-N-T-S she spelled excitedly.

H-A H-A I K-N-O-W, he replied.

You knew! Why didn't you tell me?

I W-A-N-T-E-D T-O S-U-R-P-R-I-S-E Y-O-U, he answered with a grin. H-A-P-P-Y?

Yes, very happy!

She turned back to her mother, who was reading the comments over again. "Jake knew!" Kassie told her. "He was checking the comments all along, but kept it as a surprise."

"Oh sweetie, I'm so proud of you!" her mother said, giving her an awkward hug as they both sat in front of the computer.

Kassie shrugged. "It's just something I did for class. I can't believe other people are watching it."

"You clearly care about it. I can see it in your face. You sent out a message and people responded to it."

"Yeah, I guess so," she said slowly. "I never thought of it that way." It was the first time she felt like something she had done mattered, like she made a difference, no matter how tiny. It felt good.

Later that night as they were lying in bed, she related to Jake what her mother had said and how it made her feel.

I'm proud of you too, he said.

You helped, she pointed out.

Do you want to make another video? he asked. P-U-T O-U-T M-O-R-E I-N-F-O-R-M-A-T-I-O-N A-B-O-U-T D-E-A-F-B-L-I-N-D-N-E-S-S?

Yes! Kassie sat up, electrified by this new idea. *But you should be in it, signing or typing. I'll add captions. We can make short videos about the D-B-C, or mobility, accessibility, all kinds of things!*

They talked for hours, planning what they would do, too excited for sleep.

The rest of the trip they spent writing up drafts for videos while Kassie's mother was at work. Jake took notes on the DBC. They only took breaks to cook together, or occasionally to take walks to some of the places Kassie had been to as a child. It was invigorating, having something purposeful to do together.

On Christmas day they opened presents, then sat down to the huge meal Kassie and Jake had spent the week preparing. Kassie had agonized for weeks about what to get Jake as a present. He wasn't the kind of person who cared much about *things*, the kind of useless knick knacks that filled the stores at that time of year. In the end she settled for a matching woolen hat and scarf, although she worried that it might be too boring. She felt even more inadequate when she opened his present to her, a beautiful filigree silver necklace.

Carter had helped me to pick it out, he explained nervously. *Everyone always says how pretty you are. I wanted to give you something pretty.*

It's beautiful. I love it, she told him, then put it on even though she was still only wearing her pajamas. He touched it gently with his fingertips, tracing the delicate lacy design as it sat against her chest.

Sorry my present is boring, she said.

No, not boring. I love it because it is from you, he replied.

On the evening of the last day of their visit Kassie sat with her mother at the kitchen table, picking at leftovers. Jake was in the living room, checking his email and reading the internet on the DBC. He had started yet another long-term chess game, this time with a guy in the UK. They proceeded at what seemed to Kassie like a glacial pace, only one move every day or so, but Jake was very much caught up in it.

"So," her mother said, in a tone that indicated she was about to open a serious and difficult discussion. Kassie felt her gut instinctively clench.

"What?" She was instantly on the defensive.

"You and Jake seem serious," her mother said slowly. "Are you sure this is what you really want?"

"Yes!"

"Hey now, no need to get all huffy. I like Jake, honestly. He's a great guy and I can tell he loves you a lot. But have you really thought this through?"

"What are you talking about?" Kassie mumbled, looking down at her plate and wishing the conversation was over already.

"Sweetie, he is severely disabled. It's amazing how much he is able to do, but he will always be vulnerable and dependent."

Kassie snapped her head up, glaring angrily at her mother. "So what, he's not allowed to have a relationship because he's too disabled?"

"No, of course not. But I have to think about you too. Are you really prepared to spend your whole life helping him? It's fine now when you're just visiting each other on the weekends, but if you live together it will be different. There will be times when you're too tired, or you really want to go do something else, but you can't because he will always need you. I just want to make sure you're being honest with yourself about taking on that kind of responsibility."

Kassie stared down at her lap again, picking at the chipping polish on her short, square nails. She could bluster all she liked, but she knew her mother had a point, and she knew where all this was coming from. She was silent for a long time, then finally she said, "You never know what's going to happen. I could choose an able-bodied guy who's super athletic and healthy, but then he could be injured or get sick and I'd have to take care of him anyway."

Her mother smiled ruefully. "That's true. But sweetie, I'm asking you this because I've been there. There were so many times with your father when I felt I just couldn't take it any more."

"I know," Kassie said softly. "But Mom, it isn't the same. He doesn't need me to do everything for him. Sure, there are some things he needs help with but it's not like caring for someone who doesn't even know you're there. He's not Dad. There's so much he does for me too." Her mother nodded thoughtfully. "Mom, I really have thought about this. We have been talking about moving in together, but we're waiting while he's looking for a job. He would be working and paying rent, not just sitting around all day. And he would move in with me and Erik, and sometimes Kevin too, so there would be more people to help him, not just me. Also he still has Carter as an intervener. He can still hire him when he needs to."

Her mother raised her eyebrows in surprise. "He could get a job? What could he do?"

"Everyone can do something," Kassie said with more conviction than she felt, echoing what Kevin had told her. The truth was she still had some lingering doubts, and she knew her mother was right to ask these things, but being questioned made her want to prove that it would work out.

Her mother stood up and put her plate in the sink, signaling the end of the conversation. Kassie heaved a sigh of relief. "Well," her mother said, "You know I have always trusted your judgment."

"So it's okay with you if he moves in?" Kassie found the words came out in a squeak, despite herself.

Her mother paused in clearing off the table to plant a kiss on the top of Kassie's head. "Sweetie, you don't need my permission, but yes, it's okay with me." She opened the refrigerator and pulled out the remains of a mincemeat pie. "I think it's time for dessert," she said. "I'm going to ask Jake if he wants any."

CHAPTER TWENTY-SIX

After Kassie and Jake returned to Seattle, despite all their talk of moving in together, for a while nothing changed. In the dead zone between Christmas and New Years, Kassie still had to work and Jake seemed no closer to leaving Bellevue. Erik and Kevin, on the other hand, had cemented their status as a couple by making a pledge of exclusivity.

"Except for anonymous hookups, but it has to be out of town and with someone we won't meet again. Or threesomes, that's okay too," Erik qualified.

"Lalala, I don't want to know!" Kassie spluttered at him, covering her ears. "Come on, I'm trying to eat breakfast here!"

Erik just laughed and poured himself another cup of coffee.

"So when is he going to move in here?" Kassie asked, because she really did like Kevin, even if she didn't want to know the details of her friend's sex life.

Erik shrugged. "Not yet. He has a ton of shit and there isn't so much room here. He's keeping his own place for now, since the rent isn't so bad." Even so, Kevin was spending most of his time at their house.

"So are you coming with us for New Years?" Erik continued.

"I don't know," Kassie sighed, finishing off the last of her granola and yogurt. For the past few years she had gone with Erik to a gay club, but this year she didn't really feel like dancing in front of a tower of speakers in a room full of sweaty, shirtless guys. And she couldn't imagine bringing Jake to such a place.

In the end, it was Cyndi who saved her at the last minute by announcing a party at her house. It was small, just their yoga friends and partners and a few other people Cyndi knew

from the Unitarian Church. Kassie brought Jake, and Jake
invited Carter, as a friend, officially off the clock, although he
still took over most of the interpreting. Between Carter and
the DBC, Kassie found herself free to enjoy the party, chatting
with her friends without having to worry that Jake might be
excluded. Her heart swelled to see him laughing and joking
with her friends. They were still a little hesitant around him,
but as they got used to him the number of stupid questions
decreased in favor of real conversation.

As they watched the countdown on TV, Kassie signed
the numbers to Jake and they kissed right at midnight. Back at
home later that night, they lay in bed together and did much
more than kiss. Jake no longer asked her for reassurance;
instead he had learned to read the signs of her body to know
when he was pleasing her. They had taken a break from sex
while visiting Kassie's mother, out of modesty, but now that
they were alone in the house they could let themselves go.

In the darkened room Kassie looked into Jake's face as
he lay on top of her, his features suffused with a look of
intense concentration and pleasure. His closed eyelids
fluttered, revealing the white underneath for a moment. It
didn't matter to her that he couldn't return her gaze or hear
the sound of her voice. She knew he understood her anyway.
He placed his hands under her chest, feeling the vibrations and
the force of her exhalations as he moved faster and faster, her
voice joining his guttural shout as they climaxed together.

After the start of the new year, Kassie started up her
ASL classes and yoga again. She couldn't be sure, but she
thought Ms. Hansen was actually happy to see her. Already
she was asking Kassie to promise she would take the advanced
class in the fall.

Each week she went on her rounds of work and classes, then drove to Bellevue on Friday evening to pick up Jake. He spent the entire weekend with her, until she drove him back on Sunday afternoon. Most weekends Kevin and Erik were around too. She had started running again with Tara, usually on weeknights, but sometimes on weekends as well, and Jake joined them. Kassie was starting to feel more like she and Jake were a real couple.

One Saturday Kassie came in from clearing the dead leaves out of the backyard and preparing the beds for the first early planting, and found Kevin and Jake sitting together at the dining room table, looking downright conspiratorial.

Jake has something to tell you, Kevin said with a wink.

Looking at them with some suspicion, Kassie pulled off her gardening gloves and tossed them on the table, then sat on Jake's other side and took his hand.

What?

Kevin found a job for me, he signed to her.

Kassie's face lit up with excitement. *Champ! Tell me more!*

Kevin and Jake both began signing to her in a jumble, and she had to keep slowing them down and reminding them to take turns, but eventually she pieced together the details. The job was at the city of Seattle Department of Disability Services, optimizing websites for screen readers and answering questions about accessibility by email and online chat.

It will be better for Jake to work with other D-A people, Kevin explained.

Are you sure? Kassie asked, Jake's hand still on hers, but signing wide, so Kevin could see. *They can train him?*

It's fine. Kevin tapped his thumb against his chest, his fingers spread flat, in a quick, assured gesture. *He told me about the programming he's done already. He's very talented. But understand it's only a part-time job.*

I'll go to school also, Jake added.

School? Isn't that expensive? Kassie asked.

Not university, a technical degree in computer programming, Kevin explained. *He can apply for a G-R-A-N-T from the state to help pay for hiring Carter to interpret during classes.*

Kassie repeated Kevin's signs. *You want?* she added.

Yes, Jake signed decisively. *But the office is in Seattle. Too far from Bellevue. So we live together now? Is it O-K?*

Yes yes yes of course! I want to live with you! So happy! Kassie made exuberant circles with her flat palm upward by her chest, and Jake repeated the sign. *Happy!*

All that remained was for Jake to tell his parents. Kassie agreed to come over for dinner, to be there for the discussion. At first she was elated, but as she drove with him over the bridge the reality started to sink in. She was sure she wanted this, whether it worked out with Jake in the long term or not, they at least had to try. But if his parents challenged her, she wasn't sure she could stay calm and polite.

She parked the car in front of his house and took his hand before getting out. W-H-A-T I-F T-H-E-Y S-A-Y N-O? she asked.

I-M N-O-T A-S-K-I-N-G, I-M T-E-L-L-I-N-G he replied firmly. Kassie felt a little swell of pride. He was doing this for her, pushing himself, so they could be together. She had to do the same, and be patient no matter what might happen.

They walked in the door together, but Jake didn't say anything at first. Mr. and Mrs. O'Malley greeted Kassie warmly, and they sat down to dinner. The meal passed quietly, with Kassie exchanging small talk with his parents, and Jake not contributing much. After they had finished eating, as his mother was clearing away the dishes, Jake felt his way along the kitchen counter and retrieved the DBC, then set it up on the table. He and Kassie had agreed it would be easier to use the device to converse with all of them at once, rather than relying on one person to translate. His parents exchanged a significant look as he turned the machine on and thrust the cell phone in his father's direction.

I have something to tell you, he typed. His father raised an eyebrow as he read the text. His mother left the dishes to come stand behind him, even though the machine voice was speaking the words simultaneously.

Jake continued, I've just accepted a job with the city of Seattle Department of Disability Services, in web accessibility and customer service, and in the fall I'm going to enroll in Seattle Community College to get a certificate in web development. He typed quickly, his fingers punching the keys without pause, not letting his parents respond until he had finished. Because the office and the school are in downtown Seattle, it makes more sense for me to live there. Kassie invited me to move in with her and Erik.

He stopped at last, leaning back slightly in his chair. Kassie held her breath, watching his parents. They didn't seem as surprised as she had expected, and she realized suddenly that he must have discussed at least some of this with them already.

If that's what you want to do, it's fine with us, his father typed.

"But how will you get around?" his mother burst out. His father duly wrote out what she had said.

Kassie asked Mr. O'Malley to hand her the cell phone, so Jake wouldn't be left out of the conversation. I can drive him, she typed.

His mother still looked concerned. "Isn't that a lot of running around for you?"

Kassie relayed the question, then replied, No, it's not far from where I work, or from Kevin's office. Kevin said I could park in his lot. Actually it will be faster than taking the bus like I do now. And I'm taking classes at the same place Jake will be. It's also downtown.

She handed the phone back to Mr. O'Malley. Your mother's a little nervous, but we know you've thought about this carefully. It's up to you to live your own life.

"Thank you!" Kassie exclaimed, feeling a little like she might cry, but Jake's parents were not big on emotional displays. His mother nodded seriously, and his father added, Son, we're so proud of you for getting that job. We always knew you could do it.

Kassie squeezed Jake's knee under the table. His pink-tinged cheeks raised in a wide, glowing grin.

The next weekend Kassie came by again, and they packed up her car with Jake's desktop computer, his clothes, and a few Braille books. Jake was bouncing with energy, but his parents were more subdued.

As they were leaving, both his mother and father hugged Jake tightly.

"Thank you," Mr. O'Malley said gruffly, giving Kassie a quick, manly hug along with a pat on the back.

"Thank you for getting the DBC," she murmured. "That made everything possible." He turned away quickly, before she could see his face.

Then it was Mrs. O'Malley's turn. The overpowering scent of White Linen assailed Kassie as she was wrapped in a fleshy, polyester embrace. She held on a bit longer than Kassie would have liked. "Take good care of him," she whispered, finally letting her go, and Kassie looked away as she saw tears in Mrs. O'Malley's eyes.

His mother hugged Jake again, but he'd already had enough and, disengaging himself with a grunt, he pulled Kassie out the door.

"Okay, bye! We'll be back to see you next weekend!" Kassie waved at them as she followed Jake down the front steps.

Back in Ravenna, Erik and Kevin helped them move Jake's few possessions into the house. As promised, they set up a desk for his computer in the extra room in the basement.

Then they settled down to dinner to celebrate. Erik had bought a thick salmon fillet at the Pike Place Market, and even though it was still chilly he grilled it outside.

Kassie spread a new tablecloth over the round dining room table and laid out their one good set of matching dishes. Erik poured everyone generous glasses of red wine, and led them in a toast.

I'm proud of you, Kevin signed, with Jake's hand on top of his. *I knew you could do it.*

Thank you. Jake smiled.

For a time no one signed anything more as they all applied themselves to the feast. At last Kassie leaned back with a sigh, then reached over to Jake and asked if he wanted seconds.

N-O B-U-T Y-O-U W-A-N-T T-O-S-A-Y S-O-M-E-T-H-I-N-G. I C-A-N T-E-L-L, he answered. She marveled for a moment at how he could guess her thoughts just from the feel of her hands. Erik and Kevin were looking at them pointedly, so with Jake's hand on hers, she signed to them.

I've been thinking, she started slowly. *I want to study for National Interpreter Certification.* Without waiting for a reply, she hurried on, *I know I have to study for years more, get a lot more fluent in A-S-L. But if I can get S-C-H-O-L-A-R-S-H-I-P I will reduce my work to part-time and study hard every day.*

Good for you! Kevin said, and Erik echoed him, but Kassie could detect a shadow of doubt on his face.

Later as they were washing up, Kassie cornered Erik. "I haven't made this decision lightly, you know," she said.

He nodded seriously, handing her a dripping dish. "I know, but it's tough work. You'll see the worst of humanity along with the good."

"I know that," she said, wiping the dish with a towel and placing it in the cupboard. "But I'm sick of spending all my working hours on a job that's so pointless. I want to make a difference. Getting all those comments on my video--it was incredible. I talked about it with Ms. Hansen, and she said she would help me plan what classes to take. I'm really ready to commit to this. Besides," she said, giving him a coy glance, "I have some great tutors."

Erik looped his long arm around her neck in a soapy, damp embrace. "Well, it's true you are living with the world's best ASL native speakers," he said, laughing.

Later that night as she was lying in bed with Jake, Kassie asked him again about her plan to become an interpreter. O-K? *You don't mind?*

O-F C-O-U-R-S-E O-K, he answered. Y-O-U O-P-E-N-E-D U-P T-H-E W-O-R-L-D T-O M-E. I-T-S Y-O-U-R T-A-L-E-N-T. Y-O-U S-H-O-U-L-D S-H-A-R-E I-T.

I L-O-V-E Y-O-U J-A-K-E, she spelled out, savoring each letter with a flick of her finger against his skin.

I L-O-V-E Y-O-U T-O-O, he replied, and finding her lips with his fingers, kissed her ardently.

E-N-D

Coming in February 2013 from Dev Love Press...

The Time Traveler's Boyfriend by Annabelle Costa

Tick tock, tick tock, tick tock...

Do you hear that ticking noise? I swear to God, it's like I'm going crazy, but I hear something ticking. And no, it's not my biological clock, thank you very much. Yes, my biological clock is ticking (I know, Mom), but it's not *audibly* ticking. Like, I don't walk down the street and hear it. Nobody says, "Hey, what's that noise? Is that your *ovaries*?"

So no, the source of the ticking is something less abstract than my 36-year-old eggs.

Tick tock, tick tock, tick tock...

I look around the entrance to my boyfriend Adam's brownstone, located on the Upper West Side in Manhattan. Yes, it's a great location, and no, I'm not dating him for that reason. I know something around here is ticking and I'll be damned if I don't figure out what it is. You can't be too careful these days, what with terrorism and all. Although I've heard that modern bombs actually don't tick. They vibrate. So it's easy to get them confused with... well, do I really need to complete that sentence? We all know what vibrates.

I do a 360 degree turn, keeping my eyes focused on finding anything unusual, and I don't see anything, until.... yes! Huddled near the steps to the brownstone is... a rabbit.

A rabbit. Okay, that's weird.

Let me be clear about something here. We're not in suburbia. We're not in some forest where rabbits frolic freely and play with their friends the deer and the antelope. You don't generally see rabbits wandering around the

Upper West Side. Especially a rabbit like this one, which is white as snow aside from a tiny little black patch on its back, and has a ticking timepiece hanging around his neck. No, this definitely isn't a wild rabbit. And I'll bet anything that its presence has something to do with Adam.

Tick tock, tick tock, tick tock....

I bend down near the little trembling rabbit, holding out my hand. See, Adam? I can be maternal. The rabbit looks at me curiously, sniffs with its little adorable nose, and then cowers in the corner like I'm the hunter in *Bambi*.

Okay, I'm not great with animals.

I straighten up, cocking my head at Adam's window, to see if he's watching me. Maybe this is some kind of psychological experiment he's doing and the whole thing is being filmed and will probably end up published in the Journal of Complicated Science. Knowing Adam, it's got to be some kind of experiment. I just can't imagine what.

Question: Why is there a white rabbit with a clock around its neck outside my mad scientist boyfriend's house?

a) Rabbit is looking for Alice and is very, very late

b) Adam tossed the rabbit out the window to see if time flies

c) Rabbit is some kind of cyborg created to destroy humanity before we destroy the planet

I turn back to get a closer look at the rabbit and now it's gone. Apparently, the little bugger ran off the second I turned my head. He isn't even close anymore, because the ticking has completely stopped. And as for me, I'm left staring at the steps of the brownstone, wondering if I've completely lost my mind.

"A what?"

Adam denies the whole thing. There was no rabbit, he claims. I just plain imagined it.

I am apparently that crazy.

"A white rabbit," I say again, through gritted teeth. I put down my fork into my plate of spaghetti and meatballs, and I fold my arms across my chest to emphasize the seriousness of the situation.

Adam pushes his metal-rimmed glasses up his nose and shakes his head at me across the dining table. He's really managed to perfect the disheveled scientist look over the years. Aside from the spectacles, his short light brown hair perpetually has that "just rolled out of bed" look, no matter what the time of day is. And I've never actually managed to catch him with his shirt buttoned properly. Right now, his checkered polyester shirt is off by about two buttons. I have to sit on my hands to suppress my urge to fix it.

I'm kind of the opposite. I feel uncomfortable if I have even one strand of hair out of place. The neat cotton dress shirts and fitted skirts I wear to work are what I generally wear all the time these days. If I go more than a week without a professional manicure, I start getting antsy.

"You saw a white rabbit outside my house..." Adam repeats, a mildly amused look in his soft brown eyes.

"With a timepiece around its neck," I add.

"And you think this is some sort of experiment I'm doing?" Now Adam is outright smirking at me.

When you say it like that, anything sounds stupid, doesn't it?

"Come on, Claudia," he says. "It probably belongs to my neighbor's kid or something. A pet rabbit."

"Yeah," I mumble, although it's really hard to push away the feeling that there was something very different about that rabbit, and that Adam isn't entirely telling the truth. But he won't 'fess up to me, and I'm beginning to sound crazy to my own ears.

Of course, it's pretty hard to sound crazy when you're dating a guy who calls himself an inventor.

I'm sure, in the olden days, like in the eighteenth century, being an inventor was a real career. It was something you could put on your business cards. For example, Thomas Edison and Leonardo da Vinci were inventors and nobody thought they were antisocial weirdos, as far as I can tell. But in the twenty-first century, if you go around telling people you're an inventor, people start to think you're a little off.

Not that Adam isn't a sweet guy and all. He even invented a few things for me—he rigged up a button on my wall that I could press that would make my remote control start beeping, because I complained that I was always losing it. (I called him in a panic once and made him help me comb the whole apartment until we found the remote. Do you know where it was? In the *refrigerator*. I swear, I think sometimes I'm losing my mind.)

"So it's not some kind of computer robot rabbit?" I ask Adam, because I still just don't believe him.

He grins adorably at me. "A robot rabbit?"

I shrug. "Maybe it's for kids who want a pet but not have to feed them or clean up their crap."

"Oh, I see," Adam says, still grinning. "As a kid, you always wanted a rabbit, but you were worried it was going to crap all over the place and you'd have to clean it up."

I sense he's not taking me seriously here. "No, that's not what I'm saying."

"No, I completely get it," Adam says. "For your next birthday, you want a robot rabbit. I'm on it, Claudia. You don't need to keep hinting."

Okay, that's enough of that. I swat at him with my hand, and he grabs my wrist. Our eyes meet and I get that "butterflies in the stomach" feeling. It's almost overpowering. We've been together over a year, yet I still find Adam unbearably sexy. It's weird because Adam isn't the kind of man I would have dated in my younger years—I was so immature that I probably would have seen him at a party and made fun of him behind his back. But my concept of "sexy" has evolved considerably over time.

Smart, sweet, nice looking, well-off guy who adores me = sexy

Devastatingly handsome starving artist who chases anyone in a skirt = unsexy

"Come here," Adam says softly as we continue to gaze into each other eyes.

I get up from my seat and settle into Adam's lap, feeling the tight muscles in his chest and arms against my body. He pulls me toward him and starts to kiss me in that gentle, tender way he always does, running his fingers through my ash blond hair. You wouldn't think it to look at him, nerdy science guy and all, but Adam is a really good kisser. Of all the men I've ever kissed, the kisses with him are the most intense, the ones that make my whole body tingle. Even more so than with Kyle, who had the tongue stud.

On a scale of 1 to 10, I would give Adam's kisses a 9. Maybe a 9.5 on a good day.

After several minutes of making out, Adam lifts his hands off me and puts them on the wheels of his chair so he can push away from the dining table. That's another thing about Adam that's different than any other guy I've ever dated—he's disabled. And not just a little limp or something. He needs a wheelchair. All the time. He cannot walk at all.

"I'm going to make you the best robot rabbit you've ever seen," Adam whispers as his breath tickles my neck. Okay, now I'm starting to worry he's not kidding.

"I don't want a robot rabbit," I say, pulling away from him. I try to sound stern. "I mean it, Adam. Don't make me a robot rabbit."

He laughs and tugs at a lock of my hair. "Relax, Claudia. I was just teasing you." I let out a little sigh of relief, but I shouldn't have worried. Even though he's a bit of a clueless scientist guy, he's generally surprisingly perceptive when it comes to me and what I like or want. "I've still got a few months before your birthday, and trust me, I'm going to get you something amazing."

I have absolutely no doubt in my mind that Adam will get me something amazing for my birthday. It will probably be some combination of really thoughtful and painfully expensive, if his previous gifts are any indication. Adam always gets me the best gifts.

Too bad it won't be the one thing I really want.

***

Since Adam cooked dinner, I clear the table. I take the plates and glasses, and load up the dishwasher for him.

Lately I've been spending more and more time at his house, to the point where we've started dividing the chores. I've been taking care of dishes, and he empties the trash.

I love spending time at Adam's brownstone. Despite his eccentricities, it's a very normal house, if a little messy and uninspired. His living room has a widescreen TV, a couch that's ripped and stained and far too old, but very comfortable, and a coffee table that's covered in rings because Adam's never heard of a coaster. The inventing is confined to one room of the house, and never overflows into the main living area. It's the one room I've never yet entered.

After I get the dishwasher going, I find Adam in the living room, hunched over his desktop computer. The screen is completely filled with some coding language—just looking at it makes my head ache. When I get closer, he minimizes the window on his screen. "Hey," he says. "Thanks for getting the dishes started."

"You should be relaxing," I scold him. "You've been working way too hard lately." Of the nights I've spent here in the last two weeks, he's stayed up hours past when I went to bed.

"You know I'm a workaholic," he says, winking at me. "That's why you'd hate living with me."

I wince. This is a little game Adam has been playing very recently, called You Don't Really Want to Live With Me. He takes it very seriously. It's all part of larger game called You Don't Really Want to Marry Me. I'm not very fond of this game.

Here's the deal with me and Adam: we've been dating over a year. Granted, that's not a huge amount of time. But I'm not 20 years old here. I'm 36, and as he noted, I've got a birthday coming up in a few months. If I had a baby now, I'd already be advanced maternal age. And I'm not having a baby now. I'm not even married. I'm not even *engaged*.

Adam is even older than I am. He's 38. And he's not a *young* 38 either. I'd like to think I could pass for thirty or even younger, but Adam can't. He looks 38. Hell, he looks 40, even 45, easy. Not because he's fat or out of shape or balding, because he isn't any of those things. He's slim and muscular in his upper body, and he's got all his hair, but he's got almost as much gray in his hair as he's got brown, and he's got more lines on his face than he ought to, especially around his eyes. Not that it's a bad thing in terms of his looks. He's one of those guys who, like Sean Connery, is just going to get more attractive as he gets older. When he's 70, he's probably going to have hot young 40-year-olds chasing him down, while I'll be a little old lady with a hump on my back.

His looks initially seemed like a sign of maturity to me, a sign that he was the sort of guy who was ready for a commitment. And we fit so well together, me and Adam. More than I thought we would when I first met him at a mutual friend's dinner party. He treated me like a queen, and I mistakenly got the idea in my head that if I brought up marriage, he'd jump at the idea (figuratively). But he didn't. He got quiet, just like every other freaking guy did.

And it stinks because Adam is the first guy that I've really seen myself growing old with. I can just see us at 70 years old, me still bringing him my futuristic computer when I've got a virus and he needs to get rid of it. And then I fix the buttons on his shirt with one of my arthritic hands, and bat away the hot young 40-year-olds with the other.

"I wouldn't hate living with you," I insist, for what feels like the trillionth time. "I'm practically living here already. Why don't we make it official so I don't have to feel like a nomad?"

He raises his eyebrows at me. "You feel like a nomad?"

"I'm carrying around panties in my purse, Adam," I say. I'm half tempted to dig them out and shake them in his face. "You think I enjoy that?"

"I gave you a drawer to use," he mumbles, his eyes lowered.

I don't want a freaking drawer. I want a ring. But I can't say that to him. We've had this conversation before and I know where it's headed, and it's not in the direction of the nearest jewelry store. There's no point in pushing him when he's clearly not ready. "I love you," I say instead. "I just want to be with you."

"I love you too, Claudia," he says. "But…"

Adam leans forward in his wheelchair, rubbing his knees, looking really uncomfortable. He told me once before the reason why he had trouble settling down, but I can't accept it. We're *right* for each other. I don't want to be one of those awful "ultimatum women" so I won't do that to him. But how long am I supposed to wait patiently for him to be ready?

"Don't be mad," Adam pleads with me.

"I'm not," I say. Well, I am. But I'm trying not to be. When I was in my twenties, I always pitied those women who made relationships all about pushing for commitment, yet here I am, close to doing it myself. It's something I vowed I'd never do. And I won't.

"Sit down on the couch," Adam says. "I'll go get you in the foot massager and give you a back rub."

The foot massager. It's another thing Adam invented for me. It used to be a foot bath, but he rigged it up